WITH HER SIGHT

THE UNITAM REALM SERIES

BOOK TWO

SUNNY HART

Published by Sunny Hart
In USA

Edited by Insomniac Editing Services

Cover by Cauldron Press

Created with Vellum

AUTHOR'S NOTE

This book is a Reverse Harem romance where the heroine will not have to choose between any of her men. It will feature a FMMM relationship and is recommended for 18+ due to mature content.

DESCRIPTION

In the Unitam Realm, power determines where you belong. And Claire just unlocked more of it.

More questions than answers is the story of Claire's life now. Where is she from? Who are her parents? And why was her vision the cost of binding her magic?

She survived her first year at the Academy, but someone out there seems determined she won't live to see the second one. Dark magic is calling beasts out of the Elven Forest that haven't been seen since the Great War, and they all seem to have a strange fixation on Claire.

Her Triad and friends have sworn to protect her, but Claire doesn't want to lose the family she's just found in them. She'll have to figure out how to control her rapidly growing magic if she wants to be the Champion of the Realm the Academy has called her to be.

With dark magic beasts, an over-interested Council, and magic that just keeps growing, Claire will have to venture into the Elven Forest in her hunt for answers about her parents, her birthright, and the true start of the Great War.

CHAPTER 1

Claire sat on the sofa back at the Academy next to Everett as Malcolm and Desmond paced and grumbled and shouted at each other. Her men were concerned and Claire couldn't blame them.

At the market earlier this afternoon, Claire had been drawn to a tent vendor selling weaponry. Inside, her magic had guided her to an Elven dagger and when she grabbed both the Elven dagger and the Fae dagger hanging at her hip, the rebounding effect of the magic had eaten away at the bindings around her magic.

Now her magic moved restlessly about her center, alive and nipping at her fingertips to be used. She settled it with a quiet tug. She would figure out her new magic later, right now she focused on the other thing that the breaking of the magical bindings had done.

She could *see*.

It was almost overwhelming and Claire found herself closing her eyes frequently to take comfort in the familiar darkness. It was just so bright and colorful when her eyes were open. Some of the colors she recognized from her time with Desmond but the others just caused her head to spin. There was so much to this world, so much she had missed out on. And why?

Around her, the discussion got heated once more as the men discussed what the events might mean. Claire opened her eyes again, focusing on the two daggers on the table in front of her as a way to keep from getting overwhelmed The Fae dagger on the right with its colors and masculine design and the slightly lighter, more feminine Elven dagger with its own set of colors.

Ignoring Malcolm's shouts about her safety, her dragon could get very rumbly, she leaned closer to Everett. "What colors are these?"

She lifted her chin up to his face and got distracted from her question the second she asked it. Everett's green eyes looked down at her. His hair was a light color, falling just over his ears and tousled because he kept running his hand through it. He was one of the most beautiful sights she had ever seen. Not that she had a lot of experience with this whole seeing thing.

He smiled at her clear distraction and leaned in, his voice a breath in her ear as he answered. He pointed towards the Fae dagger first, "Both daggers are a silver-colored metal. This one, the Fae dagger, has red, orange, and purple gems and colors inlaid in it," he pointed at the colors, "that one," he moved his hand towards the Elven dagger, "has inlays of blues, greens, and purple in it as well."

Claire hummed as she studied the colors he pointed out. Her face heated lightly at the memory of the color red. She traced the colors with her eyes, her hands wanting to pick them up but she resisted the urge until Desmond and Malcolm were finished.

They didn't know what handling the daggers would do to her magic just yet. Plus, this information on top of the Headmaster's earlier news that she was called to be a Champion of the Realm with the support of a supposedly neutral, sentient Academy was information overload. Claire was doing an outstanding job of shoving it to the side and studying the colors in the daggers instead.

There was a knock on the door that broke the conversation apart and drew Claire's gaze. The door was a dark brown against the grey of the stone. Her eyes ached as she took in the distance. Not seeing things in shadows was going to take some getting used to.

"It's Holly," a voice came through. "I have Bethany, Zack and Cody with me. You all weren't at the dining hall."

Claire looked around at her men. She knew they were wary of others knowing but these were her friends. She could trust her friends. "Come in," she called.

Holly opened the door and her friends stepped through. Claire took time to study them now that she could see. Holly looked like her voice sounded, warm and inviting. She had brown hair and brown eyes but it was a warm brown color not like the cool brown of the couch. Bethany was all fire and passion. She also had green eyes but they were a lighter green than Everett's were. Her golden hair was tinged with red and cascaded wildly around her face.

Zack also looked like his voice sounded, solid and steady. He stood a head taller than the girls and was leaner than her men. His brown hair was cropped close to his head and his silver eyes were hidden behind glasses. Cody was as tall as Zack was but more solid. His brown hair was curly and fell to his chin. His brown eyes were playful and tinged with a bit of gold.

"Why are you looking at us like that?" Bethany asked when the silence stretched on, her green eyes narrowing.

Claire broke out a smile, "Because I can see you."

They didn't get it. Cody, surprisingly, was the first one to realize with his widening eyes. He crossed the room, ignoring the growl from Malcolm, and picked Claire up, spinning her around. "You can see!"

"What?" Holly exclaimed as Cody set her down, ruffling her hair in a way an older brother would.

Claire laughed and held her arms out to Holly, "You won't ever have to help me match my clothes again."

Holly dove into her arms. "What? How?" The normally eloquent witch was at a loss for words.

"When?" Bethany echoed, wrapping her arms around the two from Claire's back. "Wait, the Market?"

The girls released her and Zack squeezed her softly, "Congratulations, Claire!"

Claire beamed at them, their excitement contagious. Not that her Triad wasn't excited; she didn't think. But it was kind of disappointing that for the last hour all Desmond and Malcolm had been talking about since they shoved a bagful of coins at the vendor and hustled Claire out of the market was Claire's safety and the consequences of her actions.

"Come, sit." Everett stole her out of the middle of her friends. "We'll explain what we know."

Claire smiled up at him, getting lost in his green eyes for a few moments while her friends arranged themself in the living room. Malcolm and Desmond stopped their pacing and discussions and joined Everett and Claire on the couch. Malcolm took Claire's other side as Desmond perched on the arm of the couch next to him. Claire snuggled into Malcolm's warmth and his continuous growl quieted at her touch.

"Holy shit, is this an Elven dagger?" Zack asked, leaning over the low table. "And is that a Fae dagger? Wait, that's the one you've been carrying around?"

"It is," Claire said.

"This is why you've been training more." Bethany said. "Not just because you are their Fourth."

She lifted accusing eyes towards Claire's Triad and Claire hurried to jump in. "Yes. Malcolm gave me the Fae dagger, and it reacted strongly to my magic. We didn't know what it meant."

"You all know that the Fae and Elves retreated decades ago." Desmond said, warning strong in his voice. "What we are about to discuss cannot leave this room."

"None of us would do anything to harm Claire." Holly's warm eyes flashed dangerously.

"I know," Claire said firmly, "and so does Desmond." She shot Desmond a warning look. She understood his protectiveness, but these were her friends.

"So tell us what's going on," Cody said, his normally playful voice serious.

Claire explained the bindings on her magic and how, when she touched the Fae dagger for the first time, the bindings seemed to loosen. She talked about the training with Malcolm and Everett and her newfound Energy Reading powers as well. Desmond told them about the call to the Headmaster's office earlier today and showed them the letter.

Her friends hunched around the letter reading it and looked up, more questions in their eyes. Before they could start on the questions, Claire hurried to finish the rest of the story about the trip to the market and being drawn to the Elven dagger.

"After the protective dome fell, Malcolm gave the vendor woman a bag of gold coins and had her swear her silence while Desmond and Everett got me out of the tent and back to the portal. We came straight here." Claire finished.

"By the Realm," Zack breathed out heavily, sitting back on the couch.

Holly smiled at Claire. "I always knew you were special but this is another level."

Claire smiled back shakily. Another level indeed. So many questions and not enough answers.

"So what now?" Bethany asked.

"We need more answers." Desmond stated.

Holly nodded, "Yes. So the most pressing questions right now are what does this mean for Claire's magic now that the bindings are loosened and what does being a Champion of the Realm entail?"

"Also, who are Claire's parents?" Zack added.

"And how do we keep Claire safe?" Cody said.

Malcolm growled and Claire placed a hand on his leg, "What do you mean?" Claire asked.

Cody leaned forward, his elbows on his knees and his hands clasped under his chin. Claire wasn't used to seeing the playful shifter so serious and she shifted in her seat a bit. She would not like what he was about to say and her Triad would probably like it even less.

"It feels like someone is moving pieces around. You received an invitation to the Academy, sent by an Academy that hasn't been able to do that in decades, since before the Great War. Malcolm gave you that dagger after his father saved a Fae warrior's life. Artifacts like that are usually passed from father to son which would guarantee that Malcolm would have it in his hoard when he was at the Academy. You were drawn to this Elven dagger after getting another letter from the Academy calling you to be a Champion."

Cody paused and rubbed his hand over his face. "I don't know, it just feels like the timing is weird. Like someone is moving the pieces on a chessboard. I don't know if it's the Academy or someone else. That combined with the warning from the Academy stating trouble is coming…" he trailed off. "Maybe that doesn't make sense and I'm overthinking it."

"No," Desmond said slowly, "I think you are onto something. Someone or something is moving pieces around."

"Who?" Bethany questioned, "The Academy? It's supposed to be neutral."

"If it is the Academy then, what does that say for the trouble that is coming?" Zack asked. "A neutral Academy wouldn't take sides unless the trouble coming was significant."

Everett looked over Claire's head at Malcolm. "Is the Academy going to be safe for us to stay here?"

Before Malcolm could answer, Claire spoke up, "The Academy is safe for me." she said with quiet certainty.

"What else do you know?" Holly caught something in Claire's tone.

"I can feel it." Claire admitted, finally saying out loud what she had been feeling these last few weeks. "It's like a constant current around me ever since I sent the magic blast into it a few weeks ago."

"When you sent some of your own magic into it unknowingly." Desmond finished her thought.

"I don't understand," Holly said, "students have sent magic blasts into the walls the whole time I've been here, that's what the arena walls are for."

"This was different." Desmond said. "Claire?"

"I think it had to do with my intent," Claire said. "When I sent it into the Academy, all I could think about was keeping everyone safe, keeping me safe. When I sent too much, I think I tied part of myself to the Academy." Its magic sat in her center now, in a corner, strong and steady and ignoring the wildness of her newly unbound magic.

Malcolm growled, and Claire winced. Desmond chuckled, "I thought we talked about sending magic into unknown magical objects."

Claire shrugged. It had been the right thing to do.

"What does that mean now that she's tied herself to the Academy?" Holly asked.

"It means I can feel it," Claire said. "I can feel its intent. It doesn't wish me harm."

Zack stared at her. "I think I might know who your parents were."

Desmond looked at him sharply. "You see it too?"

Zack nodded slowly, his eyes never leaving Claire. Claire's

stomach started fluttering. Answers. Something she always thought she wanted, but when faced with the possibility of them she almost wished she could disappear.

As if sensing her thoughts, Malcolm wrapped his arm around her shoulders and tucked her further into his chest. Everett tightened his grip on her hand, and the bonds between them eased her panic.

"I think your parents were Elven or Fae," Zack said, "or both."

Elven or Fae. Two races that hadn't been seen since the Great War. Two races that lived on opposite sides of the Realm. Two races that were supposed to be selfish and unwilling to work with the other races. Two races that were apparently okay with binding a child's magic and abandoning her in the forest.

As if sensing her spiraling, Holly broke in. "I think that's enough for tonight. We have the most pressing question answered, which is Claire is safe here at the Academy. We can figure out what this means for Claire's magic now that the bindings have been loosened. This summer when we train here, and starting tomorrow, we can comb the Academy's library for information on Champions of the Realm."

As Holly outlined a plan, Claire felt the nerves in her stomach ease. There was a plan. She had her friends' support and help and her Triad surrounded her. It was going to be fine. She desperately tried to cling to that last thought, but the dark, anxious thoughts still swirled in the back of her brain behind the false positive thoughts Claire tried to keep repeating.

What if the answers she desperately wanted to find weren't the answers she wanted?

CHAPTER 2

When Claire woke up the next morning, she let out a groan and threw her arm over her eyes. Why was it so bright? Was this what it was like to wake up every day for people who could see? This sucked. The room darkened, and Claire lifted her arm to peek out.

Desmond stood next to her window, having just closed the curtains. "Good morning, little witch." He said cheerily.

"Good morning, Desmond." Claire said, lowering her arm and sitting up in bed. She had asked for space last night from the Triad, and they had reluctantly given it to her. She just needed a little space to wrap her head around all of this. Not that it had done much good, as she tossed and turned all night. A yawn nearly split her jaw open, and Desmond chuckled as he came to sit next to her.

"Rough night?" He asked, reaching his hand out for hers.

Claire took his hand and got distracted from his question. By the Realm, Desmond was handsome. His messy black hair fell just over his ears, with a few stray pieces dusting his brow. His blue eyes were as soft as his gentle half smile. That smile did dangerous things to her insides and her magic.

His hand squeezed hers softly, and Claire realized she was staring. "Sorry," she said blushing, "what was the question?"

Desmond's half smile turned into a full smile, a twinkle in his blue eyes. "I asked if you had a rough night but I'm going to go by the state of your curls that it was." He reached up and tugged one of Claire's curls over her forehead and between her eyes before brushing it back, his hand soft on her forehead.

Claire reached up and touched her hair, bringing some curls to the front of her face. The brown was soft? Not warm like Holly's, but darker?

A strange sense of loss filled her. She'd missed out on so much in life. "I've never known what color my hair was," she said softly

She looked up at Desmond with a weak smile. "How am I supposed to be a Champion of the Realm if I don't even know what color my hair is?"

"Oh, Claire." Desmond shuffled them until both of their backs were against the headboard. Claire was pressed against his side as he wrapped his arms around her and tugged her gently into his chest.

"There's so much I don't know, Desmond. Basic things! Like colors and shapes and then more complicated things like how to use magic or fight. What if this is all a mistake? What if I don't belong here?"

Desmond hugged her tighter at her frustrated declaration, and Claire sagged backwards into him. "I'm not going to say you don't need to know colors and shapes, but I am going to say you know everything you need to know to do this. You have progressed so much since you first arrived here. You are developing proficiencies in all four elements and have the rare talent of being an Energy Reader. You are picking up combat skills at a pace faster than most. But more importantly, you are strong and kind and always looking for the best in people. You draw people in, make them want to know you. The Realm has had enough strong warrior champions. Maybe it needs someone who can see the best in everyone, not just the most powerful."

Claire was silent, processing his words. Power ruled in the Unitam Realm and there was no way she was going to be able to best the most powerful warriors in the realm by being kind. "Thank you for trying to make me feel better," she said finally.

"I'll keep telling you until you believe it." Desmond wasn't fooled by her words, "And remember, you have me, Everett, Malcolm, Holly and your friends. We will all prepare you and stand by you. And if it turns out you don't belong here at the Academy then we will find a new place to belong, together."

Claire buried her face in his chest and squeezed his arms.

"See, I told you sending Desmond to wake her up wouldn't work. He gets too distracted."

Claire lifted her head to see Everett standing in the doorway talking over his shoulder to Malcolm. Desmond let out a gasp of mock indignation, "I do not!"

Claire patted Desmond's arms and then wiggled her way off the bed. Everett was there when she found her feet on the soft rug covering the stone floor. "Everett," she said, stepping into his waiting arms.

"I missed you last night." Everett whispered in her ear, "No more of this space thing, okay?"

Claire pulled back and smiled at him, "Not that it worked anyways."

Cinnamon and smoke stole her away and Claire turned to wrap her arms around Malcolm, "Good morning, little treasure," Malcolm's low voice buried into her hair.

"Good morning. What was Desmond supposed to wake me for?"

"Training." Malcolm said, "Training before breakfast although there is some fruit if you want something light in your stomach."

"Can I train with the daggers?"

The men exchanged looks and Claire waited them out patiently. It was kind of adorable how much they worried.

"Let's wait a few days." Desmond said. "I'll do some research on how to use them and then you and I can practice sending and recalling magic into them before we unleash you on Malcolm and Everett."

"Ok." That made sense. Better to figure out how to work with her magic before she accidentally hurt one of her men.

Claire changed quickly and followed the men down to the Combat Arena. The Academy was slowly emptying of students so they barely passed anyone on the way. Not that Claire would have been able to see as she was walking in the center of her Triad, like they were shielding her from the world. She would have to ask if they were planning on keeping her newfound sight from the rest of the Academy.

If Claire thought having her sight would make training easier, she was sorely mistaken. If anything, the newfound shapes and colors distracted her and she groaned as she hit the dirt again. Malcolm came into her field of vision as she stared up at the blue sky. He extended a hand and she accepted his help and scrambled to stand.

"You're distracted." He stated the obvious.

Claire fought the urge to roll her eyes. "Yes. It's too bright." Was it wrong to want to go back to her world of shadows?

"You have to ignore it."

This time Claire did roll her eyes and a snort came from behind Malcolm. Desmond. "I'm trying," she said, "but it's not easy." she tried to explain.

"Let's call it for today." Everett interceded when Malcolm would have replied. Her grumpy dragon liked to push. And normally Claire appreciated that. But she just had her sight for one day for the Realm's sake. It was going to take her a little bit to get used to it.

"Yay, breakfast!" Desmond pushed off the wall he was leaning on and captured Claire's hand.

Claire let herself be tugged out of the arena. It shouldn't be harder to fight with her vision but it was and Malcolm was right. She was distracted. She could just see so much more. Even now, as Desmond tucked her hand in his arm and led her across the courtyard, she was distracted. Her head kept turning left and right as she put colors and shapes to all of the places she had walked over the last year. The dormitory buildings were the same grey stone on the outside that they were on the inside. The class buildings were a light brown stone, the same stone that the large administrative building opposite of the Combat Arena was built from.

Large trees lined the pathways, their green leaves seemed to glow in the early morning sun. There were more students out now. Some of them were carrying boxes. Claire watched one first year walk out of the dormitory with two people who must be her parents behind her. Claire's heart clenched as the mother placed an arm around the student and they both laughed at something. What was that like? In searching for all of these answers would Claire find out what happened to her own mother?

A gentle hand on her back interrupted her thoughts. She turned her head and Everett gave her a gentle smile. He always seemed to know her moods. She returned the smile and then focused on the steps to the dining hall.

A chorus of good mornings welcomed them to their table. "Can you still see?" Cody leaned forward and asked.

Bethany smacked the back of his head and watching the action that was such a familiar sound to her made Claire grin. There was no way Cody didn't see Bethany coming so he was definitely letting her smack him. Interesting.

"I can still see," she said as she sat down between Desmond and Malcolm.

"I was worried that it was all a dream," Holly admitted.

"You and I both," Claire said. That was something she wasn't allowing herself to consider just yet. Was her vision a temporary thing or was it permanent. She firmly shoved the question to the back of her mind. They had other more important things to figure out first before Claire decided to be selfish about her vision.

"How was training?" Bethany asked.

Claire could feel her lips twist into a frown and Bethany laughed, "That good, huh?"

Claire shrugged and waved her hands around, "Seeing is hard."

The table laughed and Claire smiled and played along further, "I don't know how you all focus with everything. There's so many colors and details."

Zack pushed his glasses up his nose, "I've never thought about it that way but you're right. I guess we take a lot of it for granted."

"It's okay," Claire shrugged, "I'll get used to it, I hope."

"So are we telling others that you can see?" Bethany asked.

"We will probably have to tell the Headmaster at least," Desmond said. "I would recommend that we keep it quiet from the rest of the students for now. Just till we have more answers. I don't want any more eyes on Claire than necessary. Most of the students are heading out this week or next so it shouldn't be too hard to keep it quiet."

Claire nodded. A thought occurred to her, "Wait, do you all have to go back home too?"

Her friends exchanged looks, nodding. "I have to leave at the end of this week," Zack said. "But Holly and I are going to try and work something out where I can be at Brandlevine this summer instead of Ashcraft."

Desmond nodded, "That's smart. Let me know if I can help with that."

"I was going to talk to Professor Andy today and see if Zack can do an apprenticeship with her this summer. That is, if Andy is going home to Brandlevine. She and Helene might be staying at the Academy."

"Professor Andy and Professor Helene?" Claire asked.

"Yes, they are each other's chosen," Holly said, "they keep their relationship on the down low because we have a lot of stuck-up students who believe their parents bullshit about no inter-species matings."

The more Claire thought about it the more the two of them made sense. She smiled, "I'm happy for them. I always liked both of them. I just didn't realize they were together."

"They might be good allies," Everett said quietly.

Desmond nodded. "Let's ask the Headmaster what he thinks after breakfast and then we can bring them in. Andy is a formidable elemental wielder."

"What about you two?" Claire asked Bethany and Cody.

"I got permission to stay for two weeks but then I need to go back to the pack," Cody said.

"Same for me," Bethany said, "but we can probably come back to visit. I can make up a school project as a reason to come back but I don't know if that will work for Cody."

"Hey, I could totally have a school project!" Cody argued.

Bethany rolled her eyes, "You haven't been into school since you were a pup. Your father will see right through that"

"I guess we will have to make the most of our collective brain power this week then." Holly broke in and shut down the starting argument. "And if Zack does an apprenticeship with Professor Andy then we will have next week too."

"Let's see what the Headmaster says and go from there." Desmond suggested as their food arrived.

The table broke into chatter on much lighter topics for the rest of breakfast but Claire picked at her food. Her friends had all become so important to her over the last year. The idea of facing any of this without them was weird. Could she do this without them?

CHAPTER 3

Claire felt a bit of deja vu as they exited the dining hall through the side door and walked down the hallway towards the Headmaster's office. It was only yesterday that they had done this same trip to find out she was a Champion of the Realm.

Now she walked the stone hallway with her vision and she took in the tall arching windows on one side of the hallway. The light they let enter spilled onto extravagant murals depicting what Claire guessed were scenes from Unitam's history. Witches cast spells, shifters phased in and out of their animal forms, dragons flew in the painted skies above. But no Elves or Fae dotted the mural. They had been written out of history. Their stories were as unknown as Claire's was.

Soon the hallway ended along with the mural. Desmond had insisted that the Triad and Claire visit the Headmaster alone first with Claire's friends waiting in the library. Holly squeezed Claire's hand lightly as they passed her and the Triad and headed down the opposite hallway towards the library.

A brown-haired witch with her hair pulled back in a tight bun sat at the desk in front of the Headmaster's office.

"Hi, Gwen," Desmond smiled, "is the Headmaster in?"

"Desmond." Gwen greeted and Claire recognized her voice which was warmer than her stern appearance, "Weren't you all just here yesterday?"

"You know me, always in trouble," Desmond charmed and Claire frowned. He was just being friendly but the smile that bloomed on the older witch's face had Claire's insides twisting.

"You all can go on in." Gwen said, jolting Claire from her twisting thoughts.

Now her stomach twisted for a new reason. Her Triad was so sure the Headmaster would have all the answers but he didn't yesterday when the Academy called her to be a Champion of the Realm. What difference would one night have made?

Desmond opened the door to the Headmaster's office, the thick wood sliding open soundlessly. Everett placed a hand on the small of Claire's back, the warmth a welcome shield as they stepped into the cooler air of the office. Headmaster Dorian's office was even more imposing with her vision. Floor to ceiling bookshelves lined the wall behind the Headmaster's desk stacked full of colorful titles. The windows were framed by green curtains that were drawn back to let the sunlight in. The light fell in columns against the floor, warming it but causing a disconcerting contrast as Everett guided her into the office and to one of the dark red chairs in front of the Headmaster's desk.

Headmaster Dorian himself was a tall man, even sitting behind his desk. He filled the large chair quite easily. His black hair was cropped short to his head and his short beard was trimmed neatly. He wore glasses, like Zack, but his were smaller than Zack's and he took them off as they approached the desk.

"You can see." Headmaster Dorian said, studying her like she was studying him.

Claire nodded, "I can."

"When did this happen?" The Headmaster directed the question to her men and Claire felt the slightest twinge of irritation.

"Yesterday." She lifted her chin slightly. "At the market when I touched an Elven dagger."

Headmaster Dorian smiled slightly and dipped his head at her as if in apology. "An Elven dagger?" He leaned forward, elbows on the desk, hands clasped in front of him.

"A matching set, it seems, to the Fae dagger Malcolm gifted her." Desmond said, sitting in the chair next to Claire's. That was a lot of information that Desmond gave the Headmaster in a simple sentence. The Triad seemed sure of the Headmaster's loyalty but Claire had a twinge of doubt.

Before Desmond could say more, Claire spoke up, "My Triad seems to think you are trustworthy and you will help us find answers."

Instead of taking her words as an insult, Headmaster Dorian met her gaze evenly. "And what do you think?"

Claire shrugged, "I don't know you well enough to say for certain. I'd like to believe that what my classmates and Triad say about you is true, but the information we are searching for is dangerous."

Claire could feel the eyes of her men on her but she didn't move her gaze from the Headmaster. She hoped her men didn't take this as an insult that Claire didn't believe them but if she wanted to be a Champion of the Realm, or if she didn't have a choice or not on being a Champion of the Realm, then Claire had to start standing on her own.

The Headmaster dipped his chin slightly in a nod of respect. "You have my oath as the Headmaster of this Academy that I mean no harm to you or yours. My loyalty is to this Academy and its students."

There was still room for loopholes in his statement but the thread of magic that the Headmaster weaved in his words was telling. Magical oaths were taken seriously in Unitam and not offered often. Claire called a thread of her own magic up from her center and imagined it flowing up her throat and into her voice, "I accept your oath."

"Tell me everything." The Headmaster said.

For the second time in twenty-four hours, Claire and her Triad relayed the story of the Market and Claire's reaction to both daggers.

"Who all knows about this?"

"My friends, Holly, Bethany, Cody, and Zack, you and my Triad." Claire said.

"That's a large group." Headmaster Dorian said.

"My friends are loyal," Claire said. They knew the stakes and would never betray Claire, she was sure of it.

"They might be loyal to you here but their lives are not their own until they graduate. Their coven leaders and alphas might present problems."

"What do you suggest?" Desmond asked. Claire tensed. They weren't considering harming her friends?

"They haven't left the Academy yet, correct?"

Desmond nodded.

"Before they leave, have them come to my office and I will have them swear a magical oath to the Academy. It's neutral magic should override any command their leaders will ask of them. It's not perfect but it's the best option."

"Holly was trying to get Zack an apprenticeship at Brandlevine with Professor Andy if she wasn't staying at the school." Claire suggested.

"That could work," the Headmaster said, "I'm not usually a fan of expanding the group that knows a secret like this but Andrea and Helene would be two powerful allies. I can relieve them of their duties here for the summer if needed."

"We had hoped to stay on campus," Malcolm said, "the Academy is better protected and offers more resources."

"More resources without strings attached, you mean?" The Headmaster arched an eyebrow at Malcolm.

Malcolm grumbled, "Our families are no secret to you, Dorian."

"I know them well. Yes, you have permission to stay at the Academy as long as you need. I worry though that the answers you seek will not be found within its walls."

"When that moment comes, we will evaluate where to go next." Desmond said.

Headmaster Dorian nodded. "Well, let's take care of the oaths of your friends first. I assume they are somewhere close?"

"In the library, Headmaster." Claire said.

"Perfect. Send them in so you can start hunting for answers."

CHAPTER 4

"The Headmaster knows about this?" Andy asked sharply, looking at Desmond.

"Yes." He nodded. "He knows we would benefit from your help."

Claire sat between Holly and Bethany on one of the library couches. Malcolm and Desmond stood behind them. Cody and Zack took the couch directly across from them. Everett leaned up against a bookcase off to Claire's right and Professor Andy and Professor Helene stood in the gap the couches created.

After swearing magical oaths, her friends and Triad had retreated to the library where Headmaster Dorian had called Andy and Helene to join them. When they arrived, Desmond threw up a privacy spell that Andy reinforced.

Claire took time to study her professors now that classes were over and she could see. Professor Helene was tall and willowy with soft brown hair that reached the small of her back in a loose braid. Professor Andy was shorter with fiery red hair that was thrown messily up into a bun. The women stood close together, casually brushing with soft touches.

When they learned Claire could see, both women enveloped

Claire in similar but different hugs. Claire had teared up a bit actually when Helene cupped her cheeks and told her she knew she was special.

Special was never a word used to describe Claire. Ever. Small. Unimportant. Freak. Those were words she was familiar with. The words popping up the last few weeks like special, important, destined, those were foreign to Claire.

"What do you need our help with?" Andy asked.

"Claire needs to learn to use and control her magic now that the bindings are loosened. We are also searching for more information on Champions of the Realm so we can know what to expect. The Headmaster has offered full access to the library as well as his personal collection."

"I can search my collection as well." Andy nodded. "The Stonemont Triad are powerful warriors though, what help do you need with training?"

Desmond rubbed the back of his neck. Claire had a feeling he wasn't used to having all the answers. "We've never trained or fought with Fae or Elves."

"We only taught here a few years before the Fae and Elven students were called home." Andy said.

Helene looked at Claire, "Do they know?" She was asking if the group knew about Claire's Energy Reading abilities.

Claire nodded and Helene squeezed Andy's shoulder lightly, "Claire needs our help with her Energy Reading abilities."

Andy's head snapped towards Claire. "You can read Energies?"

Claire shrugged, "Not well."

"She's being modest," Everett said, "before her sight returned, she was using her abilities to train in combat."

"You knew?" Andy asked Helene. Helene rubbed her upper back to reassure her partner.

"Claire came to me early in the year asking about it. I gave her a book but didn't think anything of it until just now. With the questions regarding Claire's heritage, it makes sense."

Helene and Andy shared a long look before turning back to the group. "We will do everything we can to help." Helene said.

"Are you staying at the Academy?" Andy asked.

"For now," Desmond said, "if we move, the Headmaster said he would release you from your summer duties if needed."

"Zack needs an apprenticeship," Claire spoke up.

Andy narrowed her eyes at Zack, "To avoid your coven leader I imagine?" Unfortunately, Zack belonged to the same coven as Brent did, the Ashcraft Coven who usually had a mixture of fire and air witches. Brent was not a nice person and Claire could only imagine what Brent's father, the Coven Leader, was like.

Zack nodded, "He's the wildcard out of all of our coven or pack leaders."

Andy nodded. "I will get the paperwork drawn up this afternoon and sent to the Ashcraft coven this evening."

"For those of us that don't always pay attention in History class," Cody said, "what baseline information do we know about the Elves, Fae, and Great War?"

Claire smiled. Cody liked to act like he wasn't smart and didn't pay attention and then turned around and used the word baseline in the same sentence.

Helene started, "The Elves and Fae have always been reclusive compared to the other races. The building of the Academy was their greatest collaborative project after the Alliance over 2,000 years ago."

"The Fae are known for their metalworking and trade for Fae weapons was highly sought after." Professor Andy said, "Even then, the Fae preferred to work with only those they trusted which meant individuals and not entire clans or covens. Some saw that as a slight to the Alliance but since the weapons were valuable, there was only minor grumbling."

"What about the Elves?" Claire asked.

"The Elves primary trade resources were their medicinal potions and salves created from plants found deep in their forests. They were also feared archers, as the Realm experienced during the Great War. Very stealthy, our warriors described them as being here one moment and gone the next."

Andy paused and Claire arched an eyebrow. "That's it?" Surely there had to be more.

Andy laughed, "Like I said, both the Fae and Elves were reclusive. When the Great War started and the Elves and Fae recalled their students and teachers from the Academy, all books and texts minus very general ones disappeared from the Academy as well. Whether it was intentional or not, it was a very smart move."

"What about during the Great War?" Cody asked, "We know that Unitam won but if the Fae and Elves were such fearsome warriors, that doesn't make sense."

"Simply," Andy said, "It was a numbers game. For all of their abilities, shifters and witches outnumber the Fae and Elves heavily. Add in that the dragons were on our side as well and that the Fae and Elven territories are on opposite ends of the Realm, it became simply a matter of time until we won."

Something about Andy's explanation didn't sit right with Claire but there was so much missing information from it that Claire couldn't narrow down what it was about that felt off. All she knew is her magic was restless and she was learning to trust in that feeling.

"Why did the Great War start? What happened to the Fae and Elves after it ended?" she asked.

Desmond answered her question, "The Fae and Elves started withholding trade and demanding a higher cost for the items. Tensions started rising and boiled over in the Market resulting in the deaths of a witch and an Elven trader. The Council tried to sort it out internally but the Fae and Elven representatives had too much pride and walked out of the negotiations. Tensions kept rising and the remaining members of the Council ordered the assets of Fae and Elven traders seized in retaliation. It all escalated from there."

Claire frowned. Again, there was something about that description that made her magic restless. It wasn't out of the Realm for what Desmond was saying to be true. As they had learned in history class this last year, each race had let pride guide them at one point or another.

"So we know nothing useful about either Elves or Fae," Bethany concluded bluntly.

"Not nothing," Holly said.

"Nothing useful." Bethany repeated. "We know why the Great War started and some basics about the Fae and Elves but nothing that answers our questions from last night."

Claire could feel Desmond wanting to argue so she spoke quickly, "We just have to look at it as one big research project with lots of pieces. We need more information on the Fae and Elves, on magical bindings of power, on Energy Readers, and on Champions of the Realm."

"Is that it?" Cody teased and Claire laughed with the others.

Desmond took charge. "Andy, Helene and I can check our personal libraries for any books on those topics. The rest of you can check the Academy's library."

Claire remembered something from a research project last year, "We won't find many books on the Elves or Fae."

"Why not?" Holly asked.

"I was searching for information on them for a paper for History class and the librarian said that most books disappeared at the start of the Great War."

Andy nodded, "The working theory on that is that the Elves and Fae took them home when they recalled their students to prevent our side from having their secrets."

Claire nodded, "That's what the librarian said. There are

only a few books left and they are all very basic. To be honest, I wouldn't be surprised if the information in them is inaccurate."

"Why would you say that?" Zack asked, pushing his glasses up on his nose.

Claire shrugged, "I was thinking about it after the paper. Some of the information didn't make sense and if I was a species with small numbers facing a massive war, I might also leave some disinformation around."

The group stared at her and Claire blushed. "What?"

"Just admiring your dark side, little witch." Desmond said gleefully.

Claire let out a nervous laugh, "It's really not that evil."

Holly squeezed her hand. "It's not evil to want to protect someone." She said, simultaneously reassuring Claire and admonishing Desmond. Claire squeezed her hand back in gratitude. Holly was always so in tune with Claire's feelings as an empath.

If she was truly Elven or Fae, she understood where they were coming from at the start of the Great War. If they were desperate to protect themselves, removing information or leaving inaccurate information would be a good trick.

Looking around at her friends and Triad, Claire realized she agreed with Holly wholeheartedly. She would gladly go over to the 'dark side' if it meant protecting the ones she loved.

* * *

Several hours later, Cody's groan echoed around the empty library. Claire would have smiled if she wasn't feeling the exact same way. She rose from the small window seat, stretching her arms over her head and twisting side to side. Everett appeared out of the bookshelves and placed a hand on the small of her back. "Find anything?" He asked.

Claire shook her head. She had found the small space and

had drawn the curtains, preferring the darkness and letting the solitude of the small window seat block the sound of her reading spell from the others.

When they had started their research hours earlier, Claire had discovered a small problem. While at the orphanage, Claire had been taught the shape of the letters and words and could write just fine but when she opened that first book to read, the small letters on the page seemed to swim in her vision as her eyes struggled to sort them into words so she could read. As if sensing her struggle, Everett had placed a gentle hand on her shoulder and then guided her to this window seat. There, she started the reading spell and practiced following along with her eyes.

She rubbed her eyes and Everett moved his hand from the small of her back to the base of her neck, fingers digging in small circles there, relieving the pressure. Claire almost forgot his question at the relief his fingers were providing.

"The book mentions different Champions of the Realm, but no specifics. It'll talk about which events they were at in history but nothing about their involvement in those events."

Claire paused and Everett waited for her to continue. "I wonder if there are personal accounts of those events we could find."

"Like journals?" He asked.

"Like journals." Claire confirmed. "They might have more details about the events and the Champions."

"It's a good idea." Everett smiled at her and Claire smiled back. His hair, which she had been informed from a whisper by Bethany, was a platinum blonde, so light it was almost white. She reached a hand up to brush a stray curl from his forehead and Everett purred softly.

His purr was interrupted by Claire's stomach grumbling, loudly. Blushing, she put a hand to her stomach and Everett laughed softly. "Come on, little mate. Let's get you fed. I think everyone's done enough research for today."

They walked back to the main part of the library where the rest of the group had gotten comfortable. Malcolm had pulled a small table with a few chairs over from another part of the library. Bethany was lying on one of the couches upside down reading from a small book while Holly took up the other half of the couch, her feet tucked up against her as she leaned against the side.

Cody was lying on the floor, his head a few feet from Bethany's head, his hand stealthily reaching out to tug on one of Bethany's curls. Claire smiled. She was going to have to corner Bethany soon about what was going on between her and Cody.

Her smile dimmed slightly. She was going to have to do that soon before her friends left for the summer. It was going to be weird not seeing them everyday. They had become such a big part of her life and helped her feel like she belonged here. Without their support, what would happen?

Bethany's shriek of outrage followed by the thump of her book against Cody's shoulders broke Claire from her sad thoughts.

"Hey, be careful with the books." Zack said from his position on the other couch.

"Careful with the books? What about being careful with Cody?" Cody complained.

"Don't dish it out if you can't take it," Zack smirked.

"Exactly," Bethany said, "You had it coming." She gracefully flipped her feet over her head and rolled off the couch. "Alright, I can't take any more studying, sorry, Claire."

"Don't be sorry." Claire said, "We were just coming to find you and see if we wanted to break for the night."

"Yes, please," Cody groaned, "I've done more research today then I've done all year."

"Why does that not surprise me, Mr. Clawmoon." Professor Andy came around the corner followed by Desmond.

"That's because I'm a straightforward person, Professor." Cody grinned cheekily.

Claire's stomach rumbled again and she blushed as all eyes turned to her.

"Sounds like dinnertime," Desmond teased as he approached, placing a kiss on her forehead.

"Have we found anything?" Claire asked.

"Helene is keeping a list of any relevant information and other resources to check into but it's a short list." Professor Andy said.

"Claire had the idea of looking into journals or other personal accounts of events involving Champions of the Realm." Everett said.

"That's a good idea, Claire." Professor Andy said warmly. "I will have Helene add it to the list."

"So we are going to be spending the next few weeks reading?" Bethany asked.

"Bethany," Holly chided.

"What? I mean that's fine but it seems that this information is being hidden maybe intentionally."

Desmond and Professor Andy exchanged looks.

"That might be the case," Desmond said, "so we might take a slightly different approach. We should still search for more information but also focus on what we can control."

"And that is?" Claire asked.

"Training you in your magic and Energy Reading." Desmond said. "That's going to be the most helpful course of action until we find more information."

"You get to spend more time with me, little treasure," Malcolm stole her into his arms and Claire smiled up at him.

"There will be a rotation," Desmond rolled his eyes. "You will continue combat training with Malcolm and Everett and your magic lessons with me. Andy and Helene are going to help us with your Energy Reading lessons as well."

Claire smiled at Professor Andy, "Thank you."

Professor Andy smiled back, "It's no problem, Claire. Now, I think you all should break for dinner before the kitchen closes for the night."

The group packed up quickly and returned the furniture to its original place before heading to the dining hall. Although they still hadn't found the answers they were searching for, at least now they had a plan.

CHAPTER 5

Claire was not a huge fan of the plan, she decided as she hit dirt again in the Combat Arena. If she thought Malcolm was tough on her before, that was nothing compared to now. Over the last two weeks, Claire had accumulated more bruises than she had ever gotten. Luckily, Professor Helene had taught her which plants were good for healing bruises during her sessions with her and Professor Andy.

She groaned as she rolled over onto her back, muscles aching. The sun overhead caused a halo-like effect on Malcolm's head, his brown hair dusting his shoulders. "I thought the point of training was to use all of my abilities including Energy Reading?" she grumbled.

"And like we've discussed, reliance upon magic in a fight is a good way to get your cute butt kicked if you ever don't have access to it." Malcolm said as he helped her up. "You almost had me that time."

Claire huffed, knowing he was trying to make her feel better. "Not really."

"You're getting better," Malcolm said.

"But not fast enough." Claire tried to keep the whine of frustration out of her voice. She could feel her body getting stronger but once up against a warrior like Malcolm, she was severely outmatched. If she truly was supposed to be a Champion of the Realm, she would be up against elite fighters all the time. There was no way she was going to be ready in time.

Everett appeared in the corner of her vision like he sensed her frustration. He always seemed to be deeply in tune with her feelings. Maybe just her in general Claire thought to herself, smiling.

"Maybe it's time for a break?" Everett suggested. Malcolm looked like he wanted to protest for a second, her dragon had been single-minded in his focus on her training.

"Fine," he conceded, "I have to reach out to my father anyways."

"Is everything okay?" Claire touched his arm.

"Everything's fine, little treasure. I usually call him once a month to update him on things here."

Claire hesitated, "Does he know about me?" Her Triad's families was a subject they had not talked about much.

"He does, and he's anxious to meet you." Malcolm pulled her into his arms. "But only when you are ready. He can be a pushy man, my mother too, but we won't let them overwhelm you."

Claire nodded, her hands tracing the stitching on his shirt. "I'd like to meet them one day, all of your families," she looked over at Everett, "but..." she trailed off. What if their families didn't approve of her or thought she was too much trouble for their sons?

"When you're ready, little treasure." Malcolm was firm.

"Okay," she said, frowning. Again, she was supposed to be a badass Champion of the Realm and her mates' families had her running scared.

"In the meantime, we can tell you more about them," Everett said, coming up behind her and placing his hands on her shoulders.

Now she was sandwiched between the two men and the bonds between them tugged with warmth. Before Claire could get lost in the feeling however, Malcolm brushed a kiss over her forehead and stepped away. She caught herself when she went to step towards him. Malcolm seemed to be holding back from her. He was the only one of her Triad she hadn't kissed yet although he gave the best hugs.

Everett squeezed her shoulders lightly. "How about a picnic lunch?"

She turned in his arms and grinned up at him, "At our spot?"

Everett smiled down at her, his platinum hair practically glowing in the sun. "At our spot," he confirmed.

"That sounds wonderful. Can I change first?"

Everett nodded, "I'll walk you to our suite and then go to get lunch."

Claire wanted to say she could walk to the suite by herself but she knew it would be wasted breath. Ever since the incident during Combat finals, the men had rarely let her out of their sight. Everett only left her alone once she was safely inside the suite.

Looking around the room, she frowned. She hadn't seen Desmond all morning and when she had gone to bed last night, the light to his workroom was still on. Bypassing the hallway that led to their rooms, she stopped outside his workroom's door and rapped lightly.

"Come in," Desmond called.

Claire pushed the heavy door open, the hinges squeaking lightly.

Desmond looked up from his worktable, smiling when he saw her. "Little witch! To what do I owe the pleasure?"

Claire smiled back at him but it was a small smile. Despite his smile, Desmond looked exhausted with dark circles under his eyes. "Did you sleep at all last night?" She asked.

Desmond looked sheepish as he sat back in his chair and

held his arms out to her. She crossed to him, settling in his lap and arching a brow at him expectantly.

Desmond smiled at her arched brow and looked back to his desk covered in papers. "I might have gotten caught up in some things."

"Desmond," Claire chided softly, brushing a hand across his brow, "you need sleep."

"I will, I will. I just need to find this one piece of information for this spell and I'll take a break."

"No, you need sleep now," Claire said, standing up from his lap and tugging on his hands until he stood. "The spell will be here when you wake up."

"Are you offering to take a nap with me, little witch?" Desmond asked, stepping closer into her space.

Claire blushed, "No. It's not that I wouldn't take a nap with you, it's just that Everett is grabbing us a picnic lunch."

"Ooh, a picnic? I guess that beats a nap." Desmond said, guiding her out of the workroom.

"Promise me you'll sleep? I'll wake you when we get back."

"Or you can crawl into bed with me." Desmond winked at her and Claire smacked him playfully on the chest.

"Only if you go straight to bed right now."

"Well now I'll have to," Desmond teased, "with the promise of you joining me later, how could I not?"

"Go!" Claire rolled her eyes playfully, watching him disappear into his room.

She entered hers and crossed over to the wardrobe. Malcolm had bought her quite the collection of clothes and ignored her protests when she found out just how many he had purchased. She had finally gotten him to agree that he wouldn't buy anything else without her.

She pulled a pair of pants that cut off at her knee and a soft green shirt out of the wardrobe. The green reminded her of Everett's eyes and she had a feeling he would be pleased with her choice. She washed off quickly, wiping away the sweat and sand from the arena.

Exiting her room, she entered the living area just in time to see Everett enter with a basket on his arm. His eyes flared as he took in her outfit, the green appearing more vibrant than usual.

"You look lovely," he said, holding the door open for her as she approached.

"Thank you," Claire smiled at him, accepting his arm as they made their way down the stairs.

Navigating around the Academy was odd now with her sight. She had relied so much on feeling before that having her sight almost made her clumsier. Stairs had been one of the most difficult things to navigate with the uneven surfaces messing with her eyes so Claire often still relied on feeling her way around.

Zack had mentioned that it was her 'depth of vision' that made it more difficult. Claire called it a good excuse to touch her Triad.

Exiting the dormitory, Claire paused for a moment, letting the sun warm her face and reveling in the cool breeze that tried to chase the summer heat away. Summer must make everything vibrant, she decided. Everything had always seemed richer to her other senses during summer and having her sight back confirmed that.

Everett led them down the familiar path into the forest. The old, wide trees standing guard around the small clearing. Claire touched one of them with the palm of her hand, feeling its ancient energy sing to her. Her magic rose inside her, dancing playfully like the leaves of the tree. It whispered up from her center dancing down her arm and into the tree, adding a musical note to the tree's song.

Pulling her hand back, Claire frowned down at it. That was the first time her magic had pushed back into something she was Reading. In her practice with Andy and Helene, they had mainly focused on Reading and identifying energies, not interacting with them. In fact, neither Andy nor Helene had even mentioned that interacting back was possible.

"Claire," Everett's voice came from behind her. She turned to see he had laid out their picnic while she had been distracted. "Is everything okay?"

Not wanting to spoil their date, Claire smiled at him, "Everything's perfect."

She crossed the clearing and knelt on the black and white checkered blanket. Everett was sitting with his back to the tree. He reached across the blanket and tugged her wrist lightly until she was resting her back against his front. The top of her head barely came up to his chin as she settled back against him, twisting slightly so she could see his face.

The greenery of the forest around them made his green eyes stand out. His strong jaw was softened as a smile stretched over his pink lips. His very kissable lips.

"What are you thinking about?" He asked, eyes dancing down at her.

"I was thinking we should switch our end of date ritual to the beginning of our dates." Claire said with a grin.

"Why limit ourselves to having it only at the beginning or the end?" Everett whispered, needing no other prompting as he leaned down and captured her lips with his.

Claire stretched her neck back, twisting in his arms so he could kiss her deeper. She sighed into the kiss when his teeth captured her bottom lip, tugging gently and causing all sorts of sparks to dance in her stomach. He traced a calloused hand up and down her forearm making her realize she was gripping his shirt in a death grip. He pulled back slightly so their breaths mixed and Claire had never felt more alive in a moment than she did right now.

"I don't think we should limit that ritual at all," she murmured.

"Is that so?"

"Mmhmm," Claire made a sound, enjoying being in his arms. He brushed his lips over hers again softly, his breath exchanging with hers and causing a pleasurable warmth to spread from Claire's center.

Unfortunately, her stomach always knew how to ruin a moment. It grumbled softly under one of Everett's hands and Claire frowned as Everett let out a low laugh.

"Let's get you fed and then we can practice that ritual a bit more." Everett said, reaching for the picnic basket and dragging it closer.

"Malcolm always says 'practice makes perfect.'" Claire smiled.

Everett unpacked the basket with one hand easily, keeping the other arm wrapped around Claire. He handed her a thick sandwich that made Claire's mouth water. The Academy kitchen was truly a marvel.

They ate in silence, enjoying the food and the sounds of the forest. One of the things that Claire liked about Everett was his appreciation for the silence. Some of her favorite memories over the last year with him was just sitting in silence, either reading or just enjoying his company.

After she finished the sandwich, she shook out the small cloth it was wrapped in and tucked it back into the picnic basket. Settling back into his arms, she asked, "Tell me about your family?"

Everett opened his mouth to reply but slammed it shut as his eyes snapped towards the forest. Immediately, every muscle tensed and Claire scrambled to sit up. Something had triggered her gryphon's senses and by his reaction something bad. Everett moved to a crouch in front of her, pressing her back into the tree behind them. After a few seconds of silence, Claire whispered, "What is it?"

"I don't know," Everett whispered back, his mouth barely moving, "But it's not the patrols."

Claire cursed her decision to leave her daggers at home. Even if she wasn't supposed to practice with them yet, she should have at least listened to her instinct and carried them. Now they were out in the forest with an unknown something lurking near them and she was defenseless. She closed her eyes and strained to hear what Everett was hearing.

As soon as her world was plunged into darkness, she took a deep breath and focused on her hearing that Cody kept telling her was as good as a shifter's.

There.

She could hear something crashing through the underbrush. It got louder as soon as she focused on it, as if the thing no longer cared about stealth. She opened her eyes as the crashing noises got closer on a path to the clearing.

Everett stood before her now, a dagger in his hand. Where did that come from? Did he call it? Claire would have to ask Desmond when they weren't preparing to face off against an unknown.

Maybe it was just a forest creature, she reasoned with herself. A deer was about to come into the clearing and then she and Everett would laugh about how they overreacted. Claire tried to breathe deeper at that thought, willing her breath to not follow the track of her racing heart.

When the thing finally crashed through the clearing though, Claire lost the battle with panic. Standing at over six feet tall, the creature stood on four legs letting out a roar that was sure to be heard back at the Academy. It shook its head at them, the jagged horns that jutted from the top of its head shining in the light that trickled through the leaves. Large gleaming teeth were bared in a snarl as the beast started to stalk closer. It's body was a reddish orange color with black stripes on its legs.

"Claire," Everett's voice was insistent, making her realize he had been trying to get her attention. "Claire, you need to get back to the Academy."

"I can't leave you!" Panic clawed at her throat. There was no way Everett would be able to take on that creature alone.

"I'll be fine. You need to run. Now."

Claire was torn. If she could make it back to the dorm to get Desmond, Everett could hold it off until then. Claire inched back a step and the beast locked onto her, letting out a roar. His red eyes tracked Claire's every movement. Well, shit.

"I don't think he cares much about you," she whispered to Everett.

"Fuck." Everett inched in front of Claire, his steps slow and seamless as to not anger the beast anymore than it currently was. "I'm going to shift and then you are going to run. Do you understand? Go straight to the suite and stay there."

Before Claire could reply, Everett exploded into his gryphon from one step to the next. Claire was momentarily stunned. She hadn't ever seen Everett shift before, she realized. His gryphon was huge, at least eight feet tall and almost solid white with black tips to his wings and the occasional black spots decorating the fur of his body. His wingspan stretched double his height as he shook them out and roared a challenge back at the beast.

Claire forgot to run until Everett's gryphon turned his head and chirped at her. She found her feet again and lunged around the tree. The beast pushed off his powerful hindquarters and leapt towards her. She let out a cry as Everett tackled it out of the air, throwing it off its course.

Both the gryphon and the beast slammed into the ground six feet from Claire. She backed away again and the beast snapped its head towards her, its red eyes locking onto hers. A deep feeling of wrongness settled over Claire's skin, like a painful itch she couldn't scratch. It let out a snarl as she took another step back and shook off Everett, kicking him away with its legs.

Claire kept backing up along the path, not wanting to give the creature her back. She tripped over a root on the path and landed heavily on her back. She quickly scrambled up. That root had not been there earlier when she and Everett had walked this path to the clearing she was sure of it. Magic was at work here.

Everett's gryphon let out a battle cry as it leapt between Claire and the beast. He spread his wings out and fluffed the fur on his back, making him appear to grow in size. Claire sucked in a breath at the intimidating sight.

One that didn't seem to deter the beast, however. He lunged again and the gryphon met him halfway. Claire scrambled to her feet again and stepped off the path towards one of the ancient trees. There was something off here. Even though Everett told her to run, Claire couldn't leave him, not when something was wrong.

She tore her eyes away from the fight to glance at the root that had tripped her. Her eyes widened. It was gone. Claire felt her body get hot as anger rose in her. Who or what was trying to keep her here? Who sent the beast and wanted her dead?

A roar forced her attention back to the fight. The beast lunged at the gryphon, swiping a paw with massive claws at the gryphon's side. The gryphon let out a shriek of pain as the claws made impact. Its white fur bloomed with red as the gryphon staggered.

"No!" Claire screamed. She fell back into the tree behind her, feeling the ancient energy dance along her back. Without thinking, she yanked on it hard, pulling it into her center. She needed Malcolm and Desmond. Everett needed Malcolm and Desmond.

She focused on the feeling for the bonds between them and yanked on them hard just as the beast launched a powerful kick at Everett's injured side, sending the gryphon crashing to the ground.

"Everett," she cried and leapt from the tree, desperate to get to him and make sure he was okay.

The beast leapt in front of her path to Everett. Claire narrowed her eyes. "That is enough!" She growled at it.

It answered her with a growl as it prowled closer to her. Her magic and the ancient energy swirled within her, trying to guide Claire to do something. But what. She took a deep breath, not moving her eyes from the beast's red gaze and dropped into her magic center. As soon as she dropped, she realized what it was trying to tell her.

When she had pulled the ancient tree's energy into herself she had tapped into a much larger network. Trees in a forest were all connected, their root systems as intertwined as their branches. By pulling one tree's energy into herself, she had gained access to that network.

She grinned as the idea came to her and the beast paused. Everett's gryphon let out a weak growl, trying to distract the beast's attention from her. Claire could also feel the bonds between her other men growing stronger as they closed the distance. The beast wasn't going to wait for them, however, and neither was Claire.

She pulled her magic up from her center, the bindings loose enough that it came easily. She layered her own magic with the tree's ancient energy and focused on the network of energy immediately surrounding the beast.

There.

She tugged hard on the energy and a root exploded from the ground beneath the beast's feet, smacking into its sensitive belly with a crack.

The beast roared in pain and jumped back. The root danced in the air, waiting for Claire's next command. She paused briefly as she thought it through. She didn't want to kill anything, even the murderous beast. There was something bigger at work here and they needed answers.

The beast looked at the gryphon and Claire narrowed her eyes. That was not an option. She tugged on the magic again and three more roots popped up from the ground between Everett and the beast. She started pulling more roots up around the beast, pulling them from the ground into the air until they reached over the beast and weaved above it.

The beast roared as it realized what Claire's plan was. Every time it lunged for an opening, Claire tugged again on the ancient network. Each root she raised though was becoming harder and harder as the network resisted. She was running out of energy and magic. Desperation pushed her as well as panic as she kept pulling up the roots, crafting a cage for the beast.

There was one opening left and both Claire and the beast saw it at the same time. The beast lunged for it and Claire tugged on the root with every bit of magic she had, it responded sluggishly and she poured all her focus into it. Desmond and Malcolm chose this moment to appear in the clearing, swords drawn and magic at the ready. Claire glanced at them briefly, her focus wavering for a fraction of a second but it was enough. Instead of the root shooting up to become the final bar of the cage, the delay caused it to pierce the beast's chest, its roar turning to a gurgle as the magic and life faded from its body.

When the last sounds from the beast faded away, an eerie quiet settled over the clearing. Claire was in shock. She hadn't meant to kill it. She just wanted it to stop.

"Claire," Malcolm's growly voice was uncharacteristically soft which added to the eeriness of the quiet.

She turned her head to look at him. He sheathed his swords at his back and approached her carefully. "I didn't mean to kill it." she said as he reached her.

"It's okay, little treasure," he said.

"I was just trying to cage it." She hadn't meant to kill it. She couldn't look away from the beast's body though. Its lifeless body.

"I know." He tugged her into his arms and that broke Claire's focus from the beast.

"Everett," she cried out and struggled against Malcolm.

"He's okay, he's okay," Malcolm kept his arms around her but moved with her to Desmond and Everett.

Desmond was crouched over the gryphon, his hands a light blue as he soaked the gryphon's side with magic. Claire fell to her knees at the gryphon's head, her hand racing out to stroke the soft feathers around his beak.

"I'm so sorry," she whispered.

The gryphon chirped softly, pushing his head into her hand.

"He's going to be fine, little witch." Desmond placed a gentle hand on her arm. "His gryphon heals fast. He'll be fine when he shifts back."

Claire was hearing his words but also not hearing them. It felt like she was in a fog.

"Everett, you're going to have to shift back." Malcolm's voice was hazy. "She's not going to believe you're okay until she sees you."

The gryphon chirped again and Claire could feel hands tugging her away as a soft white glow of magic covered the beast. She fought the hands, trying to get to Everett but they held steady. When the glow faded, Everett laid on the ground, breathing heavily.

"Everett!" She slammed into his chest and his arms caught her close.

"I'm okay, little mate." Everett's voice was a bit shaky.

Claire pulled back to examine his side and then her cheeks heated when she realized he wasn't wearing any pants. She averted her eyes while Everett's chest rumbled in a silent laugh.

Desmond's laugh was not as silent. "Let me help you out with that," he said. The soft shimmer of magic glowed again as Desmond conjured him some pants.

A shout drew Desmond and Malcolm's attention but not

Claire's as she traced the angry pink marks on Everett's side with her eyes. That had been too close. She had almost been too late.

The Headmaster, Professor Andy and Professor Helene came running into the clearing.

"The wards tripped." The Headmaster said.

"Is that a Felua?" Professor Andy stared at the beast.

Everett paused Claire's obsessing over his injuries by placing his hand over hers and getting to his feet. He placed an arm around Claire's waist, keeping her close and Claire burrowed into his side. Her brain still felt foggy, the adrenaline from the fight was wearing off leaving her shaky.

She didn't want to look at the beast again, the Felua. Didn't want to see what she had done. But Everett had almost gotten killed because of her. She could push aside her weakness and be strong for him.

She straightened from his side and Everett frowned down at her. She traced a hand over his jaw, smoothing the frown before turning to look at the beast. She tried to hold down her shudder. Up close, the beast looked even larger. It towered over her, the top of its head an easy two feet above Claire's head. Its eyes were still open, still tinged with the red even though the light had faded from them.

"It doesn't make any sense," Professor Helene stepped up next to Claire.

"What do you mean?" Claire turned to her.

"Felua are usually solitary animals. Protective over their territory but not openly hostile. They live deep in the Elven forest. We haven't had a sighting at the Academy in centuries. Not even before the Great War."

Claire turned back to the beast. What would make a solitary beast venture so far from its home. "That's why something felt wrong." she said half to herself.

"Wrong?" Desmond asked.

"Something felt wrong about it. The ferocity felt forced, unnatural." Claire struggled to find the words.

"Claire's right." Professor Andy said, standing up from where she was crouched by the beast. "This creature has been tampered with magically. Come look."

Claire pulled away from Everett and stepped next to Andy. She crouched with her and followed her pointed finger. On the underneath of the beast's belly was a black symbol that looked like it had been burned into the beast's fur. "What is that?"

Desmond crouched next to her and she turned to look at him. Her usually playful wizard was frowning deeply. "I've seen that symbol before, in books."

Andy nodded. "It's a dark compulsion symbol. It requires dark magic that is banned in Unitam. The skill required to place this spell is very rare and even then it is hard to place a regular compulsion spell. Especially on a solitary animal such as this one. From the placement, I would guess that whoever placed it, placed it in a trap on the forest floor and got the beast as it went over."

"That's awful." Claire felt sick. She placed a hand over her mouth as her stomach rolled. She had to kill a creature that wasn't even trying to hurt her.

Desmond must have read her face. He tugged her gently to her feet and cupped her face. "You had no choice." He murmured.

"Neither did it." Claire said back, stomach still churning, threatening to upheave the sandwich she had eaten earlier.

"No, but it would have killed you. Would have killed Everett. And you were just trying to keep it contained."

Claire knew he was trying to make her feel better but she couldn't shake the sick feeling in her stomach. She hadn't been fast enough, hadn't had enough control over her magic. Turning back to the creature, she forced herself to study every inch, to read the energy around it so she would never have to do this again.

"We will move the body," the Headmaster said, "and study the symbol."

He turned to the Triad and Claire. "I will up the patrol count but we might have to consider that the Academy is not the safest place for Claire anymore."

Desmond nodded. "We will discuss it in the morning." Claire could feel his worry in the bond, her awareness of the bonds seeming to have grown since she yanked on them earlier. They vibrated like a gentle tickle in her magic center.

Claire let her Triad lead her from the clearing still feeling like she was in a bit of a daze. Even when they entered the suite and she ducked into her bathroom to clean up and change, questions swirled in her mind so much that her movements were automatic.

Andy said whoever it was had to be very skilled but they must be heartless as well. Who would do that to any creature, take control of them like that and force it to leave its home and do terrible things? And why was it fixated on Claire?

CHAPTER 6

The itchy warmth that surrounded Claire when she woke up told her she had fallen asleep with her Triad. The feelings of safety that sleeping with them invoked warmed her heart but the heat they exuded was making her body uncomfortably warm and not in a good way. Like a woolen scratchy blanket. She kicked at the covers, trying to dislodge them. Instead of covers though, her feet hit someone's side and they let out a soft 'oof'.

She cracked open her eyes and then widened them. "Everett! I'm so sorry!" She said in a hushed whisper.

The sleepy gryphon smiled up at her and captured her feet, tugging the blanket off for her. "It's okay, little mate."

He reached over and nudged Desmond. "Desmond, make it cooler."

Desmond groaned sleepily but lifted his arm wrapped around Claire to draw a rune in the air. Almost instantly the air in the room started circulating and he placed his arm back over Claire, tugging her closer.

In her sleepy state, Claire had forgotten Desmond had

masteries in fire and air elements. She tried to go back to sleep with the cool air dancing over her skin, chasing the overwhelming heat away. After a few minutes of just laying there, she shifted against Desmond lightly as she rolled to her back. Turning her head, she studied Malcolm's sleeping face next to hers. His strong jaw and cheekbones made him look like he was carved out of stone, even in sleep. His lips were parted and soft puffs of breath danced across Claire's face when he exhaled. His shoulder-length brown hair laid messily across the pillow and Claire's fingers ached to push it back from his face but her arms were pinned to her side by Desmond's around her waist.

She glanced down at Everett's sleeping form. The angry red marks from yesterday's attack had faded overnight. Only thin silvery lines hinted that yesterday's events had even happened. Claire frowned. Yesterday's events shouldn't have happened. Elven beasts roaming close to the Academy was supposed to be impossible yet yesterday, someone had magically tampered with one, sending it to the Academy.

And to what end? Was Claire the target or was the Academy the target? If someone had meant to send the beast towards the Academy, were Claire and Everett just unwittingly in its path? Claire couldn't help the shiver that shook her body as she remembered how the beast's eyes tracked hers. The red glaze in them had been menacing and focused. She shouldn't kid herself. The beast had definitely been sent to look for her.

But what did that mean? Did that mean that the Elves were behind it? The beast could only be found in the Elven forests. Did that mean Claire wasn't Elven and only Fae? But then why did she have an Elven dagger? Or was that not even relevant?

"I can practically hear you thinking," Desmond's voice murmured in her ear.

She turned her gaze from the stone ceiling above their heads and met his blue eyes. This close, she could see they had hints of silver in them. "I didn't mean to wake you," She whispered. Desmond was already not sleeping enough, and was actually supposed to have been sleeping yesterday before the attack happened.

"It's fine, little witch." Desmond said, shifting closer and resting his forehead on hers. "Are you doing okay?"

This close, Claire knew she couldn't lie to him. She shook her head slightly. "I have so many questions."

"I know, little witch. Let's see if we can get some answers this morning. Why don't we wake the others and rustle up some breakfast before going to see the Headmaster?"

Claire nodded. She shifted in Desmond's arms and wiggled one of her own out of his hold. Gently, she removed the hair that had fallen across Malcolm's brow and then smoothed her thumb over one of his cheekbones. "Malcolm," she whispered softly.

His eyes opened, instantly alert, as his body tensed. When he focused on Claire, he softened. "What is it, little treasure?"

"We have to get up," Claire said.

Malcolm nodded, placing a soft kiss on her forehead before rolling away. Claire felt her lips tip into a frown. Why hadn't he kissed her yet?

Desmond must have been watching her face as he let out a soft chuckle. He placed a light kiss on her lips, kissing the pout away before also rolling away. "Wake our gryphon up, little witch."

Claire suspected that Everett had been awake since she accidentally kicked him and was only feigning sleep. As Malcolm and Desmond left the room, Claire sat up and crawled down to Everett. When she reached him, she let out a soft gasp as he rolled her underneath of him, confirming her theory.

"Good morning." She smiled.

"Good morning, little mate." Everett lowered his head and kissed her softly, brushing his lips across hers until Claire wanted to growl in frustration. Would none of her mates just kiss her already?

He pulled back and his teasing smile told her he knew exactly what he was doing. "Let's go get your questions answered."

The absence of his weight suddenly made Claire feel cold. She let herself lie in bed for another moment before heaving herself up and crossing to the bathroom.

She dressed quickly, splashing cold water on her face to chase the rest of the sleep away. When she entered the living room, smells of egg and bacon danced to her nose. Desmond was cooking in their small kitchen, Malcolm sitting at the table.

An arm slid around her waist and she leaned back into Everett. "You're sure you're okay?" She questioned him.

"I'm fine." He said as he guided her forward.

They ate quickly, the questions dancing in Claire's mind apparently also danced in her stomach and she was only able to eat a portion of what Desmond had put on her plate. Ignoring Malcolm's frown, she pushed the plate to Everett who quickly finished it for her.

It was time to get some answers.

* * *

"This isn't the first sighting of beasts that shouldn't be here."

The Headmaster's words had a heavy effect on the room. Claire could feel the weight of them settle like a heavy blanket.

"Explain." Malcolm growled. His protective instincts were probably riding his dragon hard.

"Other patrols have been reporting strange tracks and forest disturbances for a few months now."

Claire glanced at Everett. Wouldn't he have heard about this? Wasn't he in charge of patrols?

He shook his head at her look, "When we increased your

training, I handed over patrol duties to the Headmaster temporarily. I should still have been informed." He directed the last sentence to the Headmaster.

The Headmaster arched an eyebrow, "You were a little busy. Besides, we had no sighting of actual beasts. Just tracks and odd marks in the trees."

"Could you identify the tracks?" Desmond asked.

Headmaster Dorian shook his head. "We can make educated guesses but our knowledge of Elven creatures is slim."

"It doesn't make sense that Elven creatures are intruding on the Academy if Claire is supposed to be part Elven." Malcolm said.

"Maybe you are Fae and not Elven?" Desmond mused.

"But why am I called to both daggers?" Claire traced the hilts of the daggers. She had strapped them on before leaving the suite, determined to never be caught without them again.

"Another mystery to solve." Desmond smiled at her.

Claire smiled weakly back. Surely they had enough mysteries to solve without adding another one.

"Regardless, with the increased sightings combined with the attack yesterday, I think it would be prudent if you all placed some distance between yourselves and the Elven forest. Brandlevine is in the southern part of the witches' territory and has formidable defenses."

Desmond nodded. "My father has already extended the invitation."

"Claire." Everett said softly, breaking through the debate. "What do you want to do?"

I don't want you to get hurt again. I don't want anyone to get hurt again, she thought but she didn't voice those thoughts out loud. Instead, she said, "If you think Brandlevine will be a better option, then that's where we will go."

"I'll release Andrea and Helene from their summer duties to accompany you."

"You won't need them here?" Malcolm asked.

The Headmaster shook his head, "I've called for some other reinforcements. From what I hear from them, Claire's lessons are going well and I don't want to stop that progress. She might need it."

Well that didn't sound ominous at all, Claire thought. But she was glad that Andy and Helene would come with. And Zack and Holly would be there as well. Andy had sent Zack to Brandlevine last week to do some preparatory work in her workshop there.

"It's settled then." Claire zoned back to the room to hear the Headmaster. "I'll have Gwen prepare a portal for this afternoon."

Claire stood as her Triad did, thanking the Headmaster. She stayed quiet as they exited the administrative building and started walking back to their building. She let her eyes drink in the familiar sights around her. Soon they would be replaced with the unfamiliar. Claire had just started feeling like she belonged here at the Academy and now she had to leave that.

The steady thrum of the Academy's magic seemed to settle around her. She opened herself to the magic and was surprised when a small thread of it settled into her center. Her own magic eyed it curiously and then made a little bit of space for it. Claire smiled. It was almost like the Academy was telling her it would always be a part of her. She increased her pace until she caught back up with her men.

Desmond paused in his planning when she took his arm. "Is everything okay, little witch?"

Claire smiled, "Everything's fine." She knew she should probably tell her men about the new thread of magic in her center but she really didn't want to worry them. And they would worry. And then they would worry her. And there was already too much to worry about. Like this new adventure to Brandlevine.

Claire continued to watch Desmond as he planned with the others. She was going to get to see where her playful wizard grew up.

CHAPTER 7

Brandlevine was nothing like Desmond.

That was Claire's first thought as they stood before it. The imposing manor house stood on one of the higher hills in the coven, rising towards the sky with its brownstone towers. Everything was incredibly detailed and screamed importance. She looked at Desmond, trying to reconcile the playful, charming man she knew with the intensity of the manor. Desmond was watching the manor and the people coming to meet them with a mixture of expressions that flitted across his face too quickly for Claire to catch. He wiped them clean and looked down at Claire with the soft smile she was used to seeing from him. "Are you ready?"

Claire shrugged. "I'm not sure we have much of a choice at this point." She said. "Are you ready?"

"As long as I have you and my brothers at my side, I am ready for anything," Desmond teased.

Claire blushed at his cheesy words but squeezed his arm as a gorgeous couple exited the manor. Claire knew instantly that these were Desmond's parents. His father had the same blue eyes. Unlike Desmond's playful gaze, his father's was piercing, making Claire shift uncomfortably. What if his father found her to be more trouble than she was worth?

Desmond's mother was definitely who he got his warmth from. Her warm brown eyes and curly hair bounced as they approached.

"Desmond!" His mother exclaimed, holding her arms out to him.

Desmond released Claire and stepped into his mother's embrace. "Hi, Mama." He said, folding the smaller woman into his arms. "It's good to see you."

"Introduce me to this beauty!" His mother demanded, stepping back and smiling at Claire.

Desmond reached a hand out to Claire and she took it, stepping forward. She was immediately engulfed in Desmond's mother's arms. Claire tried to relax into it but the hug felt unfamiliar. When her mates hugged her, it felt like home. Claire didn't have any experience with a mother's hug though.

"Aren't you a gorgeous thing," Desmond's mother said, pulling back, "I can see why my boy is smitten. My name is Ilena."

"It's a pleasure to meet you." Claire said, warming up to the woman from her warm smile.

"This is Frederick," Ilena said, gesturing to her husband who extended a hand to Claire.

"It's a pleasure to meet you," Claire repeated to Desmond's father, trying not to shift under his gaze as she took his hand.

"It's our privilege to welcome you to our home." He said stoically.

Ilena elbowed him, "Oh for the realm's sake, lighten up or you will scare the poor girl away and they'll never come visit us." She glared up at her husband who softened at her look.

"Why don't you all come in?" Frederick said, "It's good to see you boys again." He said to Malcolm and Everett who got their own hugs from Ilena.

The group ascended the steps into a grand entryway. A dark wood staircase spiraled up at the back of the entryway and ornately carved wood trim decorated two large doorways on either side of the entryway.

"Let's go into the kitchen while the men discuss things in the library." Ilena looped her arm in Claire's.

Claire shot a look of panic towards Malcolm who was facing her. It wasn't like she didn't want to get to know Ilena more but this was a new place and she was feeling a bit unbalanced still.

"Actually, Ilena," Malcolm stepped forward. "Claire is an integral part of the discussion we need to have with you."

Frowning, Ilena nodded. She kept her arm linked through Claire's as they went through the doorways on the left. The doors opened to a large library with floor to ceiling bookshelves. The dark wood gleamed and the books looked well-loved. A few couches made a comfortable square to the left of the room, taking advantage of the large windows at the front of the house. To the right of the room, nestled in the bookshelves was a large desk that Claire guessed belonged to Frederick.

Ilena let go of Claire's arm to sit on one of the couches by her husband. Desmond tugged Claire down next to him and she couldn't help but relax into his side. Ilena watched her movements with a soft smile.

"It's not that we don't love having you visit," Frederick said, leaning forward and resting his elbows on his knees, "but what brings you home, son?"

"Before we start," Desmond said, "I need to know if you can keep the Councilmember in you separate from this discussion. We are coming to you as my father and as the Brandlevine Coven Leader."

Frederick frowned but nodded.

Desmond seemed to be okay with the nod as he began. "Claire is not only our Fourth, she is my soul flame, Everett's mate, and Malcolm's mate."

Frederick's eyes widened slightly as Ilena let out a gasp. "All of yours?" Ilena asked, a hand over her mouth.

Desmond nodded and Ilena lowered her hand to reveal a wide smile, "Oh, my sweet girl." she said and Claire smiled nervously at her.

"When Claire came to the Academy, she came from Windshire Coven." Desmond paused and looked at his father.

Frederick brought a hand to his chin, thinking for a moment, "Windshire, you said?"

Desmond nodded. He looked down at Claire, seeming to silently ask how much he could share. Claire squeezed his hand. "I've lived in Windshire for as long as I can remember. According to the coven, I was found wandering the woods as a child. I was placed in the orphanage and lived there my entire life as no one wanted to adopt a blind child with little to no magic abilities."

She couldn't look at Desmond's parents as she said that last part, unable to see the judgement in their eyes. Everett placed a hand on her leg and she grabbed onto it, soaking up all the comfort.

"But you can see now?" Ilena asked.

Claire nodded. "It's a recent development."

Frederick leaned back on the couch. "Tell us all of it. From the beginning."

Claire looked at Desmond and nodded permission at him.

"Everett and I were asked by the Headmaster to travel to Windshire and pick up a new student." Desmond began. "Little did we know we were going to pick up the prettiest little witch we had ever seen. I recognized her as my soul flame instantly and Everett recognized her as his mate."

Claire frowned slightly. They had never told her they recognized that about her that day. Everett, noticing her frown, leaned down to whisper, "It's always been you. You just weren't ready to hear it that day."

Even though she didn't like they had kept it a secret for so long, Claire agreed with Everett. There was no way she would have taken that information well. Not on the heels of an unexpected invitation to the Academy. She probably would have stayed in Windshire if they had piled on that news as well.

"Once at the Academy, Claire's abilities started to shine." Desmond kept going. "She showed a beginning proficiency in all four elements and a knack for herbology. She didn't let her blindness impede her progress at all."

Malcolm picked up the story here. "She was progressing well in Combat class. She showed an interest in short daggers so my dragon wanted to give her a gift. That's when the first piece of the puzzle revealed itself. My father had passed down to me a Fae dagger he acquired from the Great War. My dragon's instinct was determined that this was the gift for Claire even though it didn't come in a set."

Frederick's eyes dropped to the daggers on Claire's hips. Malcolm continued. "When Claire touched the dagger, the bindings on her magic loosened."

"The bindings?" Federick questioned.

"Yes," Desmond replied. "When Claire described what touching the Fae dagger felt like, I recognized it from my lessons with you as bindings. Someone bound her power at a very young age. We started training her with the excess magic that had been released."

Desmond explained Brent and Cassie's attack during Combat Finals and Claire's attachment to the Academy that resulted afterwards. "After the year ended, we were at the Market when Claire was drawn to a second dagger, an Elven dagger. When she touched that dagger, another layer of the bindings released and Claire regained the ability to see."

"Oh, you poor girl." Ilena said, "You've been through a lot."

Claire nodded. "It's definitely been an interesting time, but

I've had the best guides." She squeezed Desmond and Everett's hands.

Frederick rubbed a hand over his face. "I don't know if this is relevant or not, but powerful Elven children often had their powers lightly bound as children until they learned to control it. It's possible Claire's loss and subsequent regain of her vision had to do with her powers being bound."

"They blind their children?" Malcolm sounded outraged from his position behind her and Claire didn't blame him. It sounded like a barbaric process.

"No, the children were never blind because of the bindings." Frederick quickly corrected. "Which makes me think the binding placed on Claire was different. You said you displayed no magic capabilities when you were younger?"

Claire nodded, "Other than basic spells, I didn't show any proficiencies."

"Whoever placed the bindings on Claire did not want her to show any magic. Typical Elven bindings are placed to curb excess use of magic and wear off when children come of age at 25. This level of binding had to come with a cost and unfortunately for Claire I think that cost was her vision."

Claire was stunned. Whoever had bound her magic must have thought that the cost of Claire's sight was worth it. She wasn't sure how to feel about that.

"Who would be able to do that?" Desmond questioned.

"Only the most powerful Elven sorcerers or sorceresses could do it, possibly only their Elders," Frederick said.

"This is all interesting information, son," Frederick said, "but you know as well as I do that the Academy would have been the best place for her with its neutrality."

"There was an attack yesterday." Everett said, speaking for the first time since they entered the library. Claire squeezed his hand.

"An attack?" Ilena questioned.

"A Felua," Desmond said softly, his gaze not leaving his fathers.

Frederick's eyes widened again. "A Felua?"

Desmond nodded. "It attacked Everett and Claire yesterday in the early afternoon. It had a particular fixation on Claire. Andrea confirmed it had been tampered with magically."

"Is it dead?" Frederick questioned.

This time Claire spoke, "I killed it while trying to contain it." Best to get it out in the open.

Instead of disapproval or disgust, Frederick gave her a small nod of approval as Desmond spoke again, "Headmaster Dorian confirmed that there had been additional disturbances in the woods from strange beasts. We thought it best to put a bit of distance between Claire and the Elven forest until we could find more answers. I was hoping with Brandlevine's previous alliance with the Elves before the Great War, you might have records that others might not."

Claire looked at Desmond. He had omitted the part of the story about her being called to be a Champion of the Realm. She would have to ask him about that later. Maybe it had something to do with his father's position on the Council.

Frederick nodded. "Our alliance was based on trade only but I can search the library tonight. And of course you are welcome to stay here as long as you like."

"Come," Ilena stood, "Let me show you where you'll be staying. You've had a long few days and need some sleep." She looked at all of them. "We can pick back up in the morning."

CHAPTER 8

The next morning there were a few welcome faces at the breakfast table. "Holly, Zack!" Claire cried out a greeting, darting from Desmond's side to her friends.

Holly met her halfway with a hug. "Claire! I'm so glad you're okay!"

Claire hugged Zack next. "I'm fine, thanks to Everett."

"I heard you were pretty badass in your own right too." Zack said.

Claire shrugged. She was still having mixed feelings about having to kill the Felua. While the logical part of her brain knew it had been tampered with magically and was not going to stop, her heart still ached at the thought of taking any life. Again, not a good mindset for a Champion of the Realm. What if the Academy made a mistake?

Professor Andy and Professor Helene entered the dining area. "Professors!" Claire greeted.

"Just Andy and Helene," Andy said back. "We aren't at the Academy any longer."

Claire nodded although her nose wrinkled slightly at calling them by their first name. It just seemed so casual. Through her training over the last few weeks with them, she discovered both women were powerful magic wielders. Much more powerful than they let on during their time as her professors.

They all settled down for breakfast. A side table that ran the length of the dining room was stuffed with a variety of dishes and a buffet of wonderful smells wafted to Claire's nose. The smells were familiar to her nose but her eyes still struggled to place the look of the food with the smell it gave off. She was kind of glad she didn't have her sight when trying new things. Some of the foods that smelled the best looked the most plain.

Desmond led her to a seat and Everett placed a filled plate with a bit of everything in front of her. She smiled up at him as Desmond left to fill his own plate.

"So what is the plan for the day?" Claire asked after she swallowed a mouthful of eggs. The familiar smell matched their rich yellow appearance.

"Well, I was going to spend most of the day with my father in the library. So you all can..." Desmond said, settling back next to her.

"Oh! Zack and I can show you around the coven." Holly broke in. "You can meet my parents and we can have lunch in town."

Desmond looked a bit put out and Claire hid a smile. Her wizard liked owning the plan.

Before he could argue, Claire broke in. "That sounds lovely, Holly." She laid a hand on Desmond's forearm, "Then we can go over what you've found in the library at dinner and do more research if we need to."

Desmond smiled down at her, "If that's what you want, little witch."

"I'm impressed, Claire." Ilena said, taking a seat next to Frederick at the head of the table. "You got Desmond to deviate from a plan."

"Mother!" Desmond complained good-naturedly. "You're supposed to want Claire to like me."

"I don't think that's a question, dear." Ilena volleyed back making Claire blush.

Claire was saved from further embarrassment by Malcolm. "I'll join you all." He told Holly.

Claire smiled at her growly dragon, thrilled to get more time with him. "What are you going to do today?" She asked Everett.

"I'll go for a flight around the coven territory." Everett said. He looked at Frederick, "I know you have wards but since we are dealing with irregular magic it's best to be overly careful."

Frederick nodded. "Please keep me apprised of anything you find."

Everett dipped his chin in agreement.

"We will settle in for the day and then tomorrow, Claire, I want to continue your training." Andy said.

"We'll continue combat training tomorrow as well," Malcolm said. "I think it's time you begin training with your daggers." He looked at Desmond. "That means you will have to drag yourself out of bed."

"What is this, pick-on-Desmond day?" Desmond groused.

The table laughed and settled in for breakfast. Once she was done, Claire wiped her mouth with the cloth napkin and pushed back in her chair as Holly and Zack also finished. She stood and then bent to kiss Desmond and Everett on their cheeks. "I'll see you later." she smiled.

"Have fun, little witch."

Instead of exiting out the front of the manor, Holly led Claire and Zack down a hallway towards the back of the house. Malcolm trailed behind them and Claire threw a smile over her shoulder at him. Malcolm gave her a smile back, his golden eyes dancing with amusement.

Before Claire could ask him what was so funny, Holly

pushed open a door and bright sunlight streamed into the hallway.

"Welcome to Brandlevine," Holly said as they all stepped outside.

They had stepped onto a small stone patio. A metal table and chairs were placed off to their right with colorful cushions for people to enjoy. In front of them, a wide road came around the right side of the house and headed towards a small town although even from the distance Claire could tell it was much larger than Windshire. There were six houses on either side of the road towards town. They weren't as large as the manor but still double the size of the orphanage house at Windshire.

Following Claire's gaze, Holly explained. "Those are for the village elders and other founding families. My parents' house is the fourth one on the left. Come on, they're at the Capital this morning but they'll join us for dinner."

Malcolm pressed a gentle hand on the small of Claire's back as they descended the stairs and headed towards the town. Claire leaned back into it slightly, enjoying the steady thrum of the bond between them.

Holly launched into the tour. "Like I said, these twelve houses are for the village elders and founding families. Most of the coven lives in the town with a few of the earth witches living on the outskirts of the other side of town for space for their gardens."

"Brandlevine is known for their earth witches," Zack said when Holly took a breath. "There are witches with other proficiencies here as well but most of the founding families have earth proficiencies and masteries."

Claire nodded as they passed the larger houses of the founding families. The sounds and smells of the town increased as they got closer. While some of the sounds and smells were familiar to Windshire's village, the intensity was not. Claire winced slightly as they got closer. For some reason the intensity of it all was battering on her more than usual.

"What is it?" Malcolm's question halted Zack and Holly.

"It's nothing," Claire dismissed.

"Claire," Malcolm growled out. Claire arched an eyebrow at him. She probably shouldn't be feeling all warm and tingling at the sound of her name growled from Malcolm's lips but here she was.

"All the sounds and smells," she waved a hand towards the town, "are just a little much for my senses apparently."

Malcolm frowned. "The Market at the Capital didn't bother you this much?"

Claire shrugged. She had also thought about that but she didn't have a good answer for him.

"Maybe it's a result of your magic being unleashed?" Zack suggested. "I've been doing some reading from Andy and Helene's library here and one of the books said that Fae tended to avoid large cities because their senses were so acute."

Claire pursed her lips. That made sense. And fell in line with Desmond's theory that she was Fae and not Elven.

"We don't have to go into town." Holly said worriedly.

Claire shook her head, "No, I want to see it. I'll make do."

"I have an idea," Zack suggested. "Andy's been having me hone my control over my air proficiency. I can try creating an air current that circles you and helps push away the smells. It might also muffle the sounds a bit but I'm not sure about that."

"That would be lovely, Zack." Claire beamed at him.

Zack drew the air rune with his fingers in front of Claire and then another rune that Claire didn't recognize. Claire felt the cool brush of air on her cheeks before the smells from the town faded away.

"It worked." Claire said smiling. She hadn't wanted to disappoint Holly by not continuing with the tour but the intensity of it all would have prevented her from enjoying it.

"Great!" Holly clapped her hands together. "Let us know if it gets too much again."

Claire nodded and they continued through the town. Holly pointed out the various shops that sold everything from colorful fruit and vibrant plants to fresh baked bread and garden tools. Claire took it all in with wide eyes. Seeing everything in color was still so very new. There were colors still she had a hard time naming and she filed them away to ask later.

The bustling town made her think of the Market and her first date with Malcolm. She smiled up at him and he caught her look. "What is it?" he asked, slowing their pace slightly to put some distance between them and Holly and Zack.

"Just thinking of our first visit to the Market and wondering what it would look like in color." She squeezed his forearm as she looped her arm through his.

Malcolm softened down at her. "We will go back," he promised.

"I'm not worried about it." Claire said. "I just like spending time with you."

"Me too, little treasure."

Laying her head on his arm as they walked, Claire finally got the courage to ask the question that had been bothering her for a few weeks.

"Malcolm, why haven't you kissed me yet?"

Malcolm stumbled slightly and Claire grinned at her normally stoic dragon faltering. Feeling a bit wicked, she pressed further. "I mean I think you like me, and I definitely like you."

Malcolm righted himself, eyes blazing as he looked down at Claire. Claire sucked in a breath at the flames dancing in his eyes and had a feeling she was looking at Malcolm's dragon.

"Give us a second," He called to Holly and Zack while not taking his eyes off of Claire. He tugged them into a side alley.

As he stepped forward, Claire stepped back with a half-smile on her face. She found herself really enjoying pushing her dragon's buttons. His eyes blazed brighter and Claire took another step back feeling the stone wall behind her press into her back.

His eyes flared brighter as she realized she had nowhere else to go. She arched an eyebrow at him as if to say 'Well you caught me, what are you going to do about it?'

"I definitely like you. I more than like you." Malcolm said as he stepped closer. It took Claire a second to process his words as the answer to her earlier statement. The heat of his body so close to hers was very distracting. He placed his large hands on her hips, and Claire's breath hitched. His thumbs stroked over her hip bones and the warm tingling in her stomach grew.

"So why haven't you kissed me yet?" She meant for her voice to come out challenging but instead it was breathy, as if the air had been stolen from her lungs at his proximity.

"Maybe I was waiting for the right time?" His voice was deep and growly.

"Am I going to be waiting forever for the right time?" Claire sassed.

"Maybe I was waiting for enough time." Malcolm growled, "Because if I kiss you, I don't think I will want to stop."

"We have the rest of our lives," Claire said softly. And she desperately clung to that belief in her mind despite all the unknowns.

Malcolm's eyes blazed brighter before he groaned and closed them, resting his forehead on hers.

"Kiss me, Malcolm," Claire whispered, "please?"

Instead of waiting for him to decide, Claire ran her hands up his chest and around to the back of his neck. She pulled him down to her and kissed him. For a second, Claire thought he would pull away as his hands flexed on her hips and then he was tugging her closer.

Claire forgot they were in an alley. Forgot that Holly and Zack were waiting on them. Forgot why they had fled to Brandlevine and forgot she was supposed to be a badass Champion of the Realm. There was only her and Malcolm in this moment.

He let her lead the kiss for all of a breath before he took control. Claire sank into him, surrendering as the fire that was uniquely Malcolm swept through her. He kissed her hard, pulling back to nibble on her lower lip. Using her gasp to sweep his tongue into her mouth and tangle with hers. His hands gripped and smoothed over her hips, kneading them in a way that had Claire's stomach pressing tighter, searching for something she couldn't name yet.

Claire forgot all sense of time and place as he kissed her. Finally the need to breathe pulled them apart, their lips a breath from each other as they breathed in each other's air. At that moment, Claire understood Malcolm's earlier point. There did not seem to be enough time in the Realm for this moment.

"I think I understand the time thing now," she breathed.

Malcolm let out a husky laugh that did nothing to settle the burning tightness in her stomach.

Even though Claire knew that Holly and Zack were waiting on them, she didn't want to leave this moment.

"We should go." Malcolm whispered but also showed no inclination to step back.

"Only if you promise we can do that again. And soon." She smiled.

"You are not making this easy." Malcolm grumbled. "All my dragon wants to do right now is fly off with you to a very remote place where we won't be disturbed."

"Everett and Desmond would worry." Claire patted his chest. "But I'm sure we can carve out some alone time for your dragon and I soon."

Malcolm growled but stepped back, reaching out a hand for Claire's.

They emerged from the alley. Zack and Holly were standing a few houses up, chatting. Holly spotted them first and smirked at the two of them. Claire's lips felt slightly swollen and she knew her curls were probably a bit messier than usual. Claire just grinned back at her and winked.

"Later," she mouthed and Holly matched her grin. If only Bethany was here, Claire thought. Then the girl time would be complete.

Zack wisely didn't say anything, but he did throw Claire a playful smile. "Are we ready for lunch?" He asked.

"I know I am and I'm sure Claire's worked up quite an appetite." Holly teased.

Claire threw her head back and laughed as Malcolm grumbled, a faint hint of red dusting his cheeks. Claire looped arms with Holly. "Let's go to lunch."

CHAPTER 9

After a hearty lunch at the village tavern, Holly took them to the outskirts of the village, showing off the garden plots of the coven members. She pointed out Andy and Helene's cottage next to a large group of trees. The sun started lowering in the sky, framing the manor house in a golden glow as they walked back for dinner. Claire's hand was firmly grasped by Malcolm's and she relished the warmth radiating from their clasped palms.

Zack and Holly stopped as they passed Holly's house. "We'll see you in an hour and a half." Holly waved goodbye. Zack was staying with Holly for the duration of his apprenticeship.

It had been a lovely day, Claire thought as she and Malcolm walked the remaining distance.

"What has you smiling like that?" Malcolm asked her, regaining her attention.

Claire took a side step closer and laid her head on his arm as they walked, "Just thinking about how lovely of a day it's been."

"Oh?" Malcolm asked, "Is there a particular thing that made it lovely?"

Claire enjoyed teasing him way too much. "No."

"Claire..." Malcolm growled playfully.

Claire laughed and darted away playfully. She barely made it more than three steps before strong arms grabbed her from behind and swung her up into them. Malcolm growled playfully down at her, his eyes dancing with gold. His dragon really did enjoy the chase. She was going to have to remember that for later.

"Didn't you ever learn not to run from predators?" He asked softly.

Claire ignored the shiver his deep voice gave her, "You're saying that like I didn't want to be caught?"

Malcolm groaned and dropped his chin. "You're going to be the death of me."

"But what a lovely way to go," Claire pushed farther, laughing as she did.

Malcolm's eyes gleamed and his head descended towards hers. Claire smiled and lifted her chin, eager for him to kiss her again.

"Oi, lovebirds!" Desmond's voice broke them apart, "There will be plenty of time for canoodling later."

Claire turned her head to see Desmond standing on the terrace, arms crossed and a mischievous look on his face. Malcolm's chest rumbled. "How do you feel about only having two mates, little treasure?"

Claire laughed and patted his chest so he would let her down. "You would miss him too much. Besides, weren't you saying something about needing more time."

As she walked up the steps she heard him huff under his breath, "I would make do."

Claire walked into Desmond's arms at the top of the steps. "Did you have a good time, little witch?"

Claire beamed up at him. "I did!"

"What was your favorite part about the town?" Desmond asked.

"Getting ravaged by Malcolm in an alleyway."

Okay, Claire lied. She was really enjoying teasing all of her men. Desmond's jaw dropped and Malcolm let out a growl from behind her.

"Well can't have the dragon outdoing me, can I?" Desmond said huskily, bending down.

Claire used a defensive spin from Combat training and extracted herself from Desmond's arms, shaking a finger at him but unable to hide the grin from her face, "Weren't you just saying we were out of time for canoodling."

Desmond lunged playfully at her and Claire squealed, darting for the door. She slammed it quickly behind her, laughing breathlessly.

Everett appeared at the end of the hallway. "Are you having fun tormenting them?" He arched an eyebrow at her, the grin on her face giving her away.

Claire sashayed down the hallway to her third mate. "I have no idea what you're talking about."

Everett reached a hand out to her hip as she got closer and pulled her snug against him. His other hand cupped her jaw, his thumb tracing over her cheek. Claire relaxed into his hold, smiling softly up at him. "Are you going to torment me too?" Everett asked.

"I would never," Claire whispered.

"Somehow, I don't believe you, little mate." Everett's lips hovered above her own.

A needy sound in the back of her throat escaped. Everett's green eyes darkened and the hand on her hip tightened. "Kiss me please." She whispered.

Everett lightly brushed his lips across hers and then took a step back. Claire blinked and took a step to balance herself. Her gryphon had a wicked grin on his face. "I would, but we have no time for canoodling."

Claire groaned and then laughed. "Turnabout is fair play I guess."

"That it is, little mate, that it is. However, if you want to even out the stakes, I left a dress for you in our bedroom."

Claire raised her eyebrows, unable to keep the slightly wicked grin off her face.

"Go." Everett commanded, seeing the glint in her eyes. "Before we skip dinner completely."

Claire shrugged, "The three of you keep saying that like it's a bad thing." Although she didn't quite know what she was asking for, alone time with her very handsome, very hot mates definitely had its appeal.

"Go." Everett growled playfully, disappearing through the library doors behind him.

Claire hurried up the stairs and into their bedroom. She leaned back against the door and brought her hands to her cheeks. They ached slightly from smiling so much but she couldn't seem to find it in herself to care. She never remembered being this happy.

A long cloth bag was laid carefully across the bed. She undid the lace ties that drew the bag closed and gasped. She pulled the dress carefully out of the bag and laid it on the bed.

The entire dress was made of a pale blue, sheer lace over a base layer of the same-colored silk. The sleeves looked like a waterfall of lace folds that would cover her upper arm and brush her elbow. Embroidered flowers dotted the fabric from the waist up one of the sides, like the flowers were growing on the material. The front of the dress had a deep V that would come down to the center of her sternum. The lightest layer of a sheer material in the same pale blue went from collarbone to collarbone. While her skin wouldn't be bare so to speak, she would definitely be more exposed than she had ever been.

She left the dress on the bed and walked into the bathroom. Stripping, she threw her curls up in a messy bun on the top of her head and stepped under the spray, scrubbing away the dust from the town. She dried off quickly, rubbing some sweet-smelling lotion from one of the jars all over her body.

Keeping the towel wrapped around her body. She poked her head out of the bathroom. The bedroom was empty. Her men must be getting ready in another part of the house. A box sitting on a chair by the window caught her eye, a pair of sparkling silver shoes gleamed in the afternoon light. Claire smiled, who knew her gryphon had such an eye for fashion.

She dropped the towel at the dresser and pulled on her undergarments from one of the drawers. She felt a little bit exposed walking over to the bed in just her undergarments and she giggled at the thought. She pulled the dress on, the pale blue silk feeling like a cloud against her body. She was right, the deep V plunged to below her sternum but the material was tight and fitted and the soft overlay of the chiffon prevented her from feeling too exposed. She traced her finger over the delicate embroidered flowers, small gems blinking at her from their centers.

The dress swished along the floor as she walked over to the chair with the shoes. Claire couldn't help but let out a little giggle as she did an experimental twirl. She felt like a princess and the ache in her cheeks was back from her smile. She truly had the best men.

Darker thoughts of Claire being more trouble than she was worth from all the unanswered questions tried to creep up but Claire firmly shoved them back down. She would deal with that later. Tomorrow, they would start training again and reality would come crashing in. Tonight, she was going to enjoy dinner with her Triad and part of their family and her friends.

She placed the box in her lap as she sat down and pulled out one of the shoes to look at it. Thankfully, it was only a small heel. Claire didn't think she would be able to walk anything larger. She already had problems with the stairs just because she could see.

The shoes were high-quality leather painted sparkling silver. A strip of the silver leather ran from the piece that wrapped around her toes up to another piece that circled her ankle. She leaned down and fitted both shoes on, standing and taking a few experimental steps. It felt like walking on a cloud which was not what heels were supposed to feel like according to a few conversations Claire had overheard in the girls' dormitory building at the Academy.

She practiced her balance in the room walking a few circles. She glanced at the clock standing on the dresser and her eyes widened. She didn't realize that much time had passed. She wasn't late but dinner was about to start.

She pulled open the door and glanced down the hallway. No one was coming in and out of the rooms on either side so they must all be downstairs already. She got to the top of the stairs and grabbed onto the railing with one hand. With her other hand, she grabbed onto her dress, pulling the extra material away from her feet. Stairs were tricky enough and now she was going to have to navigate them in heels even if they were small heels.

All of her attention was focused on making it down the stairs without tripping so she didn't notice the hush in the room. Reaching the bottom, she smiled and looked up, stopping at the sight of her Triad.

They must have showered somewhere else as their hair was slightly damp still. Desmond's curls were parted at the side with one side sweeping across his face. His silver blue eyes seemed brighter than normal as he studied her with an intensity that made her toes curl. He wore a white dress shirt with a blue vest over it and black pants. His mouth quirked up in his familiar half-smile. Claire returned it and dragged her eyes to Malcolm.

Malcolm's brown hair was brushed back away from his face

and the dark suit he was wearing fit like it was made for him. It probably was with his black shirt fitting snugly over his wide chest. His brown eyes flared with gold as he dragged them down her dress.

The man responsible for the dress, Everett, studied her with an intensity that not only made her toes curl but her stomach heat with a low burn. His green eyes dragged up from her shoes, over her dress and to her eyes. His lips parted in a slow grin that did nothing to ease the burning in her stomach. His white hair was tousled, like he didn't really care about getting dressed up for dinner. He wore a grey shirt with a black vest and black pants, looking like the shadows he liked to disappear into.

"Bethany is going to be so pissed she missed this." Holly's whisper to Zack broke the spell that Claire and her men found themselves under.

Claire flashed a quick smile at Holly and Zack but her attention turned back to her men who seemed to shake themselves out of the spell. All three walked towards her and Claire forced herself not to take a step back. Individually, their focus was intense but all together their attention combined with the bonds between them had Claire speechless.

"Little witch," Desmond purred. "You look delightfully beautiful." He extended a hand to Claire and led her in a twirl.

"Gorgeous." Malcolm grunted out, like that was the only word he was capable of saying.

"All thanks to Everett." Claire smiled at him.

"I might have provided the dress but you made it stunning."

Claire's cheeks heated and she changed the subject before they could offer any more compliments. "You all clean up quite nicely as well."

"This old thing?" Desmond said, tucking her hand in his elbow as he led her towards the doors to the right of the entryway, opposite the library. "I just threw it on."

Claire laughed and then spotted her friends whom she had

forgotten about much to her chagrin. "Holly, you look wonderful and, Zack, you look very handsome."

Malcolm growled softly and Claire held back an eyeroll. Her growly dragon knew that Zack wasn't interested in Claire or any women.

Holly was wearing a dark green dress that hung off her shoulders and fit her lithe frame. Zack was wearing brown pants, a white shirt, and brown suspenders.

Holly gave her a hug. "Thank you, but the award for the best entrance definitely goes to you tonight. I've never seen them that speechless!"

Claire looked around, "Where are your parents?"

"Mom and Dad are in the dining room with Uncle Frederick and Aunt Ilena." Holly said. "And apparently a few others," she looked towards Desmond.

"Of course." Desmond said, rolling his eyes, "because it's Brandlevine and nothing can ever just be small." He was smiling when he said it but Claire heard a faint thread of bitterness in his voice. She frowned slightly but quickly smiled when Desmond looked down at her. "Ready, little witch."

"As long as I have you three by my side, I'm ready for anything." She repeated the words he had said to her yesterday when they arrived at Brandlevine.

Desmond smiled warmly down at her. Malcolm stepped forward and held the door open for them.

CHAPTER 10

The room they entered was massive. Easily forty paces long and twenty paces wide, the walls were made from the same dark wood paneling that was all over the rest of the house. Twelve tall windows ran from floor to ceiling on the right side of the room. A long wooden table dominated the center of the room and the left side wall was dotted with paintings. It was very different from the smaller dining room they had eaten breakfast in this morning.

The large room was already half-filled with people. Claire recognized Frederick and Ilena at the opposite end of the room speaking to a few older-looking people. Claire would guess those would probably be some of Brandlevine's elders.

A couple that looked like Holly walked towards them from the window side of the room. "You must be Claire." The woman said. "Holly's told us so much about you. I'm Clarissa." The woman had Holly's eyes and the same warmth to her personality.

"It's a pleasure to meet you, Clarissa." Claire took her offered hand and shook it.

"This is my husband, Benedict. He's also Frederick's brother."

Claire nodded at the man. Holly got her hair color from him. Benedict smiled warmly at her, "It's a pleasure to meet you, Claire. Good to see you again, Desmond."

Desmond returned their greeting. "We're going to get Claire something to drink and get out of the doorway in case my parents invited anyone else to this small gathering.

Clarissa let out a small laugh, "You know how your mother likes to entertain."

"All too well." Desmond's voice did not reflect his smile but Claire chose not to comment on it.

She let the men lead her to the opposite side of the room. "Do you want anything specific?" Everett's voice was a brush on her ear.

Claire tried not to let herself be distracted by his proximity. "I'm not picky. Choose for me?"

Everett nodded and stepped away with Malcolm to grab them drinks. "Is everything okay?" She asked Desmond in a low voice. Holly and Zack had stayed with Holly's parents and were chatting with someone else now.

"Everything's fine, little witch." Desmond said. "Here come my parents."

"Claire, you look lovely!" Ilena cried, eyes sparkling. The older woman was in a silver sheath dress that matched Frederick's shirt.

"Thank you," Claire murmured, accepting the woman's hug.

"Mother, Father." Desmond greeted. "Didn't realize this turned into a party."

"News travels fast, son." Frederick said. "It's not every day a Triad, especially the Stonemont Triad, finds their Fourth. People are curious. We did try to contain the guest list though."

Frederick gave Desmond a look. Desmond nodded jerkily, clearly not happy with the news but accepting it.

"Ilena, introduce me to your son and his lovely Fourth." An older woman stepped up to the group.

"Claire, this is Rosemary, one of Brandlevine's esteemed elders."

"Esteemed?" Rosemary arched an eyebrow, "At least it's better than old as dirt."

Claire couldn't help but let out a small laugh and the twinkle in Rosemary's eyes told her that had been the goal. "It's a pleasure to meet you." Claire said.

"Beautiful and with good manners?" Rosemary arched an eyebrow at Desmond. "How in the realm did she end up with you?"

"It really is pick-on-Desmond day, isn't it?" Malcolm broke in handing a glass to Desmond. Everett touched Claire's elbow and offered her a glass as well.

"All in jest, all in jest." Rosemary waved a hand. "I've known the lad since he was toddling around here."

"Practically helped raise me." Desmond told Claire.

"Took the whole village with how much trouble you were apt to get into." Rosemary said.

Malcolm chuckled and Rosemary turned to him. "Like you were much better. The three of you together ran rampant."

Claire laughed at the chagrined look on her men's face. "Rosemary, we must talk further."

"Oh no, there will be none of that." Desmond playfully tugged her away. "The two of you don't need to spend any more time together. It was a pleasure to see you as always, Rosemary."

Claire and Rosemary laughed as her men guided her away. Claire let out a small wave.

"You handled her very well, little mate." Everett whispered in her ear.

Claire raised an eyebrow. Rosemary seemed the grandmotherly type. Why did she need to be handled?

Malcolm saw her expression and stepped in closer, bending

down to hover over her ear. To the rest of the room, it might look like he was whispering sweet words but instead he explained. "Ilena and Frederick invited some important and curious people tonight. Say as little as you can about your heritage or powers."

Malcolm drew back, a smile on his lips but his eyes were worried. Claire was confused. Weren't Ilena and Frederick on their side? Or at least on their son's side? Hadn't Desmond asked if Frederick could keep his help separate from his Councilmember position. Was he reneging on his word?

All of sudden Claire felt like all of the eyes in the room were on her. She quickly glanced around to see it was only her worries causing the feeling. She caught eyes with Holly on the opposite side of the room who frowned lightly. Her friend's empath abilities must have picked up on Claire's sudden change of mood. Claire gave her a small smile and a nod before turning back to Malcolm. She kept up the act and reached a hand up to smooth his collar before patting his chest lightly and nodding to show she understood.

"We'll be with you every second of the evening." Everett assured her from behind her. "We'll guide the conversation if needed."

Ilena made her way over to them from behind Malcolm's shoulder. Claire tilted her head slightly towards her, alerting Malcolm who turned.

"Boys, you aren't mingling." Ilena smiled. "People are eager to meet Claire. How about I take her around?"

"We've got her, Mother." Desmond said lightly. "I know you are busy playing host."

Ilena's eyes narrowed slightly although her smile didn't drop. "Well get on with it then, it's better to go to people than make them come to you."

Her words sounded like a warning that Claire didn't quite catch. Malcolm must have as he nodded at her.

"Alright, little witch, we've been summoned." Desmond said, Claire's hand still firmly tucked in his elbow.

She smiled up at him, "Come now, it won't be so bad. It's just saying hello."

It probably was much more than just saying hello but if Claire thought about the politics or trying not to say the wrong thing, she would end up worrying so much more.

The first couple that her Triad introduced her to was also a pair of Brandlevine Elders. Their questions were polite but probing. Claire kept her answers vague. She was a student at the Academy. That's where she met the Triad. They were visiting Desmond's family now that school was out.

After they made their polite excuses to move on to the next group, Malcolm leaned down from his place at Claire's side. "Good job, little treasure."

Feeling a bit dangerous, Claire pushed, "I expect to be paid in kisses later."

A soft snort from behind them told her Everett had heard her teasing. Claire fought to not let her grin get too big as Malcolm's eyes flared. He dropped his lips to her ear, "I think we can negotiate something." Did he just nip her ear? Claire fought to keep her expression neutral as heat flooded her core.

"Will you behave?" Desmond hissed at Malcolm and then groaned softly. "How in the realm did you get me to be the rules enforcer? I'm supposed to be the one misbehaving with Claire."

Claire let out a quiet giggle and Desmond threw her a mock glare. "You're a terrible influence, little witch."

"Oh, to be young and in love." A voice from in front of them said.

Claire looked away from Desmond to see a stately older woman in a deep red gown walking towards them. Her arm was linked with an equally stately older man, white hairs peppering his beard. Something about the woman's tone was... off? The words were meant to be sweet but the tone didn't match the words.

"Councilwoman Merda." Desmond greeted politely, if not a bit stiffly, telling Claire her instincts were right.

Councilwoman? What were Desmond's parents up to?

"Oh, it's former Councilwoman now. Just Merda is fine." The woman raised a hand. Claire didn't know if former Councilwoman was any better than current Councilwoman.

They exchanged pleasantries before Merda asked a question. "So Frederick tells me you show aptitude for all four elemental proficiencies?"

Claire was glad she wasn't drinking like Desmond was when Merda asked that. Desmond coughed lightly to clear his throat. Claire simply smiled at Merda. "Beginning proficiencies, yes."

"That's very unique." Merda said, her eyes calculating.

"It is," Claire said before raising her glass to her lips.

It was clear Merda wanted to ask more questions but a tinkling of bells from the front of the room indicated dinner was about to be served. Claire looked over to see Ilena by the server holding the bells. Did she have him ring them because they were talking to the Councilwoman? Even after Ilena invited the Councilwoman?

Sitting in the middle of her Triad, Claire was sure the food was great but she had trouble tasting it as it felt like she was put on display. Although having food in her mouth was a great excuse to just nod or shake her head.

She was much less likely to accidentally give something away if she could only give yes or no answers. Like, "Did you meet at the Academy?" Nod her head. "Are you from Brandlevine Coven?" Shake her head. "Are you staying at Brandlevine?" Nod her head again.

After dinner, it seemed like most guests moved over into the library for evening drinks. Desmond made polite excuses to his parents and the other guests within earshot that Claire was still tired from the journey yesterday. As soon as they could, they escaped up the stairs to their room. Desmond threw up a privacy spell around the boundaries of the room so they could talk freely.

"Your parents shared a lot of information about us tonight." Claire said casually, leaning against the dresser.

She didn't want to upset her Triad at her negative thoughts of Desmond's parents, but she was a little irritated because it felt like she and her Triad had been thrown into the deep end of the lake with the display.

The dramatic groan Desmond made Claire realize she shouldn't have worried. "I don't know what their game was."

"It was actually a brilliant political play." Malcolm admitted. "By admitting what they did it kept everyone focused on Claire and not asking questions of her heritage."

"It's only a matter of time before those questions start." Everett commented. "People are going to want to know where she comes from. The Council, specifically, so they can tap into more power."

Claire asked the other thing that had been bothering her.

"Earlier this evening, what did you mean when you told Clarissa you knew all too well that your mother liked to entertain?" Claire asked as she tugged off the shoes.

"What do you mean, little witch?" Desmond paused in unbuttoning his cuffs.

"You smiled when you said it but your voice didn't match your smile." Claire said.

Desmond exchanged a look with Malcolm who shook his head. "You could tell that from my voice?"

"Yes," Claire was getting a bit frustrated with his avoidance. "Why did you look at Malcolm?"

"Because next to Desmond, I'm the most-versed of the bunch in political bullshit. We monitor our expressions and tones closely in order to not give anything away that could later be used against us. I didn't catch anything from Desmond tonight. I would have only known about that comment because I know his history."

Claire frowned. What kind of politics did Unitam have that required you to so thoroughly hide oneself? Windshire had sheltered Claire and the Academy seemed to have as well.

"You said his tone didn't match?" Malcolm prompted gently.

Claire nodded, "I don't know how else to explain it." She shrugged. "There was just something off about your tone."

"Maybe it has to do with your blindness?" Everett suggested, "You are probably used to catching those things."

Claire shrugged. Maybe.

"We can figure it out later." Desmond said, rubbing his face. "Let's go to bed. I'm much too tired to think."

"That's a first," Everett teased and Desmond tossed a pillow at him that the gryphon caught easily.

"Take the bathroom first, Claire." Malcolm said.

Claire pulled some sleep clothes out of the dresser and crossed to the bathroom. She carefully took off the dress. A knock on the door had her pausing. "If you give me the dress, I'll put it away for you." Everett said through the door.

Claire cracked the door open a bit and handed Everett the dress through it.

She dressed quickly and washed her face. As she stepped out of the bathroom, Desmond passed her, dropping a quick kiss onto her forehead as he entered the bathroom.

Malcolm had already changed and was lying on the bed. He held an arm out to Claire and she snuggled up to him. Everett claimed her other side as Desmond came out of the bathroom.

As Desmond laid on Everett's other side, Malcolm spoke, "Don't forget we are getting up early for training tomorrow."

Desmond groaned and Claire giggled. Desmond reached over Everett to tickle Claire's sides and she squealed, trying to squirm away. Malcolm groaned and Claire looked up to see his eyes dancing gold.

"Sleep." He growled at all of them and the bed shook with Desmond and Everett's silent laughter.

"Good night." Claire whispered into the darkness, falling asleep almost instantly.

CHAPTER 11

"Okay so before I unleash you on Malcolm, let's talk about how we infuse magic into objects."

Desmond sat cross-legged in front of Claire in Brandlevine's small training center. It was half the size of the one at the Academy and much cozier. The Fae and Elven daggers lay on the ground in between Claire and Desmond.

Claire nodded and Desmond continued. "Anyone can infuse magic into an object. They usually have to be touching the object while they do. Not everyone can infuse magic into an object and have it hold its magic when they aren't touching the object. There are certain objects like your daggers and others that are created to be magic reservoirs but they are rare. They usually take the shape of charms."

"What about the mark on the Felua? That was a compulsion rune, right?"

Desmond nodded. "It's similar to infusing magic in an object but different. The person who did that infused magic into the rune, definitely, but there has to be a cost, usually blood or life energy. That's why the practice is forbidden by the Council because it's so dangerous and comes at a high cost."

Claire frowned. That was a high cost for that particular rune magic but someone had been willing to pay it.

"Back to infusing magic. Like I said, anyone can infuse magic into an object. This is because the process is fairly simple. The trick is wielding the magic through the object. We are talking about wielding it through weapons but there are many witches who use it for more everyday tasks."

"Like what?"

"They might use it as an extra set of hands in a workroom or kitchen. If something needs constant stirring, they might infuse the spoon with magic to stir while they do something else."

Claire was impressed. "Can you do that?"

Desmond smiled at her. "I can. It's definitely a big help in my workroom."

"Okay. So what do I need to do to infuse magic into the daggers?"

"Hold on, little witch, not so fast. Like I said the trick is wielding the magic through the object. Before we go sending magic into objects or taking strange magic into our centers." He paused and gave her a pointed look as if referencing the first time Claire touched both daggers and when she took in the Academy's magic. "We need to be clear on the intent."

Claire rolled her eyes playfully and Desmond pretended to be offended. Giggling, she waved her hands at him to continue.

"What do you think your intent should be with the daggers?"

"To use them to defend myself." Claire said, slightly confused. What other intent would there be?

"That's one part of it." Desmond nodded, "but what about also to help attack? And 'defend myself' is very broad. Do you need them to shield against blows, to deflect attacks, to counter-attack? The more specific you can make your intent, the easier it will be to wield the magic. Eventually you will be able to send and change your intent seamlessly."

Desmond rose to his feet and helped Claire to hers. "Pick up the daggers now and we will practice infusing the magic into the daggers before I unleash you on Malcolm."

From his spot on the side of the arena leaning next to Everett, Malcolm scoffed. Desmond and Claire exchanged mischievous glances. Their growly dragon would learn not to underestimate them.

"Okay so reach into your center and pull out a small thread of magic. It doesn't need to be a large amount at all."

"Shouldn't I hold the daggers?" Claire gestured to where they still lay on the ground between them.

"Not yet. Let's practice calling the magic and weaving your intent into them before you send it into the daggers."

Claire nodded and took a deep breath, sinking into her center. She ignored the Academy magic in the corner and focused on her magic. The bindings were still there but they looked like a patchwork quilt. She called it to her and widened her eyes when it rushed towards her. Holding up her hands, she halted it. It had always been so hard to call it most of her life. Having it respond this easily to her was strange. She took another breath and got more specific. She focused on pulling the smallest thread of magic to her and felt it warm her palms.

"That's it." Desmond's warm voice said. "Now focus on your intent. We will start with the intent to shield against blows. Envision your magic creating a shield everytime someone strikes at you."

Claire felt a little silly as she envisioned it but she trusted Desmond. She focused on an image of one of the metal shields that hung on the wall at the Combat Arena at the Academy.

"That's perfect." Desmond said. "Now here's the important point. Release the magic back to your center."

Claire frowned. She had just called it and now he wanted her to release it?

"Releasing the magic is one of the most important parts. You must control your magic. It cannot control you. Release it."

Claire tried to release it and like her, the magic seemed confused. It stayed in her palms. That didn't work. She tried to coax it back to her center and it remained stubborn.

"Don't panic." Desmond's voice was soothing. "Our magic responds to our emotions. Focus on releasing it and telling it you're safe."

"We're safe." Claire thought, feeling silly as she tried to coax it back to their center. Her magic wavered slightly and Claire repeated the thought to it. She brought up the feeling of safety she felt this morning, waking up among her Triad. Her magic wavered and then released, going back to her center.

She opened her eyes and grinned at Desmond, "I did it!"

Desmond smiled at her. "You did. Now do it again."

Desmond had Claire practice calling and releasing her magic a dozen more times until the magic obeyed her seamlessly.

"Okay. Now you are ready to practice with the daggers."

Claire leaned down and picked them up. The Fae dagger in her left hand and the Elven dagger in her right hand. It was strange but the daggers felt at home in her grip. She gave them a few experimental twirls like she had been practicing with Malcolm. The daggers were perfectly weighted for her and sliced the air easily.

"Okay, my little warrior witch." Desmond teased. "Let's focus."

Claire smiled sheepishly. She had gotten carried away with the feel of the daggers.

"Call your magic again."

Taking a breath, Claire focused on calling her magic again. The magic came rushing to her call, the daggers in her hands seeming to amplify the magic and glowing at the impact.

"You just need a small amount of magic." Desmond chided softly.

"That was a small amount of magic," Claire protested. "I

called the exact same amount as before. The daggers are making it easier."

Desmond frowned, the crinkle in his forehead telling Claire he was puzzling out this new development.

"Release the magic." He said firmly.

For a brief second, Claire worried that the magic wasn't going to listen to her. That the way the daggers amplified it, also meant that she would struggle releasing it. But as soon as she released the magic, it retreated to her center almost instantly.

Now it was Claire's turn to frown. "That was almost too easy," She murmured, studying the fading glow of the daggers.

"I wonder if the daggers are some form of conduit for your magic," Desmond said thoughtfully.

"A conduit? Is that different then just sending magic into an object?"

"It is. They're in the same family so to speak but different. Conduits are specially designated to a magic user and make using magic much easier. That would confirm what we already thought, that the daggers were made specifically for you."

"That's good, right?" Claire asked. If the daggers were specifically made for her, maybe her parents did care enough to give her some tools.

"It is good, but also rare." He shook his head smiling, "I always knew you were special."

Claire mirrored his smile even as her thoughts twirled. So many questions and so few answers. And it was like every answer they did find led to more questions.

"Alright, let's do it again."

For the rest of the morning, Desmond had her practice calling magic and releasing it. Once Claire had mastered the intent of shields, she also practiced deflecting attacks and doing a few offensive moves.

"Now you're ready to take on Malcolm," Desmond smiled. "But maybe not today," He said as she dropped her arms in exhaustion. Controlling and releasing her magic was more exhausting than physical training it seemed.

Claire laughed. "I don't know about that," She said, "I don't know if I'll ever get to Malcolm's level."

"He is a great warrior, but I'll deny saying that if anyone ever asks." Desmond teased. "Come on, we are all finished for the day."

Claire carefully sheathed the daggers and secured them around her hips. She took Desmond's outstretched hand and they started walking back to the manor house.

"Did you find anything in your father's library yesterday?" Claire asked.

"Nothing that we didn't know from the Academy's library already. Although we only got through a fraction of his books. I was planning to spend the rest of the afternoon going through more."

"Do you want any help?" Claire asked.

"I'll always take your company, little witch. Let's go see what we can find."

Hopefully some more answers, Claire thought. She had a feeling they were running out of time.

CHAPTER 12

It had been a long morning in the library at Brandlevine. Desmond and Claire hadn't found anything yesterday so Claire was back at it this morning, though without Desmond, who was patrolling with Malcolm.

Instead, Claire was sitting in the library with Desmond's father, Frederick. Everett was somewhere, likely in the shadows close by, but she hadn't seen him since breakfast.

Claire closed the book on her lap with a frown. They had been finding scraps of information all morning but nothing that fit all of the pieces together. They needed a personal account of some sort. Directly from a Fae or Elf. A thought struck her.

"Were any Elves or Fae Champions of the Realm?" Claire asked.

"Why do you ask?" Frederick looked up from his own book. His glasses were perched on the edge of his nose and they softened his features. In that moment, she could see what Desmond would look like in the future.

Claire had forgotten he didn't know she was supposed to be a champion. She thought quickly. "In History class, the Champions of the Realm were mentioned briefly and our professor said they often kept journals. If there were any Fae or Elves, maybe they wrote some secrets down in the journals?"

Frederick nodded slowly, "And those books wouldn't have been recalled as they live in the Council's archives. Good thinking, Claire."

Claire smiled weakly at him. She had almost blown their secret. "Can we get access to them?"

"The general public does not have access but luckily for you, I do. I'll reach out to the Council Archive's scribe and make the request. I'll say it's for a research project or something."

The smile Claire gave him this time was more genuine. "Thank you."

"You're very welcome. I'll go do that right now." Frederick left the library and Claire heaved a sigh of relief.

"You handled that very well." Everett's voice behind her made her jump slightly.

She turned and smiled at him as he stepped out of the shadows of the bookshelves. Her sneaky gryphon was never far from her side. "I almost blew it," She admitted, stepping forward into him.

His arms wrapped around her lower back and he tilted her chin up towards him with one hand, "But you didn't. You thought quickly on your feet."

"I know why we are keeping it a secret but it's hard remembering some time who knows what. And he's Desmond's dad. Shouldn't he be invested in helping us."

"He is Desmond's dad but he is also still a Councilmember. We took a risk by sharing your possible heritage with him. He can get away with not sharing that with the Council as you're family. But the Champion of the Realm is a different story."

"Why is that?"

"A Champion of the Realm would affect the Council directly. Champions are only called during times of great unrest and as far as the Realm knows, we are actually in a peaceful state right now. Whatever is not right with the Realm, it's hidden under the surface."

"And you think the Council is involved?" Claire felt sick. The most powerful among them could be the ones hurting the Realm.

"I don't know for sure, but I would never chance you." Everett's eyes were intense. "None of us would ever risk you like that so for now, Frederick can't know."

"Okay," Claire said softly. She agreed with Desmond but she was worried. The Council was powerful and surely had ways of finding out all sorts of information. How much longer until they found out about her?

* * *

Claire ate lunch with Everett, enjoying a sandwich that was as big as both her fists combined. Afterwards, Everett walked her to training with Andy and Helene and he was promptly shooed away by Andy.

"Go. She's safe with us. You three are always distracting her." Andy waved her hands at him.

Everett rolled his eyes but let himself be ushered out the door. "I'll be back to walk you back to the manor for dinner." He threw over his shoulder.

Claire waved goodbye as Andy shut the door and turned to her. "Come, let's go out back to the garden. Helene is waiting for us there."

Claire followed Andy through their cottage and back into the garden. Technically, Andy and Helene qualified to live closer to the manor house but they preferred to be back on the outskirts. Claire wondered if it had to do with Helene being a Dryad.

"How are you, Claire?" Helene greeted warmly.

"I'm doing good." Claire said, "A little overwhelmed but good."

"That's to be expected." Helene replied. "You've had a lot to deal with. What's on your mind?"

Claire hesitated. There was something that she hadn't really said to her Triad that had been bothering her. It wasn't that she thought her Triad wouldn't care, but they always were wanting to protect her.

"I'm worried after the attack at the Academy," Claire confessed. "I almost didn't get that final root up in time and if I had been faster I wouldn't have killed the beast but my magic levels were so low. I don't want that to happen again."

It had been a powerless feeling and Claire still carried immense guilt from killing the Felua. Her Triad kept telling her that she did what she had to do but if only she had been a bit faster she could have saved it. And probably prevented the attack completely and saved Everett from the injury.

"That's to be expected," Andy comforted, "but you accomplished an incredible feat of magic for one as young as you are."

Helene was silent and had a look of contemplation on her face. "What is it, love?" Andy placed a hand on Helene's knee. Claire marveled at how in tune with each other the two women were.

"Just thinking." Helene said, "I wonder, Claire, if it wasn't your magic levels that were low but instead your energy levels?"

Claire wrinkled her nose, puzzled. "I don't understand?"

"You described tapping into the energy of the trees and weaving it with your magic. I have no doubt your magic was helpful but I wonder if it was the energy that was low. It sounds like the tree gave its energy to you and access to the network but… did you actively try to draw energy from it?"

Claire was confused. "No, I just used what was there."

"I think you used what was offered. I think you could learn to pull on additional energy if you needed it."

"Pull on additional energy? Like from the tree?"

"From anything." Helene's voice turned serious. "In the Great War, it was rumored that the Fae could drain magic or energy from anything and anyone."

"Anyone? Like from people?" Claire was shocked and slightly horrified. You could kill someone by draining their magic. She should know. During Combat Finals, her magic had been drained dangerously low from deflecting the magic attack into the Academy.

"Yes, from people." Helene nodded.

Her expression was serious as she took one of Claire's hands in hers. "I tell you this, because I know you understand the consequences and wouldn't do it lightly. But if your energy ever became that low, you could draw from living sources around you, including plants, animals, and people."

"I could never do that." Claire pulled back, horrified at the thought of unknowingly killing someone.

"You will never know the situations you might find yourself in." Andy said. "That's why we are going to practice how to do it safely. So if you are in that situation, you can do it to protect yourself, your Triad, and your friends."

Andy had her there and she knew it. Claire would do anything to protect her Triad and friends. She took a deep breath, trying to settle her stomach and push the horror aside. "Okay. Tell me what I need to know."

"We'll start with plants." Helene waved a hand in front of her and a flower blossomed from the ground.

For the rest of the session, Claire practiced pulling energy off of the flowers and bringing it into herself. She nearly cried the first time she pulled too much and the flower died but Helene quickly brought it to life again.

Eventually, Claire was able to find the balance of how much energy she could take before doing serious harm. All living things had excess energy that rolled off of them. Claire had to get very precise with her focus in order to define what was excess energy and what was critical survival energy.

By the time Andy called the session, Claire was exhausted. She leaned on Everett on the way back to the manor, brushing off his concerned gaze. She opted to skip dinner, instead going straight up to their bedroom. She was too tired to eat. Everett left the room briefly and when he returned, Claire could hear Desmond and Malcolm with him but she didn't open her eyes. Sleep pulled heavily at her as her Triad settled in next to her. Energy Reading was hard work. Maybe she wasn't as good at it as everyone thought she should be.

That night she dreamed about the Felua. Instead of attacking her, it was running away from her as Claire tried to suck the magic from it.

CHAPTER 13

The problem, Claire decided, wasn't that Claire couldn't see Malcolm's sword coming down towards her, it was that she couldn't get her tired body to move fast enough to react. Choosing a defensive option, she rolled out of the way, barely dodging the sword that landed on the ground next to her shoulder.

Malcolm frowned down at her. "That was sloppy. What's wrong?"

Claire pushed herself to her feet, "I'm just tired today."

Everett stepped up next to Malcolm, "From yesterday?" His observant eyes traced Claire's frame.

Claire shrugged and gave a little nod. The energy work she had done with Andy and Helene yesterday had drained her more than she thought. When she had woken up this morning, it felt like there was sand in her eyes and her bones had turned to weights. Her muscles moved with an ache that Claire didn't even know existed.

"What did they have you do yesterday that makes you look like you went two dozen rounds with Malcolm?" Desmond called from his place sitting on the arena wall, a book open in his lap.

"Just some Energy Reading," Claire said, unwilling to share the actual work with them. She didn't want her Triad thinking she was a monster with the ability to drain someone's energy or magic completely from them.

Instead, she glossed over the details, "We worked on manipulating the energy, drawing it and sending it. I guess it was tougher than I thought it was going to be."

"Can you draw energy to you?" Everett asked, "Would that help you this morning?"

Claire froze briefly. What if she drew too much? "I don't know," She said carefully, "I only just learned how. I don't want to hurt anyone accidentally."

Desmond hopped down off the wall. "What if you didn't take it from a person but from an element?" He asked, crossing the distance to stand with them.

Claire frowned, "What do you mean?"

"I mean like drawing energy from an element like fire?"

Claire tilted her head thinking. Would that work? In theory, it made sense. Elements had their own energy.

"Maybe?" She said tentatively.

"Let's try it. If it doesn't work then we know." Desmond said.

He conjured a ball of fire in his hands and nodded at Claire. She stepped up, lifting her hands to cup the ball. She focused on feeling the energy of the fire, the space it was taking up, the warmth in her hands. Then she imagined drawing that energy in towards her, imagining the fire coming inside of herself. Her throat burned and it felt like her insides heated dangerously. She dropped her hands, coughing, trying to suck in the cooler air.

"What's wrong? What happened?" Everett slipped a hand around her waist and rubbed the other over her back, soothing the tight muscles there.

Claire straightened, frowning. "I think I did it wrong," She rasped, the feeling of smoke still in her lungs.

Malcolm handed her a canteen of water and Claire took grateful small sips.

"What do you mean?" Desmond had dropped the fire and stepped up, taking her hands with his once she was done and sending a healing spell through her that cleared the burning in her throat.

"I imagined the fire coming into me and I think it did it quite literally."

"What do you mean?" Malcolm growled out.

"It felt like I pulled the fire's heat into me and not the actual energy." Her men were silent as they took in her words and Claire's lips twisted as she thought. "I want to try again."

"Absolutely not," Malcolm growled.

Desmond frowned, "Maybe we should wait. Talk to Andy and Helene."

"Let's try one more time?" Claire looked up at him, "And if it doesn't work we can stop. I'm not going to do the same thing. I'm going to try something different.."

Desmond studied her face for a few seconds before sighing, "Okay, little witch, only because you know we can't resist you."

Claire laughed softly but stepped forward as Desmond conjured the fire.

Claire had a feeling about where she went wrong the first time. She had focused on bringing the fire inside of her, not the energy of the fire. This time when she laid her hands around the fire, she went deeper than the first energy layer she found. The first energy layer was directly around the element and felt like a searing heat. This was the layer Claire had tried to pull inside her. She pushed deeper into the energy, looking for the feeling of pure energy she had felt yesterday in her work with Andy and Helene.

There. Deep under the heat of the fire, a second layer of

energy danced against her searching magic. Not wanting to be wrong again, she didn't pull all of it into her, just the smallest piece. She wrapped her magic around the small piece and pulled softly. She knew the moment it worked when the energy expanded out of her center, soothing down her aching muscles and feeling like a breath of crisp fall air in her lungs. She opened her eyes and saw Desmond's grin.

"You did it!"

Claire smiled back at him, "I did?"

Everett cupped her cheek and turned her to face him. He studied her face, "The shadows under your eyes are lighter." He commented.

"I didn't want to take too much in case I was wrong." Claire felt a bit lighter, like the fog of exhaustion had lifted from her brain. She still was tired, but this was much more manageable.

"Let's keep going." She turned to Malcolm.

Malcolm nodded slowly, "If you're sure, little treasure."

Claire nodded and drew the daggers from their sheaths again. They discovered that the daggers always returned to their sheaths even if Claire dropped them. A handy trick for sure.

"Let's run through the pattern again," Malcolm instructed, "you need to get the rhythm down."

They had been working on a fight pattern that Malcolm taught in advanced combat classes. Claire was still struggling to find the rhythm for the movements.

She dropped into the stance again, her right leg back and to the side, daggers raised in front of her to block Malcolm's first strike.

He started with an overhead strike that required Claire to cross the daggers and drop to a knee. She shoved the sword off to the left and spun with it to get back up to her feet. Malcolm came at her again with a diagonal blow. Claire used the Fae dagger in her right hand to push the blow away and then darted in with the flat part of the Elven blade to tap Malcolm in the side.

He grinned at her in approval, his eyes tinging gold as his dragon rose to the fight. This next part was the part Claire had been struggling with. It was a quick set of blows in multiple directions that required precise footwork to keep her balance.

Malcolm thrust his sword forward towards her chest. Claire's instinct was to step backwards, daggers crossed in front of her. As soon as Claire stepped backwards though, she groaned at her mistake. The impact of the sword against her daggers sent her sprawling backwards to her back.

"You've got to step to the side," Malcolm chided gently, helping her to her feet. "There's too much force in a straight blow to absorb going backwards."

"I know," Claire said, frowning. She knew, but she was having problems getting her body to know in the heat of the fight. She was just reacting when she needed to be taking into account the force and direction of the blow and flowing it into her next movement.

"You looked good to me," A new voice called from the arena door.

Claire turned to see Bethany and Cody standing in the doorway with Holly and Zack behind them. She squealed and sheathed the daggers, running towards her friends. Bethany met her halfway, the feline shifter's arms wrapped tight around Claire's middle.

"You're here!" Claire pulled back, her own smile matching Bethany's grin.

"We're here!" Cody confirmed, wrapping arms around both Bethany and Claire and swinging them around slightly.

"Cody! Put us down," Bethany growled but it was playful.

"But how? When?" Claire didn't think she would be able to see her friends until the Academy started back again in the fall.

"I think you broke her," Zack teased.

Claire freed an arm from Bethany's embrace and swatted at Zack who danced away.

"Holly's parents invited us formally to Brandlevine's Summer Solstice celebration tomorrow."

Claire had forgotten the Summer Solstice with all of the training and researching. "I'd forgotten about that," Claire admitted.

"I can't imagine why," Cody said, "It's not like you have anything else going on."

Claire laughed, "I'm so excited to see you all."

She turned to Malcolm who read the question in her eyes. "Go," He said smiling, "Enjoy time with your friends. We can train later."

She broke away from her friends to go to Malcolm, throwing her arms around him in a quick hug. He wrapped his arms around her, squeezing gently, his eyes glowing gold. "Go, before we get selfish and keep you for ourselves."

"You aren't selfish," Claire protested lightly.

"We are very selfish when it comes to you." Malcolm kissed the tip of her nose. "But your friends are important to you."

Claire pressed a kiss to his cheek, ignoring her dragon's playful growl. She skipped to Everett for another hug and kiss on the cheek. Desmond was ready for her and caught her in his arms with a kiss on her mouth. Claire sank into him, getting distracted for a few seconds before Desmond pulled back, grinning at the dazed look on her face.

Claire rolled her eyes at him and wriggled out of his arms. "Be good." She instructed, waving a finger at him.

The grin Desmond gave her was wicked, causing a flutter in her stomach. "For you, always," Desmond said.

"Come on, Claire!" Bethany shouted from the door, "You can kiss your men later!"

Laughing, Claire turned to catch up with her friends,

looping her arms through Bethany and Holly's as Cody and Zack walked ahead.

"I can't believe you're here," she said, leaning her head against Bethany's shoulder briefly.

"We wouldn't have gone the whole summer without seeing you," Bethany said, "I'm just sorry it took so long. Tell us everything."

All the way to the village, Claire filled them in on the last few weeks from the Felua's attack to the awkward dinner Desmond's parents had surprised them with, to her idea yesterday about finding an Elven or Fae Champion's journal.

"Sounds like you have a good handle on things." Cody said as they sat down at the same tavern that Holly and Zack had taken her and Malcolm to their first day here.

They had passed the same alleyway and Holly had given Claire a sly smile that Bethany had caught. "Girl talk." Holly had mouthed at Bethany, who's eyes gleamed with questions.

"It doesn't feel like it." Claire admitted. "There's still so much I don't know."

"Give yourself a bit of a break though," Holly said, "You are learning everything at an accelerated pace compared to others your age."

"You'll be so far ahead of everyone at the Academy this year, even us," Zack agreed.

Claire frowned. She had forgotten about the Academy to be honest. They would be expected to attend this year as well but what if they couldn't find the answers by then? Would Claire's new magic and increased skills cause her to be more of an outsider at the Academy?

"You'll be able to stick it to Vivienne!" Bethany crowed. "No more witch bitch."

"Bethany," Holly chided.

"Come on, no one likes her," Bethany said, "Although I'm surprised she hasn't tried to come here this summer."

"What do you mean?" Claire asked.

Holly frowned at Bethany but filled Claire in, "In the past, Vivienne would often spend part of summers at Brandlevine with the hopes of spending time with your Triad. I think her father was responsible for those visits to be honest but Desmond, Everett, and Malcolm never looked twice at her," Holly tried to assure her.

Claire frowned down at her plate as hot feelings of jealousy and self-doubt swirled in her stomach but she pushed them away. She couldn't judge her Triad on things that had happened in the past.

Bethany squeezed her hand, "I'm sorry, I didn't mean to upset you. You have absolutely nothing to worry about though because as soon as those men met you, they've always looked at you like you hung the moon."

"You know, I've never understood that phrase." Cody said, "How in the Realm would one hang the moon? How does one even get up there?"

Bethany smacked Cody's arm but his words had their desired effect as the table laughed at his questions.

They ordered food and spent the afternoon around the table talking and catching up. Bethany and Cody filled them in on their respective pride and pack's comings and goings. Later that night, Holly, Bethany, and Claire hauled extra pillows and blankets into Holly's room for a sleepover.

Her Triad had been less than thrilled that Claire wasn't sleeping in the manor house and had even offered the girls their bedroom. Holly told them that one night wouldn't kill them and when that didn't work Claire batted her eyelashes at them like Bethany had taught her to.

Everett's lip twitch almost gave Claire away to Malcolm and Desmond so Everett had offered the concession that the men would take turns standing watch in the area. So now the girls were settling onto the nest of blankets they had made on the floor of Holly's room.

The scene was familiar to the sleepovers they had at the Academy. Claire smiled at the thought. Those sleepovers, especially the first one after Claire had found out she was the Triad's Fourth.

"Ok," Bethany said, settling on her stomach, "tell me everything you couldn't say in front of the boys."

"Claire got kissssssed," Holly said dramatically, throwing herself back onto a pillow.

"What?" Bethany cried. "Why in the realm didn't you lead with that?"

"And say what?" Claire laughed. "Hey Bethany. Great to see you. Malcolm kissed the soul out of me the second day we were here."

"Yes! Exactly that!" Bethany said indignantly.

She tugged Claire down next to her and Claire landed on her stomach with an oof. "Tell me every detail!" Bethany demanded.

Holly rolled over on her stomach, "Ooo don't forget when they eye-fucked you when you came down in that dress."

Claire and Bethany stared at Holly in shock before bursting into giggles. Holly was not normally that crude.

Bethany hit Claire's shoulder playfully, "And they eye-fucked you!!! Tell me everything! Now!"

Claire groaned, her cheeks burning. "Stop, they did not eye-..." she trailed off, unable to say the word.

"Awww you're so cute and sweet, you can't even say it." Bethany teased, "That's okay, I'll say it for you. They totally eye-fucked you. They do it all the time when you are in regular clothes so I have no doubt they did it when you were in a stunning dress."

"They do not." Claire protested weakly.

"Sorry, Claire, they totally do," Holly chimed in, "but in like the cutest way."

"And they better be doing it in a respectful way too or I'll have to have a word." Bethany grinned.

"Stop, they have been so good to me."

"And hopefully made it good for you." Bethany teased.

"You are both terrible," Claire complained but she was giggling. By the Realm, she had missed her friends.

"So what happened first? The soul-sucking kiss or the eye-fucking?" Bethany asked, laughing.

"Stop," Claire giggled, "or I'll never be able to tell you the story."

"Okay, I'll behave." Bethany wiggled her eyebrows at her.

"No, you won't," Holly said, also giggling.

Claire's stomach ached with all the laughter and she took a deep breath trying to stop giggling. She described Malcolm's reluctance to kiss her that resulted in Claire teasing him. Bethany practically swooned when she told them how Malcolm dragged her into the alley and kissed her until Claire forgot where she was. Holly helped Claire describe the dress Everett had found and Holly described the 'eye-fucking' in great detail much to Bethany's delight.

"That is the most adorably cute thing I have ever heard." Bethany said, groaning. "All the sweetness is going to give me a toothache. Do you have any bloodthirsty stories?"

Claire laughed, "I mean, not really? Training stories but nothing bloodthirsty yet." She brushed away the images that came to mind about the dead Felua.

"Boring," Bethany complained.

"I'm sure we can get up to some trouble now that you're here." Holly teased.

Bethany sprang up on her elbows, her eyes gleaming, "Now that's an idea!"

"Oh no, look what you've done," Claire jokingly complained to Holly.

"Hey, I make your lives interesting, admit it." Bethany protested.

"You definitely do." Claire reassured her.

"Make them interesting tomorrow though," Holly said yawning, "so we can keep up."

"Fine. Ruin all my fun," Bethany teased as she snagged a pillow, her own yawn betraying her.

Claire fell asleep with a smile on her face and her bonds thrumming faintly as her men kept watch outside.

CHAPTER 14

The next morning they all sat down for breakfast at the manor house.

"I'm glad you are all here." Ilena said over breakfast the next morning. "We need some help finishing up preparations before the festival."

"We'll be happy to help," Claire said, speaking for all of them. Ilena and Frederick had extended so much hospitality to them, the least they could do would be help with the festival.

Windshire had celebrated the Summer Solstice but she knew it was probably nothing like how Brandlevine celebrated it.

"Thank you, Claire," Ilena smiled at her and Desmond let out a groan.

"Now you've done it, little witch," he teased, "she'll have us slaving away all day."

Ilena rolled her eyes, "The dramatics. It won't be all day. Just until it's done."

"That means all day," Desmond winked at Claire who laughed.

"It won't be that bad." She reassured him. "Besides, we'll get to do it together."

"Ugh, the sweetness," Bethany teased from across the table.

Desmond went to retort but Ilena clapped her hands together, disrupting what was sure to devolve into an argument. "If you're done here, you can head into the village and find Clarissa. She has the task list that still needs to be done."

They walked to the village, Claire's smaller hand folded in Everett's calloused grip. She exchanged a small smile with her quiet mate as they listened to the others chatter. The best part about Everett, in Claire's opinion, was his surety of himself and the comfortable quiet and steadfastness she found in him. He was always there, always. Instead of feeling creeped out by it, Claire found a lot of comfort in his slightly stalkerish presence.

"What are you thinking about?" He rumbled.

"How I don't mind you stalking me." Her thoughts came out of her mouth before she could stop them. And the best part? It was right during a pause in the others' conversation.

Desmond guffawed out a laugh in a way that was unlike his polished self. Everett grinned and ducked his head, ears slightly red. Malcolm just looked at them as if he was thinking, "of course stalking someone was fine." Claire rolled her eyes at Malcolm's expression, possessive dragon, and squeezed Everett's hand.

"I really don't." She insisted softly, "It makes me feel safe."

"I would never let anything happen to you," Everett promised softly.

"Don't say that." Claire said, "There's no way to guarantee that."

"But it's true," Everett insisted, slowing his pace so they fell behind the group. Desmond and Malcolm continued with the group but kept glancing back towards them.

"It places a burden on you I don't want you to carry," Claire was firm, "I could trip tomorrow over a stone and hurt myself and I don't want you beating yourself up over accidents."

"I wouldn't do that," Everett grumbled, looking away.

Claire arched an eyebrow and waited until he looked towards her again.

He sighed and drew her into his arms, "I just don't want anything to happen to you."

"I'm supposed to be a Champion of the Realm." Claire kept her voice hushed, "Things are bound to happen to me. How about you just promise to always be there with me."

"Even if it's by stalking you?" Everett teased.

Claire rolled her eyes, "Yes, even if it's by stalking. I thought we covered that I'm strange because I don't mind it."

"Not strange, just perfect for us."

"You can canoodle with your mate later!" Bethany yelled, someone clearly having filled her in on Claire's use of that word with Malcolm and Desmond the other day, "This festival won't set up itself."

"Is that a possibility?" Cody wondered.

Bethany smacked him on the shoulder lightly and the two started bickering as Everett and Claire caught up with the group.

"Oh good, there you are!" Holly's mother, Clarissa, said, rushing up to them. "Malcolm, Everett, I need you over there with the other men finishing putting together the tables. The rest of you, follow me. We have more decorations to hang."

Clarissa led them down the main road a bit farther. A few crates with colorful decorations spilling out from the tops sat outside a shop door and two wooden ladders leaned against the side of the building.

"These garlands need to hang across the road and then these decorations need to decorate the shop doors," Clarissa gestured to the crates respectively.

Ever the planner, Desmond immediately started organizing, assigning Zack and Cody the task of being on the ladders with Bethany and Holly handing them the decorations. He gave Claire the task of decorating the shop doors and windows.

Claire smiled internally, Desmond might laugh at Everett's protectiveness but he was just as bad.

They had moved a few doors down when two women walked through the group. "Never thought I would see the day when shifters attended a witch festival, it's just unnatural. I don't know why Frederick would allow it." The one woman remarked to her friend as they passed underneath the garlands.

It was said loud enough that Claire was sure she had wanted them to hear it loud and clear. She frowned darkly at the woman's departing back and took a step forward.

"Leave it." Holly touched her arm gently, "That's Matilda. She is still stuck in the past."

"The far past," Bethany growled, "she forgets the shifters fought alongside the witches in the Great War."

"If they did, then why is she so... hateful?" Claire asked. The woman didn't even know her friends and yet was making comments like that. "Doesn't that mean the shifters and witches were allies?"

"Allies is a loose term." Zack remarked from up on the ladder. "It was definitely born out of necessity rather than a true willingness to work together."

"What do you mean?" Claire asked, picking up the next garland and helping Bethany untangle it.

"Well when the Elves started demanding higher prices for their medicinal treatments, the other races knew that they had to band together and refuse to pay those prices until they were lowered. That forced the shifters and witches into a trade alliance at least." Zack explained.

"So how did the Fae and Elves become allies then?" Claire asked. There was something they were missing. Something that could explain all of this. Why would the Elves withhold the treatments otherwise when for thousands of years they had held to the Alliance?

"That was a surprising development," Desmond said, "At

least according to Father. The two races lived on opposite sides of the Realm yet when the first attack happened, the Fae came to the Elves' aid."

"The Elves attacked first?"

Desmond nodded but Zack broke in, "Actually, I don't think that's true. At least not according to the Dryad's journal I was just reading. It was the witches who attacked first in a surprise attack on an Elven village close to the border."

Desmond frowned, "That's not what the records say."

Pursing her lips, Claire thought about the differing accounts. "I think," She said carefully, looking around to make sure their group was alone, "I think we should maybe consider that everything you've been taught about the Great War is wrong."

"Why do you say that?" Holly frowned as they all paused, turning to look at her. Claire took a deep breath, keeping her voice even but low. She didn't think her friends would judge her words but the other witches in Brandlevine might take it the wrong way.

"All the official records are written by the witches, shifters, and dragons, correct?" Claire asked.

"Yes," It was Desmond who answered her this time.

"Wouldn't they want their stories to be told? Or at least the stories from their perspective?" Claire arched an eyebrow, "And isn't it convenient that there are no records from the Fae and Elves."

"I thought you thought the Fae and Elves recalled the records?" Bethany asked.

Claire shrugged, "I did and I do think that. I'm just also wondering if there's more to it that we don't know. Would the Council keep records from the other side's perspective? Especially if those records didn't fit the story they were sharing, like the book Zack read."

The group was silent and Claire gave them time to process as she fiddled with a decoration. At Windshire, they had never really talked much about the Great War and any learning Claire did was self taught. As a result, she had a more unbiased view of the Realm as she hadn't grown up with those stories or with family who had fought in it. Well, maybe she did have family who fought in it but she wouldn't know.

"I think you're onto something, Claire," It was Cody who was first to speak, "I think it's time to consider that everything we've been told might be wrong."

"But that would mean the Council…" Bethany trailed off but the rest of her statement hung heavy in the silence. That would mean that the Council had been lying to everyone.

Desmond swore softly and looked around them, the distant chatter from the village center catching his attention. "We can't talk about this here and now, out in the open like this."

"Later," Claire agreed. She didn't want any of her friends getting hurt.

"After the festival tomorrow, before Bethany and Cody have to go back," Holly said, her face pale.

They finished the decorations in a somber silence until they headed back to the village center. There, they pasted smiles on their faces like their whole worlds hadn't just been turned upside down. Claire would have felt guilty putting those expressions on their faces if she wasn't worried they would need to know to face what's ahead.

CHAPTER 15

Claire wasn't sure what to expect from a Summer Solstice festival as she had never been to Windshire's. She knew there was always a celebration of some sort around it, but the orphanage had rarely been invited to participate. She had no idea of what to expect but the morning started bright and early with Desmond surprising her with a pair of lightweight white summer pants and a dark red blouse.

His eyes sparkled as he showed her the shirt and Claire blushed, thinking back to the time that she had asked him to describe the color red to her. That had resulted in him stealing a quick kiss before Holly and Bethany had arrived to get ready together. Watching Holly shoo Desmond out the door with a petulant look on his face had Claire bending over in laughter.

"Those men are obsessed with you," Holly said, smiling even as she shook her head, turning away from the door..

"Ya know, there are worse things in life." Bethany commented, "Especially when they provide cute outfits."

The girls laughed and chattered as they got ready, nervous excitement swirling in Claire's gut. When they opened the door, Claire's Triad stood in the hallway sending the girls into more peals of laughter as the Triad watched them with confused amusement.

"Obsessed," Holly mouthed at Claire as they headed down the stairs.

Claire rolled her eyes and giggled, accepting Malcolm's arm and enjoying the heat in his eyes as he took her in. They ate a light breakfast and then headed down to the village. The festivities would go on all day.

The village was alive with all sorts of sounds and smells. Lively music threaded through the crowds as children shouted and squealed, darting through the legs of the adults with colorful streamers clenched in their sticky fists. The sweet, tangy smell of hot sweet buns was almost drowned out by the savory smell of meat roasting over multiple fires.

Malcolm accepted two sweet buns from one of the women at a table and handed one to Claire. She brought it up to her nose and took a deep whiff of the honeyed sweetness before biting into it. As the flavors exploded on her tongue, she sighed. This was almost better than the sweet buns she and Malcolm had at the Market.

As they munched on the sweet buns, the group threaded their way through the crowd. Bethany and Holly stole her away from Malcolm for a bit, pressing a glass of sweet smelling liquid in her hand. The three girls toasted and drank the sweet wine quickly. It warmed her insides and Bethany put a finger to her mouth in a shushing motion with such a devious smile on her face that Holly and Claire collapsed into wordless laughter, their sides aching. When the men found them, they stared at them in amused bewilderment before Malcolm stole Claire back into his arms.

Bethany and Holly broke off to chat with Holly's parents and Cody and Zack got roped into playing a kickball game with the children. Their excited shouts as the older boys joined the game made Claire smile and she stayed to watch the game with

Malcolm for a bit. She laughed as Cody let himself get tackled by a few smaller boys, falling to the ground dramatically with exaggerated shouts of defeat. The little ones piled onto him playfully, crying out in victory at having taken down the 'big bad wolf'.

Everett appeared at her other side with a plate of savory smelling meats and fresh vegetables. He held up a piece to Claire's mouth and Claire blushed, either from the wine or from being slightly embarrassed at being fed like an infant in public. When her mouth closed around the juicy meat and Everett's fingers, she understood the power she had here. Keeping eye contact with Everett, she sucked the juices from his fingers, feeling indescribably pleased when his eyes darkened. Both Everett and Malcolm groaned when she licked her lips and she fought not to let her smile get too big. She was more sure of what she was asking for now. Bethany and Holly had made sure of that, but Claire also knew that over half of what her friends had described could not be done in a public place.

"What?" She fought to keep her voice innocent, "It's good."

Malcolm's hand snaked around her stomach and tugged her back into his chest, "You play with fire, little treasure."

"Good thing you're fire-proof," Claire teased back.

Malcolm groaned but found them a quiet corner for Everett to finish feeding her. Claire tried to keep her teasing to a minimum but couldn't resist. That's how Desmond found them.

"Why are you making me the rule-follower?" Desmond's grumbling caused Claire to break her intense eye contact with Everett, "We are in public for the realm's sake."

Claire couldn't help but laugh at the put-out expression on Desmond's face. His eyes brightened at the sound.

"Are you laughing at me, little witch?" He closed the distance between them, a familiar wicked gleam entering his eyes.

"With you?" She offered, unable to hold her grin in as he

formed the third side of the triangle that was her Triad. She giggled at the thought.

"Have you tried a little wine, little witch?" Desmond arched an eyebrow at her.

"I don't know what you're talking about," Claire smiled innocently, not betraying her friends, "But I would like to try some now."

"Mhmm," Desmond raised his eyebrows at her and Claire looked up at him with her 'pleading eyes' as Bethany called them. "Fine, we'll get you some to try."

"Is that wise?" Malcolm asked from his position behind her as her seat-back.

She twisted in her seat to give him a grin, "I think it's a brilliant idea."

Everett backed her up with a small chuckle, "She's safe here with us."

"No one would attack a coven on Solstice anyways," Desmond said.

Malcolm grumbled but nodded. Perfect timing too as her friends were weaving through the crowd, cups in their hands.

The sun was setting and the evening air was starting to cool but when Claire took a sip of the sweet wine that Bethany had pressed in her hand, her insides warmed comfortably. Around them, parents were gathering the children closer, the youngest ones were going inside to bed while the older ones fought to stay out longer.

The music changed and the crowd started shifting outside the village towards the field behind it. "What's happening?" Claire asked, lifting on her tiptoes to ask the question to Desmond's ear.

"They are about to light the bonfire," Desmond said, smiling fondly down at her, "And there'll be dancing until we release the light orbs."

"The light orbs?" Claire questioned.

Zack, overhearing her question, answered, "They are balls of fire and air that the witches conjure to release into the sky to celebrate the Solstice. Each member of the coven gets one. You're supposed to make a wish on them or give an intention to think about for the rest of the year."

Claire frowned, "I never heard of those in Windshire."

"They require witches with both fire and air proficiencies," Desmond told her, "Covens who don't have witches with both use candles typically."

Claire wanted to ask more questions but they had gotten to the bonfire that was now raging cheerfully to the sky. The pile of wood was taller than Malcolm even and clearly meant to go all night. The music had changed to an upbeat song and several people were already dancing.

Bethany and Holly dragged her into the dancers and Claire tried to copy their movements, laughing with them when she stumbled. The girls toasted and drained their glasses and the warmth that settled into Claire's bones helped her move with the rhythm although she still struggled.

Light hands landed on her hips and the scent of spearmint had Claire leaning back into Desmond. "It's like those warm-up forms Malcolm loves so much." His voice a soft breath on her ear. "Think of it like a rhythm that way."

Claire didn't know if it was Desmond's advice or his warm hands on her hip that helped Claire sink into the beat but she didn't care. There was no Champion of the Realm here, no questions about who her parents were, or what to do with her growing power. Surrounded by her friends and Triad, she danced and let go of everything else.

Hours later, sweaty and breathless, the music softened, taking on a softer, almost haunting, tone. Desmond smiled and broke away from the group, leaving her in Everett's arms. He, along with a few other witches, including his mother Ilena, started conjuring. They mixed air and fire into a glowing orb and then dispersed it. It was orderly, and almost eerie as no one spoke, the music softening to haunting whispers that spoke of a season ending and beginning. The coven patiently waited for their orbs, the older children shifting excitedly when they received theirs while their parents looked on with gentle amusement.

When most of the crowd had received their orbs, Desmond returned to their group. Conjuring orbs, he gave them to Claire, Malcolm, Everett, Holly, Bethany, and Cody. Bethany and Cody had hesitated when he went to hand them theirs. Claire wondered if they were thinking of that woman's words from yesterday. Desmond didn't say anything to break the silence, just smiled and offered the orb.

"Family, friends, coven mates," Frederick's voice rang out. Claire turned to see him standing before the fire on a raised box, his own orb in his hand.

"Tonight we gather here to celebrate the Summer Solstice, the longest day of the year and a symbol of our power and continued growth. The sun has blessed the Realm and us through the spring bringing us another season of prosperity. The seeds we plant here tonight will grow into a plentiful fall harvest but only if we tend to them. Tonight, we celebrate its life-giving warmth and turn our intentions and sights towards the rest of the year. As we whisper our wishes and intentions into these orbs and release them into the sky, we renew our commitment to them."

Claire was startled. She had been having so much fun she hadn't even thought about what wish she would release. The most obvious wish that came to mind was wishing for answers on where she had come from or who her family was but…

She looked around her circle, her Triad and friends and their unrelenting love and support. Isn't this what family was? She was hit by such an overwhelming wave of love and adoration for these people around her who had been with her through every up and down over the last year. Tears filled her eyes at the thought of doing this without them. She knew what her wish would be. Whoever her parents were, whatever was out there waiting for them, this group right here was Claire's family.

Let me always be able to protect them, she pushed her wish into the orb with a small strand of magic. The orb glowed brighter for a second before settling, the light fuzzy from the tears filling her eyes. She blinked them back though, as happy as those tears were, tonight was not the time to cry.

Looking up, she met Everett's concerned eyes at her tears. She smiled at him and pushed a wave of love and reassurance towards him down their bond. His eyes widened as if he had actually felt it. She felt the question in her own eyes and he nodded minutely. She looked deeper at the feeling and realized that the faint bonds with her Triad had grown stronger. She could actually feel the bonds tying her to her Triad in her magic center.

They had always been there, Claire had just never recognized them that clearly before. She pushed a wave of love down all three and Desmond and Malcolm's eyes snapped to her as well. She grinned at them, loving the smiles that grew across their faces in response.

Frederick called for them to release their orbs to the sky and Claire lightly tossed hers up. It joined her friends and the steady stream of orbs crawling up towards the stars. Everett pulled her back into him, and she reached out hands for Desmond and Malcolm to take as they tracked the orbs in the sky until they couldn't see them anymore.

Claire dropped her eyes to her family and vowed to make her wish come true. Whatever it took.

CHAPTER 16

Sleep eluded her that night, worry about her wish and how to keep it had her tossing and turning until finally, Claire slipped from the bed. With soft feet and years of practice of being invisible, she slipped from the room and out of the manor, making sure to keep the sensitive bonds between herself and her men quiet and calm. The horizon was lightening from the midnight blue of the night to a soft purple as the sun started waking up.

Claire's bare feet hit the wet grass and the coolness of the dew sent a shiver up her spine but she pressed forward. Ever since getting her sight, Claire tried to watch as many sunrises and sunsets as she could. She climbed a small hill off the path towards town. Frowning down at the wet grass, she thought for a moment before rolling her eyes at herself. Conjuring a bit of magic up from her center, she drew an air rune and used the breeze to dry the grass on top of the hill. She sank to her knees just as the sun peeked out from the horizon.

Entranced, her eyes watched the colors that began to dance across the sky as the sun rose above the horizon to dance with the clouds. Reds, oranges, yellows, purples, and blues, wove together in a beautiful masterpiece as Claire sat completely enthralled. There were so many colors.

She frowned, heart heavy as the colors also reminded her of everything she had missed out on. She had missed out on this her entire life because someone thought the price of Claire's vision was the price to pay for binding her power. But if that was the price, what was the cost if they hadn't?

In the distance, she could hear the men calling for her from the stone patio but she didn't answer, lost in her own thoughts and in the beauty in front of her. She knew Everett would find her shortly anyways, probably aided by their newly strengthened bonds. The man had an uncanny sense for where she was at all times.

Not more than a minute later and her view was only made better by the sight of her men.

Everett stole the space behind her before Malcolm could, ignoring the dragon's rumble. He nuzzled in on Claire's neck and left a trail of soft kisses to her ear. "Good morning, little mate." He said.

Claire sighed and leaned back into him. "Good morning." She whispered into the quiet morning air.

"So this is where you ran off to," Desmond said, taking a seat next to her and beating Malcolm to it. Malcolm just grumbled at him and sat down on her other side.

"Couldn't sleep?" Malcolm asked, his tone worried. Claire shifted slightly in Everett's arms so she could see his face. His eyes matched his tone as they traced her face.

Realizing she hadn't answered his question, she shook her head, "Something woke me up so I came out to watch the sunrise. It's beautiful."

"Not more beautiful than you," Desmond said, winking at her and causing the other men to groan with his cheesiness.

Giggling, Claire held a hand out to him and beckoned Malcolm with the other. Surrounded by her mates, they watched as the sun came up. A new day dawning.

As the sun rose higher over the horizon, it was like Claire's magic woke up with it. Twirling around and softly beating at the dome of bindings that still covered it like a patchwork quilt. Her magic was awake and wanted to be let out.

As if he could sense her restlessness, Malcolm got to his feet and extended a hand down to her. "Come. It's time to train."

Although Desmond groaned, he joined the rest as they got to their feet and headed to the training arena.

Claire unsheathed her daggers when they arrived and began working through the warm-up forms. Remembering what Desmond said last night, she tried to think of them as a rhythm not just a sequence of movements. The form flowed and the daggers became an extension of her body as she found the rhythm that had been missing the last few weeks.

When she was done, she turned to face Malcolm who was watching her with a quiet, proud smile. "Let's begin." He motioned her forward, drawing his own sword as he did so.

Claire struggled to keep that same rhythmic feeling she felt during the warm-up form for her spar with Malcolm though. Her movements flowed more smoothly but she still struggled with the speed and power to deflect Malcolm's blows. After about twenty minutes, Malcolm had her spar with Everett so he could watch Claire's form and make suggestions.

Everett fought differently than Malcolm did, moving faster and almost melting from one place to the other like the shadows he liked so much. The one similarity between the two of them was the power behind his blows. Neither of her mates went easy on her nor did she want them too. If she was going to keep her wish from last night and keep them and her family safe she had to learn this.

A particularly powerful downwards blow from Everett sent

her stumbling backwards. She frowned. It didn't seem to matter how fast she moved, the sheer power from the blows of a warrior like Malcolm or Everett could knock her off her feet.

"I've got an idea." Desmond announced from his place leaning against the wall. Claire hoped his idea wasn't just switching out with Everett. He sometimes joined their sparring sessions and his lithe frame was no less powerful.

"Spit it out before it dies of loneliness," Malcolm grumbled. Claire swiveled her gaze to Malcolm, eyebrows raised. Did her grumpy dragon just make a joke? Before breakfast?

From the affronted look on Desmond's face, he must have. Pushing down her laughter, she tried not to let the smile on her face get too big and broke in before Desmond could retort.

"What is it?" She laid a hand on his arm.

Desmond frowned at Malcolm before breaking into a wicked smile. He grabbed Claire's arm gently and ushered her a few paces from Malcolm. "Well now, it's not for the class to know." He threw over his shoulder before throwing up a privacy spell so his conversation with Claire wouldn't reach the others.

Claire laughed then at the mischievous look in his eyes. "What do you not want them knowing?"

"A way for you to knock Malcolm on his ass." Desmond waggled his eyebrows at her, making her laugh harder.

"Desmond, there's no way I can do that. As you all keep pointing out, I'm little and you all are big."

"It's not about the size of the warrior, it's about the power in the blow."

Claire raised her eyebrows at him, he wasn't making a lot of sense. Seeing the look on her face, he continued. "The power behind their blows is just energy. What if you absorbed the power the same way you absorb energy and redirect it back at him?"

Claire thought for a moment. It could be possible, she

guessed. But she would have to react fast enough to yank the energy and then send it back. That would be faster than she's ever directed Energy before

"Remember that time when you closed your eyes and felt the energy of the staff and surrounding air?" Desmond asked.

Claire nodded. "It's the same thing." He continued. "It will happen faster but think of it as a faster rhythm and be firm with your magic. Don't ask. Tell it what you want. Demand it if you have to."

"You really think that's going to work?"

Desmond grinned, "I do. If I'm wrong, I'll owe you as many sweet buns as you want."

Claire smiled, "And if you're right?"

Desmond's grin turned a different kind of wicked, "If I'm right, then you owe me a different kind of sweetness."

Claire's breath caught as she understood his meaning. She let her own grin spread across her face, "Then I hope you're right."

The surprise in Desmond's eyes was evident but the smile on his face told her he enjoyed her teasing. He dropped the barrier, "Prove me right, little witch."

Malcolm watched Claire approach with a small frown, but matched her stance when she dropped into it. Claire focused on opening her Energy Reading ability wider than it had ever gone. Her magic answered her call, swirling at her fingertips and all over her body.

It felt like Claire's skin was hyper-sensitized, every touch of air brushing energy down her spine. She spun out of the way of a blow and focused on absorbing the energy of it and aiding her spin. The energy came easily and Claire twirled twice from the power. She caught her balance again and grinned. Malcolm gave her a wary look but continued with the match. She waited for his next downwards blow. She didn't want to hurt him, so she adjusted the magic in the

Elven dagger to a shield, keeping the Fae dagger on the offensive.

Malcolm liked the powerful downward blows and sure enough, his next move was one of those. As the sword descended, Claire didn't dodge as she normally would have. She met his blade with the Fae dagger, focusing on yanking the powerful energy from the metal. She didn't ask, she just demanded and the energy came at her demand, vibrating her body from the force of it but only for a second as she pushed all of the energy into the Elven dagger and thrust it towards Malcolm's middle. The energy left as quickly as it was called and Malcolm went flying backwards at the unexpected force, crashing to his back.

The arena was silent for a breath before Desmond let out a whoop and ran to Claire, lifting her up and spinning her around.

"Desmond!" She exclaimed, struggling to get out of his arms, worry for Malcolm at the forefront of her mind. "Let me down. I've got to check on Malcolm."

Everett was already helping Malcolm to his feet, unable to contain his own chuckles as he dusted off Malcolm's back.

"Malcolm, are you okay?" Claire ran up to him and then squeaked as Malcolm drew her into his arms suddenly.

His golden eyes glowed with his dragon and he let a wide grin take over his face. "I am so proud of you."

"But I knocked you down!" Claire protested. Quite forcefully too, she added silently.

"Yes, and that was good." Malcolm reassured her. "You did exactly what you needed to against an opponent of my size."

"I know that." Claire admitted reluctantly, "But I don't want to hurt you."

"You didn't hurt me," Malcolm said.

"I just want to say," Desmond broke in, "that this was all my fabulous idea."

Malcolm rolled his eyes as Claire giggled. She wiggled out of his arms, ignoring his rumble and danced to Desmond. "It was, and it was a brilliant idea."

Desmond smiled down at her, looping an arm around her waist. Her Triad was always holding her but as Claire snuggled in next to him, she found she didn't really mind.

"Good job, Claire!" Everett affirmed.

Claire's stomach interrupted her reply with a loud grumble.

"I'm sorry, was that Malcolm in there?" Desmond teased.

Claire rolled her eyes and shoved him away playfully. He fake-lunged towards her and she squealed, dancing away and hiding behind Everett who crouched down so she could hop on his back.

Everett carried her out of the arena, Malcolm and Desmond close behind. As they exited, they ran into Claire's friends.

"Good morning!" Holly greeted, "We were just coming to watch training."

"We just finished," Claire said, "We had a bit of an early start."

"You missed Claire knocking Malcolm on his ass." Desmond said, throwing an arm around Holly's shoulders as the group turned towards the manor house.

"Aww, we missed *that*?" Bethany complained, ignoring Malcolm's rumbly growl.

"That's what you get for lazing the morning away like a cat." Cody teased Bethany, running around the group to avoid her returning blow.

"It was one time," Malcolm grumbled.

Claire's friends laughed with Desmond and Everett and Claire reached out to squeeze his shoulder, "It's okay," she said, "you are still my big strong dragon."

Malcolm smiled and shook his head at her, "Thank you, little treasure."

"Malcolm," Claire complained, teasing, "You have to stop calling me little now. You're going to ruin my rep as a badass!"

"Never, little treasure, never."

CHAPTER 17

Back at the manor house, Claire slid off Everett's back. "I'm going to go clean up before breakfast." She said, calling over her shoulder as she ascended the stairs.

"Do you need help, little witch?" Desmond asked.

"No." Holly answered for her, "Because if you go up there we will never be able to have that conversation we all need to have before Cody and Bethany have to leave." She reminded them of the conversation they had about the true start of the Great War.

The mood sombered at her words and Claire hurried up the stairs and into their bedroom, closing the door behind her. They would need all the time they could get for that particular conversation.

Turning around, Claire froze.

Lying on their bed was a creature Claire had never seen before. It was small and could probably fit in Claire's arms if she wanted to lift it. Soft furred ears stuck out from the top of its head. The ears were large and a dark grey that blackened at the tips. They swiveled as Claire took it in, as if they were tracking the sounds from all around them. The fur on its face was a soft grey that lightened to a white chest. Feathery grey wings speckled with black spots stuck out from its back and four soft clawed feet belayed the fierceness of this animal. A small beak similar to Everett's gryphons but much daintier stuck out between large black eyes. Large black eyes that glowed red that instantly threw Claire back to the forest at the Academy. And if that wasn't enough, the same wrong energy that had surrounded the Felua poured out of the creature.

Dark magic.

Claire opened her mouth to yell for her Triad and the creature pounced. With a speed much faster than Claire was expecting, it hit her chest and Claire fell back expecting to hit the door. Instead she hit the ground. Sitting up, she realized the creature had transported them to somewhere else.

Brandlevine was nowhere in sight. She was on her own.

Scrambling to her feet, Claire whirled around trying to locate the creature who disappeared as fast as it appeared. Movement on her left caught her eye and Claire barely had time to call a shield spell before the creature pounced again. Her shield spell was half formed and only barely deflected the creature. Claire stumbled backwards from the force of the pounce and drew her daggers, thankful she hadn't taken off the sheath yet. Panic clawed up her throat but Claire tried to force it down. Panic would make her freeze and she couldn't freeze. She was on her own, no Triad or friends to save her. She had to do it on her own.

The creature circled Claire as she held her daggers out in front of her. She called her magic up like she practiced with Desmond and focused her intention around the magic on a shield. She didn't want to kill it like she had killed the Felua.

When the creature sprang at her again, its eyes red from the dark magic, she realized the creature didn't have the same reservations about killing as Claire did.

She absorbed the force of the blow and danced away from the creature, avoiding its sharp beak that snapped just inches from her side. She shoved the creature away and spun to face it.. She was going to have to figure something out. And fast. She was already tired from not sleeping. That combined with a training session this morning and Claire could feel her muscles burning. If only she could release the creature from the hold the dark magic had on it.

Her eyes widened. That was it. She could pull the dark magic from the creature's Energy.

She pulled the magic back from the daggers, reforming the intention to stunning instead of shielding. The next time the creature sprang, she lifted the Fae dagger up and let the force of the stunning spell fall down on the creature's head. It dropped to the ground instantly and Claire winced. Hopefully that wasn't too much for the small thing.

She held the daggers in front of her for a moment longer and then dropped them when it didn't move. Only the rise and fall of the creature's stomach told her she hadn't killed it. She would have to act quickly though as she had no idea how long the creature would be out.

Claire sank to her knees as she sank into the creature's energy, easily finding the dark magic that tainted it. It coated the creature's natural energy like a black sludge, so deeply intertwined that Claire struggled to tell where it ended and where the creature's Energy began. Whoever did this didn't want the creature breaking out of their hold anytime soon. She didn't have much time to analyze though as who knew when the creature would wake up. Ignoring the nerves that tightened her stomach, she took a deep breath and began pulling on the tainted energy, coaxing it away. It resisted at first, stubbornly clinging to the creature's Energy but the more she tugged on it the easier it came away until it swirled in a black ball in front of her., thick and oozing.

She held it between her palms as far away from her body as she could.

Claire didn't want to take it into her center but also didn't want to release it into the air or into the earth. But how to get rid of it?

The creature was shifting in front of her and Claire knew it was beginning to wake up. One of the edges of the dark magic flickered like a flame and a thought came to Claire. What if she could burn it? Burn the dark magic away?

She called on her magic and drew a bigger fire rune than she usually did. As the fire grew in her palms, she lifted her hands around the ball of dark magic and commanded the fire to burn it away.

It fought back at first, trying to jump to her palms and into her center. Claire slammed her defenses down and sent more magic into the fire. She held her breath until ever so slowly, the ball of dark magic started shrinking, slowly burning away until not a speck of it remained. Claire released the fire and fell forward, catching herself with her hands as her head spun and her magic moved sluggishly in her center from the overuse. She was never going to a training session without breakfast again. Claire took a few more deep breaths and then lifted her head to check on the creature. She sucked in a breath when intelligent golden eyes stared back at her.

At some point, the creature had regained consciousness and was watching her. Its owl-like head was cocked curiously, its body still lying on the ground. The rapid rise and fall of its stomach indicated it was still trying to recover from the stunning spell Claire had administered.

Claire tentatively extended a hand towards it, palm up in a nonthreatening manner. The creature dragged itself up onto its feet and shuffled towards her. Pausing a breath away from her hand, it studied her with its eyes, waiting for something.

"It's okay," she said softly, "it can't hurt you anymore."

The creature chirped back, pushing its soft feathery head into her hand. As she stroked her fingers through the greyish-black feathers, a small strand of magic crept up from her center and pushed softly into her hand. It began to glow and the creature lifted its head to look at her. The creature's body began to glow a pale blue and Claire felt its own magic push at hers. Her magic retreated and the creature's magic followed, taking its place in her center next to her magic and the thread of magic from the Academy.

She really needed to stop accepting strange magic. Desmond was going to have a kitten when he learned about this.

Claire stood and dusted off her knees. The creature had teleported them somewhere into the countryside. Grassy fields as far as Claire could see stretched out in all directions. Not a tree or building interrupted the view and definitely not Brandlevine's manor house. Claire frowned and bit her lip. This was not good. She had no idea where she was, where Brandlevine was, and there wasn't another soul in sight except for the creature at her feet. Forget Desmond having a kitten, Malcolm was going to have a fit. Everett probably too.

The creature chirped at her from the ground. Claire looked down and the creature extended its wings and jumped up towards her chest. She wrapped her arms around it with a soft 'oof' and adjusted her hold on it.

"I don't suppose you know where you took us?" Claire asked. "I need to get back to Brandlevine before my Triad realizes I'm gone."

The creature just chirped at her and settled into her arms as if teleporting them here and getting the dark magic extracted had taken everything from it. Claire rolled her eyes while fighting a smile at its antics. Of course it was too much to ask to take her home or to know where they were.

Well if every option looked the same, then any option would do, she thought as she chose a direction and started walking. Maybe she could find some familiar landmarks.

After thirty minutes of walking, Claire had not found any

landmarks and the creature was fast asleep in her arms, apparently worn out. Claire couldn't blame him but wondered when it was going to be her turn to be carried and to sleep. Claire shifted its weight, her arms beginning to ache slightly and wished she had a summoning orb to call her Triad.

Claire stopped walking. She was so stupid. She didn't need a summoning orb. She had the bonds. Closing her eyes, she felt inside her for the bonds linking her to her Triad. She had completely forgotten about them in the rush. The bonds felt chaotic and worried and Claire had a feeling her disappearance was noted. At least a few hours had to have passed since she ran up for a quick shower. She plucked at Everett's bond, then Desmond's, then Malcolm's. The chaotic energy stilled for a second before exploding with more worry. Claire winced at the bombardment and tried to send soothing feelings down the bonds to let her Triad know she was okay.

The bonds settled but Claire had a feeling it wasn't because her men were calm. An image came to mind in response of Desmond pacing in the library with Everett and Malcolm hunched over a map. Could she push images at them now? It was worth a try. She really needed to ask Desmond more about what Fourth's could do with their Triads.

She pushed an image of the map back at them with a feeling of negativity. She didn't know where she was. She tried pushing an image of the landscape around her. Fields of flowing grass with rolling hills as far as she could see.

The next image she got was the men outside, stripping off their shirts. Claire got slightly distracted by the image before she realized Everett and Malcolm were stripping to shift. They must have shifted as the bonds between Everett and Malcolm grew wilder as their animal sides came forward.

She could feel Desmond's worry and frustration about being left behind and she pushed soothing feelings down the bond again. She also pushed an image of the creature in her arms and felt his surprise. His whisper of worry now across the bond seemed like he was asking if it was dangerous. She sent him the image of the dark magic and burning it away.

A warm feeling flowed down the bond and Claire realized it was pride. She stopped walking, feeling a bit overwhelmed and grateful for such wonderful men. She pushed the gratitude back at him before pushing an image of the sky at him. She was going to start keeping a lookout for Malcolm or Everett.

It would probably be best if she could see a bit more of her surroundings, she decided. A larger hill rose to her right and Claire adjusted her course. She panted slightly as she reached the top, the extra weight of the creature beginning to drag on her. She gently set the creature on the ground, running a hand down its fur as it stirred before straightening. She scanned the skies around her, trying to spot Malcolm or Everett. It would be so much more helpful if she had any idea of where she was.

She scanned the skies again, turning in a slow circle. The bright sun caused her eyes to ache and she lifted her hand to shield them from the worst of the rays. A small black dot caught the corner of her eye. She squinted at it, trying to make out what it was. She wanted to shout and wave, but who knew if it was actually one of her men or if it was whoever had cast this spell on her creature?

The dot got larger until Claire could make out wings and the color red. It definitely wasn't Everett but the bond that was growing stronger between them told her it had to be Malcolm. At least she was pretty sure. She plucked on the bond between her grumbly dragon and her, pushing an image of her looking up at the sky at him.

Joy filled the bond as Malcolm's dragon caught sight of her. He dove towards her from the sky. Her eyes widened as the approaching dragon got bigger and bigger. Claire quickly scooped the creature up so it wouldn't get smushed. Right before the dragon hit the earth, he extended out his ruby red wings, sending a gush of wind blowing Claire back a few steps, as he roared with victory from having found her. She also had a feeling Malcolm's dragon was showing off for her.

And he had reason to show off. This close, he towered above her, half the size of one of the dormitory buildings at the Academy and nearly twice as long. Claire had a feeling he would take up a good chunk of the Combat Arena with his size. Ruby red scales glittered in the sun as he snaked his head down towards Claire. Great golden eyes scanned her for injuries as he settled his head next to her. He eyed the creature in her arms and let out a rumble that shook the ground slightly.

"It's okay," Claire said, "it's a friend now."

The dragon rumbled again but didn't move. Claire gently deposited the creature at her feet and stepped towards Malcolm. "Malcolm, your dragon's amazing!"

Her dragon huffed as if to say, "of course," but pressed his snout into her hand as she approached. His red scales darkened into a deep black at the horns that protruded from his nose and the crown of his head. Darker red scales dotted down the back of his neck to match the color of his wings.

His tail snaked around his body and wrapped around her waist gently, careful not to poke her with the sharper spikes at the end. Claire squeaked as it lifted her onto Malcolm's back, right behind his head in a groove between the darker scales.

"Wait, don't leave him," Claire pointed at the creature. Even if a strand of the creature's magic didn't reside in her center, she knew the creature was going to be important to her.

Malcolm's dragon huffed but snaked his tail towards the creature. The creature squeaked agitatedly and dodged the tail. Instead, it extended its wings and leaped towards Claire, batting its wings twice to land softly in her lap.

Claire looped one arm around the creature and the other arm around one of Malcolm's scales.

"Don't let me fall." She teased softly, knowing Malcolm

would never let that happen. Relief had her body sagging in exhaustion though and Claire was worried she wouldn't be able to hang on.

Malcolm's dragon huffed in exasperation and rolled a great golden eye at her before Claire felt his muscles bunch underneath her. One second they were on the ground and the next those muscles uncoiled with a powerful leap sending them soaring into the air. The wind from Malcolm's wings buffered her slightly and Claire shrieked. The creature on her lap adjusted itself so Claire felt a bit more secure and then they were off, flying in the complete opposite direction from where Claire was heading. *Sigh*. Of course.

They had only been flying a few minutes when a piercing cry cut through the air. Claire shifted as much as she dared to look over her shoulder. Everett's gryphon had caught up to them. Claire took the time to appreciate the sight before her. During the attack in the forest, Claire had barely any time to truly take in Everett's gryphon.

His brilliant white body practically glowed in the afternoon sun. The perfection of his wings darkened to black wing tips giving him a fierce look. His beak was a solid black and he opened it to roar another cry that echoed the joy Claire felt down her bond. She laughed and waved as Brandlevine manor came into view.

Malcolm and Everett's strong wings made quick work of the distance. There was no way Claire would have found her way back here by herself and definitely not any time soon. Especially not heading in the complete opposite direction.

A lone figure paced the front of the house and as they got closer, Claire made out Desmond shoving his hands through his hair as he watched their approach. Despite his size, Malcolm's landing was as soft as the feathers on Everett's wings. As soon as his wings stopped, Claire slid down his neck. The creature chirped in annoyance but sprang softly to the ground as Claire ran to Desmond.

Desmond's hug was fierce, fiercer than anything Claire had ever felt from him before. "I'm okay." She said, trying to reassure him even as she sagged in relief herself.

"I know, but give me a few moments and we'll both feel better about it."

Claire didn't have any trouble snuggling into his arms and letting him hold her for a few moments longer, especially as the exhaustion caused her to lean against him heavily.

"Don't hog her," Malcolm grumbled from behind her, having shifted back.

Claire turned and threw herself at Malcolm who caught her. "Your dragon is so pretty!" She exclaimed.

Malcolm rolled his eyes and hugged her tight, ignoring Desmond and Everett's laughter. Everett tried to steal her from Malcolm who just growled so Everett stepped up behind Claire, pressing his chest to her back.

He pressed a soft kiss to the base of her neck, making Claire shiver. "You had us worried, little mate."

"I didn't mean to," Claire said, "he just transported us so far and I didn't know how to get back."

"He?" Desmond questioned, as Malcolm released her reluctantly.

Claire looked down and found the creature at her feet. It chirped and leapt up to her chest. This time, Claire was ready for it and caught it easily. "This little guy." She explained as she turned to her men, leaning against Malcolm for support.

"Claire, do you know what that is?" Everett asked her.

Claire shrugged, "No. Why?"

"It's a Notus," Desmond started to explain but was cut off by a shout.

"Claire!" Holly and the others came running from the village.

"There you are!" Bethany exclaimed as they got closer. "Where have you been?"

"Is that a Notus?" Zack asked.

Her friends' questions were rapid-fire and threaded with worry.

"We sent Holly and the others into the village when we couldn't find you in the Manor." Desmond murmured to Claire. To the group, he said, "Let's take this inside. We can talk there."

Once inside, they all piled into the library and Claire recounted the last few hours starting from when she entered the bedroom until Malcolm found her.

"I couldn't kill it." She said softly, looking down at the Notus in her arms which chirped softly at her, "So I had to save it. I pulled the dark magic out of it and burned it."

"You broke a dark magic hold?" Desmond asked, shock evident in his tone.

Claire shrugged, "I mean, I guess? It didn't feel that difficult." It hadn't been truly, once she had figured out what to do. Remembering she could manipulate Energy had taken the longest.

"Didn't feel that difficult?" Desmond fell back into his seat, the words whispered as if he hadn't meant to say that out loud.

"What my usually eloquent cousin is trying to say," Holly said, "is that type of magic is almost impossible to break unless it's done by the person who cast the original spell."

Claire frowned, concern for the Notus filling her, "Do you think whoever cast it will know I broke it?"

Everett stood up straight, frowning at Desmond, "Would the spell caster have known?" He repeated Claire's question with a lot more force, concern layering in his voice.

Desmond rubbed a hand over his face, "I don't know. There's not a lot of research available on this type of magic for a reason. The only stuff that exists, exists in the Council's archives."

And they didn't want to look there. Claire stood, careful of the Notus in her arms and met the eyes of her concerned friends and Triad. “What’s done is done.” She stated firmly. “There’s no point worrying about it now. Let’s get some lunch. I’m starving.”

Her Triad jumped up as they realized Claire hadn’t eaten and the fast pace at which they disappeared towards the kitchen was almost comical.

Holly reached out to squeeze Claire’s arm, one eye on the creature as she did so who did nothing more than nestle further into Claire’s arm. “I’m glad you’re okay.” She said softly.

“Us too,” Cody said, “you had everyone really worried.”

“Sorry,” Claire felt bad, “I didn’t have much of a choice thanks to this guy.”

“We know.” Zack said, “But we still worry. We’re family.”

Zack looked a bit surprised at his words but smiled warmly when Claire looked at him. She met his smile and looked around. Her family. The Notus purred in her arms and Claire had a feeling her little family just got one member bigger.

CHAPTER 18

"So, what is a Notus?" Claire asked as Everett placed a plate with a huge sandwich in front of her. The creature in question was lying over her feet under the table, content with the bites of turkey Claire was sneaking it.

"A Notus is an Elven creature." Zack answered her. "They are solitary creatures that live in the Elven forest but they are usually pretty curious and sociable by nature. They are high-energy creatures and it's rumored that they are the creature of choice for Elven familiars."

"Familiars?" Claire thought about the strand of magic from the creature that now resided in her center next to the Academy's magic. Oops.

"Yes, familiars. They help magic users absorb and channel large amounts of magic. They act as a grounding mechanism of sorts. There is not a lot of data on them as there aren't a lot of familiars. I think one of the Councilmembers has a raven familiar."

Claire hummed, feeding the Notus another chunk of turkey and thinking. Was that magic from the creature familiar magic?

Desmond narrowed his eyes at Claire, "What did you do?"

"Me?" Claire tried to play it off. The last time she had taken in strange magic, Desmond had scolded her for it.

"She bonded to it, obviously." Bethany, as blunt as ever, said.

"Claire!"

"Bethany!"

Desmond and Claire spoke at the same time, both in exasperation.

Bethany laughed, "It's Claire, what did you expect? Naturally, the only answer after breaking the dark magic was to bond with it."

Her friends laughed and Claire rolled her eyes. That wasn't her only answer but it was what happened.

"It just kind of happened." She said to Desmond, laying a hand on his arm and trying to comfort him.

"It forced a bond on you?" Desmond asked, worriedly

"No, I accepted its magic."

Desmond sighed and leaned back in his chair, "I thought we talked about sending and accepting strange magic from creatures."

"No," Claire teased, "we talked about sending and accepting strange magic from objects, not creatures."

The table chuckled as Desmond looked gobsmacked.

Claire squeezed his arm again, giving him a small break. "I didn't realize it was a bond but I don't regret accepting it. If he meant me harm, my magic would never have accepted his."

"Now that we've established that the Notus is Claire's familiar," Holly said smiling. "What about that spell? Was it familiar to the one with the Felua?

Claire thought of the red eyes and shuddered. "Yes, it had the same tainted energy. This one seemed a bit different in the intention, maybe?"

"What do you mean?" Everett asked.

"It could have killed me here in the room but I think it intentionally teleported me away from the Manor house, away from you all." Claire shuddered softly. Now that it was over and she had a second to breathe, her stomach turned at how vulnerable she had been. It was easy to talk about now that it was over but if the person controlling the Notus had shown up...

"It learned from the attack in the forest." Everett summarized grimly, looking at Malcolm and Desmond. "It wanted you isolated from us or anyone who would protect you."

"She was still in witch territory but close to Fae lands." Malcolm said, looking at Desmond. "Does that mean anything to you, genius?"

"As much faith as you have in my abilities, unfortunately I don't have all the answers. It's definitely an interesting piece to the puzzle though."

Before they could puzzle anything more out, Desmond's parents, Frederick and Ilena entered the room, drawn by all the noise. The Notus, spooked by the new arrivals, leapt onto Claire's lap from under the table and then leapt onto the table, hissing with wings spread and fur puffed in a defensive position in front of Claire.

The group sat stunned by the speed and nimbleness of the Notus.

"Well, I guess that answers the question of whether or not it's Claire's familiar," Cody drawled.

"You have a Notus as a familiar?" Frederick asked sharply, "When did this happen?"

Desmond sighed, "This morning. You missed quite the adventure."

"The Council called an emergency meeting." Frederick said sharply. "Reports of other creatures not seen since the Great War are surfacing."

"Other attacks?" Claire asked quietly, feeling a bit ill at the thought that people were out there getting hurt possibly because of her.

"No attacks, just sightings." Frederick answered her, "Like they are looking for something. Or someone."

Looking for her, is what he implied. Claire sat back and worried her bottom lip. It was Desmond's turn to squeeze her arm softly. Warm feelings of reassurance flowed down the bond from him and Claire smiled gratefully up at him. He was trying to make her feel better and it was working but it didn't change the fact that something was stirring creatures that hadn't been seen since before the Great War.

"Can we sit?" Ilena asked cautiously, eyeing the Notus. The Notus had stopped hissing but hadn't relaxed his stance.

Claire stood up and reached for the Notus, soothing the fur on his back before picking him up like an overgrown housecat and setting him back on her lap. "Sorry." She apologized to Ilena who waved her off as she took a seat.

"What happened?" Ilena asked after Frederick took his own seat.

For the second time that day, Claire recounted the morning's events. When she finished, Frederick and Ilena were silent, exchanging a long look.

"What other creatures have been sighted?" Everett asked, leaning forward in his chair causing his forest smell to be stronger to Claire's nose.

"A variety of lesser creatures," Frederick said, "nothing that's showed any aggression, birds with too intelligent of eyes, the occasional Notus. Ashcraft Coven reported sighting Felua tracks near their village but I'm less inclined to believe that one."

Claire frowned, "Why not?" The fearsome creature they encountered in the forest was no joking matter.

"What Coven Leader Brandlevine probably can't say," Zack spoke up, "is Coven Leader Ashcraft is a bit of a storyteller who likes to build his own importance up."

Frederick dipped his head in acknowledgement. "Either way,

these reports are concerning. And they have reached the Council's ears. They are particularly curious about Claire."

Desmond sat up straighter as Malcolm let out a low growl, "What did you tell them?"

"I was as vague as possible simply saying Claire was your Fourth and a student at the Academy from Windshire Coven. They asked questions about her heritage but I answered them truthfully that I didn't know it because we don't."

Frederick arched an eyebrow at Desmond. "Don't forget, son, she's going to be my daughter as well. I wouldn't jeopardize her safety."

Desmond nodded at his father and relaxed back into his chair slightly. His hand found Claire's under the table and gripped it tightly. Claire held onto him just as hard. She had been taken before they had been able to have the conversation about the Council but the timing was all a bit too convenient.

"That being said," Frederick said, "I wouldn't be surprised if the Council made a 'surprise visit' here in the next few days to meet Claire and see for themselves. The addition of the Notus will definitely complicate things."

"If we have enough advance warning, maybe we can hide him?" Holly suggested.

Frederick nodded, "That would probably be wise."

Claire studied the Notus in her lap wondering how in the realm they were going to hide it. Feeling her eyes on him, the Notus lifted his head and met her gaze with his own golden one. He chirped softly at her as if telling her not to worry about it.

"What are you young ones doing for the rest of the afternoon?" Ilena asked.

Holly looked around the table, "I think we were going to spend some time with Cody and Bethany before they headed back."

Bethany nodded, "Thank you again for having us."

"It's been no problem at all. Give your fathers my best," Frederick answered.

* * *

"So what are you going to name it?" Cody asked as they settled onto the same hill that Claire had watched the sunrise on this morning.

"Can I name it?" Claire asked, "Isn't that... I don't know, disrespectful?"

"I don't see why not?" Bethany said, "I mean if you pick a name it hates then he'll probably let you know by pooping on your bed."

"Gee, thanks, Bethany." Desmond said drily, "What a wonderful thing to look forward to. You see, Claire, this is why we don't accept strange magic from objects or creatures."

Claire laughed and leaned back against Everett, the Notus sitting next to her, preening its feathers. She stroked its head. "Would you be okay if I named you?" She felt strange asking but didn't want to be disrespectful.

The Notus paused in its grooming and chirped softly, pushing its head into her palm briefly before going back to its feathers.

"Well, it's not a no," Cody pointed out and they all laughed.

"Let's table that discussion for later." Claire suggested, "We have other things to talk about now."

The cheerful mood settled like a rock at the bottom of a well as their thoughts turned to the conversation from only a few days ago. So much had happened since then, Claire thought. So many changes. Would they be able to keep up?

Desmond and Zack threw up a privacy spell that shimmered in the air. Claire was briefly distracted watching the shimmer until Everett nudged her leg with his softly.

"What are we really suggesting here?" Zack asked, voice hushed even with the privacy spell.

Ever blunt, Bethany answered him, "That everything we've been taught about the Great War is wrong."

"What does that even mean?" Cody asked, "Like all of it is wrong?"

"That's what everything means," Bethany shot back.

Before it could escalate further, Claire broke in. "Yes and no," she said carefully, "I think the biggest thing we should reconsider is what actually started the Great War. Who attacked first? Why did the Fae come to the Elves' aid?"

"Well to answer your second question," Zack said, "The journal I'm reading right now is from a cousin of Professor Helene's. She was a Dryad who also lived among witches. According to her, the witches attacked the Elves first. A small border village on the edge of the Elven Forest."

"And according to the official records," Desmond said, "the Elves attacked first in retaliation."

"Retaliation for what?" Claire asked.

Desmond frowned, "Come to think of it, I don't know if it says. It's implied that it was because of Elven goods being seized after the Fae and Elf Councilmembers walked out of negotiations to try and de-escalate the tensions."

"If Fae and Elven goods were seized, why didn't the Fae attack too?" Bethany pointed out. "Were the goods really that valuable? What even were they?"

"It would have been everything at the Market," Everett said slowly, "maybe everything meant the people as well?"

"Like the merchants?" Desmond asked, the wrinkle in his forehead creasing deeper as he considered the implications.

"That would have definitely provoked an attack," Malcolm said, "but Zack's journal says the witches attacked first."

"You said that alliances were born out of necessity," Claire pointed out, "what if both were true? What if it was the Council's decision to seize the goods and maybe the people but the witches' decision to attack the Elven village?"

"There's some merit to that." Zack said. "Historically, the witches have a terrible track record of working with others."

"Which coven was it that attacked?" Holly asked.

"It was the Flamell Coven if I remember right."

Desmond huffed, "Well according to Father's descriptions of that coven growing up, that would not be surprising. They were all wiped out during the Great War, correct?"

"All of them?" Claire asked, shock and horror spiraling through her. Even the children?

"A village for a village," Malcolm said grimly. "If the Flamell coven wiped out the Elven village in a surprise attack then the Elven warriors would not have rested until every member of that coven was dead."

"But the children," Claire whispered, horrified. On both sides there had been children.

The somberness settled on the group like a woolen blanket, heavy and uncomfortable.

"Unfortunately, that's war, little witch. The Great War was named aptly for a reason," Desmond said softly.

"So the Council seizes Elven and Fae goods including the merchants. The coven wipes out the Elven village prompting the Elves to retaliate. The shifters come to the witches' aid and then the Fae join with the Elves," Cody summarizes.

"But even before all of that," Bethany said, "there's one more lie we should consider. The story is that the Elves started to demand a higher price for medicinal treatments, what if that wasn't true either?"

Desmond rubbed his temples, "What do you mean?"

His voice sounded tired and Claire felt a twinge of guilt. If she had kept her mouth shut the other day, they wouldn't be having this conversation and her wizard wouldn't be looking like the weight of the world was pressing in on his temple.

"I mean, that if the Council is lying about the start of the Great War then they are probably lying about the cause of the Great War."

"I don't know if we are going to ever know that," Holly said, "unless we find an account that says differently. Besides, even if the Elves raised the price on medicinal treatments, what if they had to? What if there was a scarcity of an ingredient or something."

"That's a possibility." Malcolm nodded, "The ingredients only grew in the Elven Forest and the Elves were fiercely secretive and protective of the forest."

"So even if we don't know the true story, let's assume they lied about the cause and start of the Great War for expediency's sake," Cody countered. Claire smiled and shook her head, there her jokester friend went again, throwing out bigger words casually.

"The real question is why?"

"Why did the Council lie? Why did the Fae come to the Elves' aid? Why did they suddenly disappear? Was it actually a numbers game like Professor Andy said or was it something else?" Holly ticked off the questions on her fingers, ever organized.

"And how does it all relate to Claire?" Bethany added.

"So many questions," Cody groaned dramatically, throwing an arm over his eyes and falling backwards.

The laughter that his actions caused lightened the mood of the group and Claire smiled gratefully at him. He was right, there were too many questions.

"Good questions though." Claire said, leaning back into Everett, "And all questions I think we need the answers to but not today. It's too much for today. Let's just enjoy the rest of the afternoon. We only have so much time left with Bethany and Cody before they have to go back."

"Stellar idea, little witch." Desmond grinned.

"So... what are you going to name it?" Cody asked, taking the subject change and running with it. He gestured towards the Notus who had finished preening his wings and had curled into a ball next to Claire. It lifted its head at Cody's question.

"I have no idea," Claire admitted, laughing, "It's not like I woke up today and was like I'm going to get a familiar and it'll need a name."

"Hmmm what about Jeoffrey?" Cody suggested.

"Jeoffrey? Really?" Bethany screwed her nose up in disgust.

"Well let's see you do better, miss feline," Cody shot back.

"I'm sure I can do better than Jeoffrey," Bethany said.

"Well let's hear it?"

Bethany floundered for a few seconds, "What about... Sunny? For its yellow eyes?"

"Bethany, we'll come back to you," Desmond informed her with a fake-serious expression on his face, blue eyes twinkling.

Claire laughed and Bethany rolled her eyes before laughing with her.

"Alright then, genius," Malcolm said, addressing Desmond, "What's your name idea?"

"Easy," Desmond said confidently, "Desmond Junior."

The Notus squawked and clacked its beak at Desmond.

"I'm pretty sure that's a no," Everett observed solemnly, a twinkle in his eye as he winked at Claire.

Claire giggled, breathless with laughter as the group continued to throw out name suggestions, each more ridiculous than the last. The Notus squawked at the particularly ridiculous ones, letting his disapproval be known.

By the time Cody and Bethany had to leave, Claire was no closer to naming her new familiar than when she had found him. But the ache in her cheeks and belly from laughing almost drowned out the seriousness of the day. Things were rapidly changing in her family's lives. Would she be able to keep up and protect them?

CHAPTER 19

A few days later, her Notus familiar had a name. Puck meant a mischievous sprite as Ilena had informed her. It was a name that fit the creature who had shown his personality under Claire's care, often hiding things from the men around the manor house including Desmond's favorite pair of shoes.

She hadn't practiced using her familiar to ground or use magic yet, as Desmond wanted to research it before she did. That wasn't going to happen until later though. Desmond was supposed to be taking a nap right now as Claire caught him early this morning over his books, having never gone to sleep last night.

She had put Malcolm in charge of enforcing that nap, much to Malcolm's delight and Desmond's chagrin. And then Everett had walked her over to Andy and Helene's cottage for another Energy Reading lesson, Puck in tow.

Helene was very impressed with how quickly Claire had picked up on drawing and sending Energy. Andy was as intrigued as Desmond was with Puck and how he could amplify Claire's Energy Reading abilities in addition to her magic. Andy was in their cottage now, searching for any books from her library on the subject.

Helene was sitting next to Claire, watching Puck play with a small piece of fuzz he kept batting around in the wind.

"How are you handling all of this?" Helene asked Claire softly, her willowy voice a soft music in the morning stillness.

Claire sighed and thought for a second. She didn't want to be purposefully obtuse and ask Helene what she meant but the truth was she wasn't feeling very confident that she was handling any of it.

"I mean, training is going well, with both you and Malcolm, so that's good." Claire started out with the positive.

"That is good," The older woman waited for Claire to continue, a patient and steady presence next to her, feeling much like her tree back at the Academy. Claire wondered if they had been going back to visit it or if Dryad's didn't need constant contact with their trees. She could ask the question and change the subject or she could grow up and answer it.

"It just feels like there are so many more questions than answers," Claire said, "every new answer leads to more questions. Dangerous questions. It's just..."

She paused and looked around for Everett. She couldn't see him, but that didn't necessarily mean anything. She plucked at the bond between them curiously and felt his response. He was close by but not within earshot. She sent a thrum of reassurance in response to his questioning feeling and smiled when she felt the bond settle. She had been playing with the bonds the last few days with her Triad trying to figure out just how much they could feel or send down the bond towards each other.

"It's just?" Helene's gentle prompting brought Claire back to the present.

"Is it all worth it?" Claire admitted, "Am I worth it? All this danger and secrecy? What's the cost of finding out these answers?"

Instead of responding to her questions, Helene simply said, "This has been weighing on you."

"It has," Claire plucked a piece of grass and rubbed it between her fingers. "I've just found this amazing family here, that a year ago I never dreamed of having. My Triad, my friends, you and Andy... what if I risk it all to find these answers?"

"You're right," Helene agreed, "these are dangerous questions with most likely dangerous answers. What do your Triad and friends think? They should have some say, correct, if you think they are at risk?"

"They want to find the answers." Claire admitted, "They want to help me find who my family is. I just..."

"You worry," Helene said.

"Yes," Claire nodded, "I worry." She worried so much it was keeping her up at night.

"Worry is natural," Helene said, "I would be worried if you weren't worried."

Claire let out a soft laugh at her play on words.

"My advice to you?" Helene said, "Let yourself be worried. Worry will keep you sharp, it'll keep you asking questions and observing details. Details that'll help you protect your Triad and friends."

"My Triad would say that's their job, to protect me," Claire said.

"You protect each other." Helene said, shrugging, "You are their Fourth, their nucleus. You give them a reason to fight and they give that same reason to you. You are a family."

Claire was thoughtful. Growing up, a family was all she had wanted. When no one came for her at the orphanage, she had resigned herself to living there always. When the invitation for the Academy came, she thought she would get a good education and then find a quiet corner of the Realm to live out her days at. Now she had a Triad and great friends. A family and a place to belong. Could she be content with never having the answer to any of her questions?

If it meant protecting what she had here, Claire knew she would walk away from her questions in a heartbeat.

"Thank you, Helene." Claire said, lifting her head to smile at her professor.

"You're very welcome." Helene assured her, "It looks like Everett is searching for you."

Claire turned in the direction Helene indicated. Everett had just walked around the side of the house, his face serious.

"What is it?" She asked, her breakfast from this morning churning lightly in her stomach.

"The Council just arrived." He said, taking Claire's hand in his. He looked at Helene. "Can Puck stay here?"

"Of course," Helene nodded. She crossed to the cottage and opened the back door.

Claire bent down and released Everett's hand to cup Puck's face, "Stay here with Aunt Helene and Andy please," She pleaded softly with him.

Puck chirped and his magic in Claire's center twirled restlessly as his tail lashed.

"It'll be safer for you *and* me if you're here." Claire explained. "If the Council learns I have a familiar, they'll be even more curious. Please? For me?"

Desmond had teased her about speaking to Puck as if he could understand her but the intelligence in Puck's eyes had Claire genuinely believing he could understand her. A fact that he proved now by growling softly but nodding his grey head. He padded past Claire and through the door Helene held for him. He looked back and chirped sadly and Claire gave him an encouraging smile. It was time for her to protect her family.

She took Everett's hand again and gave him a small smile as they walked back towards the manor house. She was thankful for the quiet and used it as time to take deep breaths and settle her magic and her face into a pleasant, yet neutral expression.

Just days earlier, Claire and her friends were talking about how the Council had been possibly lying to them all. Now Claire was going to have to face that same Council and not let any of that show on her face.

Everett and Claire entered the manor through the back patio door and made their way down the darkened hallway towards the voices from the library. Everett tucked her hand in his elbow and guided her closer to his side before knocking on the library doors. Malcolm opened them, his face serious but his eyes softening as he saw Claire. She gave him a small smile and proceeded into the room with Everett.

Desmond and the others sitting around the couch including Frederick stood when she entered. Desmond broke from the group and Claire stepped forward into his arms, ignoring the other occupants of the room. She smoothed a hand over his hair, the slightly rumpled ends had her smiling as it appeared that up until the Council arrived, he had actually been sleeping.

He shared her smile, rolling his eyes at her playfully, guessing the direction of her thoughts before turning and presenting her to the room.

"Councilmembers, this is my lovely soul flame, Claire. Claire, this is Councilmember Roland and Councilmember Vanya, and of course, you know my father, Frederick, as well."

Claire nodded her head at them and was proud when her voice was even. "It's a pleasure to meet all of you."

"Ours as well," Councilmember Roland said formally, his eyes traveling up and down Claire and she fought not to fidget. Did she have dirt on her pants? Or worse, on her face? Surely, Everett would have told her if that was the case.

"Come sit," Desmond guided her to sit between Malcolm and him with Everett standing behind them.

"Are you enjoying your time here at Brandlevine?" Councilmember Vanya had thin features, almost bird-like. She wondered if this was the Councilmember who had the raven familiar. Or maybe he was a bird shifter. Why hadn't she asked more about the Council before now?

"I am." Claire said, "It's been nice to meet my Triad's family."

She was glad her hands were hidden in Desmond's and Malcolm's so the Councilmembers couldn't see them shake as she met the Councilmember's eyes. Malcolm squeezed her hand softly and Claire tightened her own fingers around his and took another breath.

"I was under the impression from Headmaster Dorian that you all were staying at the Academy this summer?" Councilmember Roland said, his dark eyes staring at Claire and she fought not to fidget.

"I didn't know the Council kept such a close track of our whereabouts?" Desmond said lightly but a thread of steel was woven into his voice.

"Your Triad is one of the most powerful assets to the Realm." Roland said, "Of course we like to make sure you have everything you need and are safe."

Claire wasn't sure how much of the Academy attack was general knowledge but it sounded like Roland was working his way up to something.

"The Academy was lovely." Claire said, "But my Triad promised to introduce me to their families as well."

"And what about your family?" Councilmember Vanya asked. "Would you not go back to see them?"

Claire was almost positive that the Council knew she was an orphan but she answered with a soft smile on her face. "I'm an orphan actually. I grew up at Windshire Coven but I have no family there to speak of."

"She's a part of our family now." Frederick spoke for the first time since Claire entered the room. The same thread of steel that Desmond had spoken with also threaded through Frederick's voice. A warning to the other Councilmembers to tread lightly.

"I'm sorry to hear that." Councilmember Roland said, not sounding very sorry, "You are welcome to come to the Capital and hunt through our archives to find more information on them."

"That's a kind offer," Claire said, "but I couldn't be rude to Frederick and Ilena's hospitality."

"Nonsense," Councilmember Roland waved his hand, "Frederick knows the importance of knowing your family. I insist."

His voice sounded more like a demand than an invitation and warning bells started going off in Claire's center as her magic flared nervously. Why was he insisting on them going to the Capital?

Desmond spoke, "Thank you for the offer, Councilmember Roland. I'm sure we will take you up on the offer soon."

"Why wait?" Roland said, his dark eyes staring at Claire. "Don't you want to know who your family is?"

I've already found them, Claire wanted to say but she knew that wouldn't help. She wasn't sure what would help to say though. Why did Roland want her at the Capital so badly? Did he know more than he was letting on or was he truly trying to be helpful? The conversation from a few days ago played in Claire's mind where they had suggested that the Council had seized Elven and Fae merchants as well as their goods. Did they want Claire too?

Claire was so in her head that when Malcolm spoke she startled slightly and shifted to try and hide her reaction.

"We appreciate your offer, Councilmember," Malcolm said, "but I promised my father a visit after we left Brandlevine."

"I see," Councilmember Roland's voice was displeased but he didn't press further. What about Malcolm's father made him back off? Claire knew he was appointed as the second dragon Councilmember after the Great War but had recently stepped down. Claire kicked herself mentally for not asking more about Malcolm's family.

The subject dropped, the Councilmembers chatted with her Triad for the next half hour about trivial things from Claire's perspective. She wondered if it was another tactic by the Councilmembers to try and draw out information. Bore their audience so much they slipped up. Frederick broke up the gathering by inviting the Councilmembers to stay for dinner. Much to Claire's relief, they declined and departed shortly afterwards.

"That invitation from your father isn't going to hold them off forever," Frederick said to Malcolm after they left.

"No, but it gives us some more time. Time to figure out what they really wanted."

"Sightings of the Elven creatures are increasing and the one new variable in the Realm is Claire's presence at the Academy and your lives. Those two will probably be searching for answers as intensely as you are."

"What should we do?" Claire asked quietly. The last thing she wanted was those Councilmembers coming back and poking around their lives.

"The simple answer is to find the answers to Claire's heritage," Frederick said, looking at Desmond, "I know you have theories you haven't shared with me. That's smart because I'm not allowed to lie to the Council that I sit on but if you have any theories or wild ideas, you probably need to consider pursuing them."

Desmond held his father's eyes but kept his face blank. "We'll take that under advisement."

Frederick rolled his eyes and Claire let out a short laugh at how similar he looked to Desmond in that moment. Frederick smiled at her and dismissed the group.

* * *

"I THINK COMBINED with the Felua and the Notus, our next step should be heading into the Elven Forest." Desmond said quietly, sharing a wild idea that Frederick had referenced earlier. "Someone there doesn't want Claire associated with the Elves."

They were lying on their bed in the manor house after dinner. Claire was lying against Malcolm, Everett's head on her stomach and her feet in Desmond's lap. Puck was curled up next to her like a little heater against Claire's side. She was so comfortable she was almost asleep when Desmond spoke.

"So naturally, into the heart of their territory is where you want to head?" Everett shifted to frown at him.

"Think about it. She was found close to Fae land and someone is intentionally spelling Elven creatures. I think whoever it is knows Claire will find answers in the Elven Forest and is trying to dissuade her from venturing near there."

"And again, you want to head straight into the danger?" Everett repeated.

Desmond shifted to look at Claire. "I don't suppose there's any way we can convince you to stay here?"

Claire huffed out a short laugh, "Being that I'm the reason why you would be heading into danger, absolutely not." There was no way she was going to let her Triad go into the Forest by themselves when Claire was the whole reason for this mess. She didn't want them getting hurt because of her.

"What if we just stopped searching?" She asked softly, staring up at the ceiling.

"Stop searching for what?" Desmond asked, rubbing her feet.

"All of it. For my parents, into the Council and Great War, all of it."

She kept her gaze firmly on the ceiling, thoughts of her conversation with Helene from earlier drifting in her mind. If she had to give up answers to keep them safe she would.

"Why do you say that, little treasure?" Malcolm cupped her cheek so she had to look at him.

"I just don't want you all to get hurt trying to find answers for me." Claire said. She would walk away from this fight if it meant keeping her new family safe. "I have a family here with you, who needs anything else?"

Malcolm's golden eyes softened down at her and his thumb stroked her cheek. "You don't need to worry about us."

"But I do," Claire pointed out, rolling her eyes at him with a smile.

"I hear your concerns, Claire, but if the Council has truly been lying about the Great War then people deserve to know. And even if they aren't, you deserve answers." Desmond said.

"I don't want answers if it means that one of you will get hurt." Her eyes landed on Everett thinking of the slashes against his side by the Felua. He grabbed her hand on her stomach and squeezed.

"Give us a bit more credit, little mate." Everett said softly. "We are trained warriors and one of the most powerful Triads in the realm."

Claire frowned. She understood what Everett was saying but she still didn't want to lose them. If she let them go into the Forest alone, she would lose them. She was sure of it.

"Let's sleep on it." Malcolm suggested, "We can make a decision tomorrow."

"Tomorrow," Desmond agreed, looking at Claire.

"Tomorrow." She nodded, stomach still twisting with nerves long after she closed her eyes and searched for sleep. If they insisted on searching for answers then Claire was going to do her best to protect them.

CHAPTER 20

When Claire woke the next morning, Desmond was curled around her but the rest of the room was empty. She stayed still, watching Desmond sleep. His face was relaxed, his dark curls strewn across the pillow and over his forehead, messing from sleep. The dark circles under his eyes made Claire frown. Her brilliant wizard really needed to sleep more.

Closing her own eyes, she snuggled against his chest, avoiding the temptation to run her hands over his bare skin. He must have shed his shirt during the night. Four bodies and a Notus in the bed generated a lot of heat. She dozed off and on until his chest moved underneath her.

She lifted her head to meet his sleepy blue eyes. "I didn't mean to wake you." He whispered into the quiet morning.

"I woke up a bit ago," Claire admitted softly, "I've just been dozing and enjoying the morning."

"Is there something in particular you've been enjoying?" Even sleepy her wizard liked to tease.

Claire could tease back though. She let her hand that was curled under her chin, move across his chest, sifting through the soft dark curls she found there. "Maybe." She said, letting her lips lift in a small grin.

"Just maybe?" Desmond shifted slightly so he was on his back and Claire was pressed up against his side, her head still on his chest.

Claire let her hand travel lower, across the muscles of his stomach and then back up. "Maybe I require further exploration." She said as his breath hitched when she trailed a finger around his nipple.

Curious, she did it again, and Desmond let out a soft groan. "Am I going to survive the exploration?"

Claire shrugged one shoulder, "Undecided yet."

Desmond just groaned and Claire smiled, feeling more confident from his reactions. She sat up and threw a leg over his stomach so she was straddling him. Desmond's eyebrows raised but when his hands came to sit on her hips, Claire shifted slightly. His thumbs stroked the sensitive skin where her nightshirt had ridden up and Claire shifted again. Desmond groaned and gripped her hips a little tighter.

She had use of both hands now and she brought them to cover his hands on her hips, trailing them down his forearms and over the muscles of his upper arms that were usually hidden by his dress shirts. Desmond was quiet, allowing her exploration but Claire studied his face for the small reactions that he was enjoying this.

There was a certain kind of power in this position, she realized. Claire hadn't had enough one-on-one time with her Triad and she knew she was still very inexperienced but now, with Desmond underneath her, Claire knew she was going to have to figure out how to do this more often.

Her hands trailed lower on Desmond's stomach and he removed a hand from her hip to grab her wrist lightly, "A man only has so much willpower."

Claire arched an eyebrow and then smiled. If he didn't want her to use her hands...

Desmond's entire body stilled as she leaned forward and placed a soft kiss on his chest. When he didn't move to stop her, she pressed another kiss on his chest and then began trailing kisses along the same path her hands had just taken.

Even though Desmond was rock still underneath her, the slight hitches in his breath and the pleasure radiating down their bond told Claire he was enjoying it. When her lips caught his nipple and sucked gently, Desmond broke.

Claire let out a squeak as he rolled her underneath of him, her wrists in one of his hands held above her head, his weight settled on her. Claire shifted as their hips collided and let out a soft moan as something hard pressed up against her center causing heat and butterflies to erupt in her stomach.

"My turn," Desmond grinned down at her, his blue eyes totally awake and focused on her in such a way that made Claire squirm.

He leaned down to press a kiss softly to the corner of Claire's mouth. Claire's eyes fell closed as he pressed another kiss to the opposite corner. She lifted her chin slightly trying to get him to actually kiss her and he acquiesced to her silent demand. The hand holding her wrists slid down to cup her jaw as Desmond devoured her mouth in soft, slow kisses that sent a burning warmth through her that pooled in her core.

She whimpered as he pulled back slightly but groaned as his warm lips found her jaw line. He traced warm, soft kisses, achingly slow up to her ear and then down her neck. Claire felt her body flush with heat in a way that was different than anything she had felt before.

Desmond tugged at her nightshirt gently and Claire hesitated before lifting her arms and helping him pull it off of her. She felt unbearably shy for a few seconds as Desmond took her in but when he lifted his eyes to hers, she gasped softly at the heat that reflected in them. His eyes almost looked like how Malcolm's looked when his dragon was too close to the surface.

"Beautiful." He whispered, holding her gaze, his blue eyes almost glowing as he lowered his head. She sucked in a breath as his mouth met the skin of her chest just under her collarbone. He pressed open mouth kisses down the center of her chest as his one hand came up to cup one of her breasts, thumb stroking the soft underside

The warmth of his hand seemed at odds with the shivers that broke out in Claire's body as his mouth nipped softly at her other breast. She gasped as his mouth covered her sensitive nipple, sucking hard before laving it with his tongue. Her hands threaded in his hair and she was torn between pushing him away or pulling him closer.

He sucked at her nipple again and Claire gasped, rocking her hips up and gasping for a different reason when her sensitive center met the heat of his body.

"You doing okay, little witch?" Desmond lifted his head, her hands still in his hair and his thumb stroking over her other nipple, causing it to pebble into a hard point.

Was she okay? She could barely think.

"Do you want me to stop or should I continue exploring?" Desmond's finger and thumb caught her nipple and rolled it in a way that had Claire bucking her hips. Oh yes.

"Keep going." She gasped softly, desperate for more of the sensation.

Desmond obliged and lowered his head back to her breast, taking the nipple he had just been teasing with his fingers into his mouth. The hand that was on her breast moved downwards, flattening over her stomach in short strokes that burned.

His hand reached the edge of her soft sleep shorts and he paused, stroking the sensitive skin along the hem. When Claire lifted her hips, he slipped his hand into her shorts cupping Claire's most sensitive area. The heat of his hand spread a fire through her, originating from her center and making her legs weak.

"Desmond," She gasped. She rocked her hips up and moaned when the pressure increased causing sparks to flash in her vision.

"Maybe we should stop, little witch?" Desmond teased, lifting his head from her breast.

"If you stop right now, you won't have to worry about the creatures in the Elven forest," Claire gasped, hips shifting restlessly, "you'll have to worry about me."

"We can't have that now," Desmond kissed up her throat reaching her mouth just as one of his fingers slipped inside Claire.

Her cry was swallowed by his kiss as she bucked her hips, trying to gain more friction from the delicious unfamiliar feeling. He obliged her movements, twisting his wrist until his thumb pressed against a spot that had Claire seeing stars. Her entire body locked up and then relaxed as what felt like an explosion rocked through her, sending her skyrocketing. When she floated back down to earth, Desmond withdrew his fingers and brought them to his mouth, sucking them clean.

Claire blushed and ducked her head and Desmond lifted her chin for another kiss. "Don't be embarrassed, little witch. You taste as sweet as I imagined."

Claire rolled her eyes but allowed him to cuddle her close and wrapped her arms around his stomach as he held her for a bit longer that morning.

* * *

CLAIRE WAS sure that everyone would know what they had been up to and wore a blush as they descended the stairs to the dining room. Thankfully, it was empty as she and Desmond entered. He laughed softly at her relieved expression and left to grab them both some food.

Malcolm entered the room as Desmond was placing a plate of food before her. Claire instantly blushed and focused on her food. Malcolm arched an eyebrow at her and then let out a throaty chuckle. He wisely didn't say anything that added to Claire's embarrassment but took a seat next to her.

She squeaked when he pulled her over onto his lap and slid her plate of food in front of them. When it became clear he just wanted to hold her, Claire relaxed back into his chest and started eating the bread roll.

"Holly was looking for you," Malcolm rumbled, "I told her that I would bring you to the village for lunch after training."

Claire nodded, swallowing her bite. "Where's Everett and Puck?"

"Everett shifted to patrol the area and Puck went with him. Last I saw them, Puck was trying to dive-bomb Everett's gryphon."

"Oh good." Desmond said, digging into his own plate, "We're free from that little scoundrel for a bit."

Claire smiled and shook her head. Puck loved playing with all of her Triad although he especially loved picking on Desmond.

"We're training this morning?" She asked, confirming the plan.

"Yes. Especially after yesterday." He grumbled and Claire squeezed one of his hands that laid across her stomach. Her growly dragon was protective on his best day so she could only imagine that the Council visit combined with Puck's actions only a few days prior was stressing his dragon.

"I want to spend more time with your dragon soon," Claire said.

Malcolm looked down at her and smiled, "He would like that."

"What about this morning?" Claire suggested. It wasn't that she didn't want to train, but that seemed to be the only way she spent time with Malcolm these last few weeks.

"You're not getting out of training." Malcolm was firm.

Claire wrinkled her nose but didn't press. If training made Malcolm feel better, then they would train.

* * *

CLAIRE REGRETTED that decision as she sat down in the chair across from Holly and Zack letting out a soft groan as her muscles ached in protest. Malcolm had been particularly difficult this morning, trying to cram decades worth of training into a single session, his dragon riding him hard from the last week. Logically, Claire knew she was improving. Illogically, she was really done with training. She would have to push back harder the next time Malcolm wanted to do that instead of having a lazy morning with her and his dragon.

"That bad?" Holly asked, frowning.

"Well it's never easy," Claire said, "but there seems to be a single-minded focus on training these days." And it wasn't just Malcolm, Desmond and Everett were just as bad.

"Where would you rather be focused?" Zack asked.

"Maybe a little more time spent with you all and just hanging out rather than training with Malcolm, using magic with Desmond, and discussing strategy with Everett."

"That's a lot," Holly said, placing a hand over Claire's.

"They're just worried about you. We all are," Zack said.

Claire nodded. "I know, but we don't know what's going to happen or if anything's going to happen. I just don't want every second of the time we do have together to be spent planned out."

"I thought you wanted to find answers?" Holly asked.

"I mean I do, but not at the cost of my relationships with you all or my Triad. What we are looking into is dangerous. What if the answers aren't worth it?"

"What does your Triad think?" Zack asked.

"They think they are powerful warriors and that I'm crazy for worrying." Claire rolled her eyes. She understood half of their point but they were facing a lot of unknowns. Claire's magic rolled restlessly in her stomach, reacting to her emotions and Claire couldn't bring herself to calm it down.

Holly laughed, "I don't think it was those words exactly but they're not completely wrong."

"Desmond wants to leave me behind and the three of them head into the Elven Forest alone." Claire pointed out, frowning.

Holly and Zack mirrored her frown. "Leave you behind?" Zack confirmed.

Claire nodded, trying not to let her frustration at the situation turn into anger at her men. She understood the protectiveness, she did, but she didn't like it.

"That doesn't seem very smart. To separate like that," Holly said.

"I don't think so either," Claire shrugged, "but I'm not sure how I can convince them."

"What if you came to a compromise?" Zack suggested.

"I feel like this is pretty black and white. Either you go into the Forest together or you don't," Holly said, wrinkling her nose.

Zack smiled and adjusted his glasses. "Not if you switch out the location. I just finished reading that journal I was telling you all about, from the Dryad. The Elven village was right outside the Elven Forest. It's abandoned now, but there might be some lingering clues?"

Claire thought about it. "I mean that would be a good place to look but Desmond seems sure we have to go into the Elven Forest."

"What if that's exactly what they want you to do?" Holly pondered, forehead creasing. "You could go right into a trap."

Claire hadn't thought about that but Holly was right. What if the Forest was more dangerous than it was already fabled to be?

"The village is sounding like the better option then," Zack said, "I mean you might still have to go into the Forest eventually but this trip will give you more clues and show them that it's better if you all stay together."

"I'll bring it up to them this afternoon." Claire agreed. For the first time that week, Claire felt a small bit of hope that they might have some answers soon.

"Hopefully, we find some answers quickly." Holly said, "It's hard to believe that the Academy will be starting back up in a month."

"Time has flown by," Zack agreed, "it's been a wild summer."

"I'll drink to that," Claire joked, holding up her glass.

The friends laughed and toasted. Someone called her name, and Claire turned in her seat.

"Claire!" Everett wove through the crowded village center, his expression fierce. Puck was balanced on his shoulder.

Claire felt her stomach drop. Something was wrong. "What is it? Are you okay? Malcolm? Desmond? Puck?"

Puck chirped a greeting and leapt from Everett's shoulder to the table as they got closer. Claire rose to meet Everett who gently grabbed her elbows as she reached for him.

"I'm fine. Desmond and Malcolm are fine too."

"What happened?" Holly asked as Claire's eyes traced over Everett, making sure he was actually in one piece.

Everett's face was grim, his mouth drawn into a tight line. "The Academy. Headmaster Dorian just sent word that an Academy patrol was attacked. Three injured."

"Oh, Everett," Claire wrapped her arms around him. Everett had led patrols frequently at the Academy and the odds were that he knew some of the injured.

"The creatures reportedly attacked and then something called them off. The patrol leader made it sound like they were hunting something as they left."

"And you think they were hunting me?" Claire asked.

Everett nodded. "That doesn't make a lot of sense," Claire continued, "Puck found me here in Brandlevine easily. Whoever was responsible for them should know I'm here."

Everett frowned, "You're right. I don't like it."

Claire let out a small smile at his fierceness. He was always going to be protective over her. They all were. But this new information of a new attack also offered some perspective. Whoever was behind this was not going to stop or wait around for Claire to find answers. They were still attacking regardless and if Claire wanted to protect her family she was going to have to be as relentless in their search for information to figure out who was behind this.

"Let's go tell Desmond and Malcolm." She said, stepping back. She gave Holly and Zack a quick hug and then threaded her arm through Everett's. "We have some things to finish discussing."

Holly met her eyes, a sad smile on her face. Her friend was worried. Claire gave her a warm smile back, trying not to let her own worry echo in her eyes. Knowing Holly's empath abilities, she could probably feel it either way but Claire could put on a brave face.

"I'll see you both later," She promised before calling to Puck.

Puck spread his wings and leapt into the air, seeming content to fly in small circles above their heads as Everett guided her towards the manor house.

* * *

"YOU WANT TO GO WHERE?" Malcolm growled.

Claire brushed off his growl and the tingling it caused,

deciding to explore that later. "To the Elven village Zack told us about the other day." She repeated, knowing he heard her perfectly well the first time.

"Why?" Desmond questioned.

"Zack seemed to think we could glean a few answers from the village before we head into the Elven Forest." She kept her hands clasped in her lap as she sat on the couch in the library. She delivered that statement with a calm firmness. Her men would argue with her on this because they were worried about her safety and they did not disappoint.

"That's an easy flight for my dragon," Malcolm said, "I can go and check it out and be back for dinner."

"We can go check it out," Claire corrected gently.

"Claire, we don't know what waits for us there. What if that journal was planted so Zack would tell you about it and it's actually a trap."

Claire raised her eyebrows at Desmond, allowing a small smile to play on her lips as she waited for him to realize how ridiculous that theory sounded.

He grimaced and ran a hand over his face, "Okay, I agree, the journal being a plant is a bit far-fetched but it could still be a trap."

"At this point, it doesn't look like I'm safe anywhere." Claire gently pointed out, ignoring the growls from all three men. "Whoever this is has proven that they can get to me at the Academy and at Brandlevine. I don't want to spend my life with you all running away from this. We need the answers and I think that if we get proactive about this we can ensure that we all stay safe."

She paused and looked down at her hands. This was a change of heart from last night and she recognized that. But if finding answers would protect her family then she would face the danger that finding those answers would bring.

"I don't want to lose any of you any more than you want to

lose me. I want this. I want this family we are building. But I'm getting tired of people getting hurt because we don't know what we are facing here."

There was silence following her statement before the air shifted and Malcolm's cinnamon and smoke scent grew stronger. He picked her up and sat back down, settling her in his lap and ignoring Puck's squawk as he displaced the Notus from the arm of the couch.

"We can't lose you," Malcolm growled, golden eyes flashing.

"You won't lose me if we all stay together. You aren't wrong, you are all great warriors. I have the bruises from combat training to prove it." Claire teased lightly, laughing softly at the rumbly growl Malcolm let out.

"But I also have powerful magic I've been getting better at controlling. I'm not the helpless girl I was when I entered the Academy last year."

"We hear you," Desmond sat down on the low table in front of the couch and grabbed Claire's hand, "we do. But we worry."

"And you think I don't?" Claire raised an eyebrow at him, "You think I wouldn't worry any less if I had to stay behind while you three went into the Forest and Realm-forbid something happened to you?"

Desmond winced at her chiding tone but nodded his head. "You're right, I'm sorry."

"So we go to the village?" Everett was standing next to Desmond, arms crossed and a frown on his face.

"We go to the village." Claire nodded. "We see if we can find any clues there. If we do, great. If we don't, we make a plan to go into the Elven Forest."

Malcolm grumbled, "I still don't like it."

"I know," Claire raised her free hand to cup his jaw, "it's not my ideal plan either. But they aren't going to let us just walk away from this."

“It would be a lot easier if we knew who ‘they’ was.” Desmond did his own grumbling.

“Maybe we’ll find that out too,” Claire suggested, aiming for an optimistic tone. Maybe she was dismissing the danger, maybe this was all a mistake. But she knew splitting up was a bigger mistake and she didn’t want this to be held over their heads forever. Even if she didn’t like the answers she found, at least they would find answers.

CHAPTER 21

Claire laughed gleefully as the wind beat against her face. Malcolm was right, it was only a short flight to the village for his dragon. His ruby red wings buffeted them from their place behind his head and Desmond gripped Claire a bit tighter as she shifted slightly.

She looked back at Desmond and he forced a smile on his face. Her wizard wasn't thrilled at riding Malcolm's dragon form and from the slightly green look on his face Claire wouldn't be surprised if her air wizard wasn't a bit scared of heights.

With the roar of the wind past their ears as Malcolm's wings carried them over the terrain, Claire couldn't offer any words of comfort so she snuggled back into his chest. Placing a hand on his own which were wrapped around her stomach, she squeezed lightly.

A flash of white caught the corner of Claire's eyes and she turned her head to the right, ignoring Desmond's grumble. Everett's gryphon coasted on the wind next to him, the white of his feathers glowing in the afternoon sun. His black spots matched Puck's. Puck's smaller wings were no match for Everett's or Malcolm's so he had taken to teleporting into the air in front of them as they traveled, divebombing Everett's gryphon as he did so. Claire was sure Everett's gryphon would have rolled his eyes if he could as he dodged the hyper Notus.

Claire laughed as Puck narrowly missed landing on Everett's wings. The gryphon let out a cry of annoyance and dove towards Puck who squawked and blinked out of the space, appearing on the other side of Malcolm moments later.

If they weren't traveling towards the village to find answers, Claire could almost imagine they were just out for an afternoon flight having fun in the air. But all too soon, Malcolm's dragon let out a roar that was echoed by Everett's answering cry and they began descending. The flat plains of the witches' territory merged into a Forest that seemed endless, even from the air. This was the Elven Forest.

Although this Elven village was outside the Forest's boundaries, it was still unnervingly close. The trees that scattered through the witches' territories paled in comparison to the massive trunks of the Elven Forest. Their branches were so intertwined that Claire couldn't see any of the Forest floor from the air. Something that was a defense mechanism no doubt.

They landed about one hundred yards from the Forest's edge, next to a lightened patch of earth. As they landed, Claire realized that this lightened patch of earth was once a road. Now the grass had overtaken it but the difference was there. As Desmond helped her down and Malcolm and Everett shifted back, Claire spun in a slow circle, taking in her surroundings. Remnants of a stone wall were being swallowed up by the earth as they crumbled. As if the earth was trying to reclaim all signs that a village was once here.

It was eerie.

A soft touch on her arm had Claire turning to look at

Everett. He was fully clothed and smirked at her slight pout. She had been so distracted by her surroundings that she had missed the men shifting back. She rolled her eyes playfully at him and then dodged away from his playful swat to her bottom.

"Focus, children." Desmond chided teasingly, looking much better now that his feet were on the ground.

The look that Everett shot her promised retribution and she was looking forward to it. But now, they had a job to do.

Malcolm tucked her between Everett and himself as they walked down the forgotten road towards the crumbling village. Puck darted ahead of them, flapping his wings as he floated in circles above the ruins. He banked and returned towards them, aiming for Claire. She caught him as he hit her chest lightly. That thread of magic from him in her center sparked slightly and then feelings of safety rose from it.

"It's safe." She told her men, giving Puck a soft kiss on his furry head and then throwing him back into the air. His wings caught a breeze and he floated above them, chirping down at her.

She caught Desmond staring at her. "What?"

"Nothing, little witch, but it would probably be a good idea to start learning more about familiar magic when we get back."

Claire nodded. She would add it to the ever-growing list of things she had to accomplish so she could protect her family.

They reached the outskirts of the village, the crumbling stone of the houses that once stood there falling into the roadway. The wooden roofs had long deteriorated leaving only the stone shells of the houses. Moss covered most of the stone that was still standing as if the earth was trying to make the stone disappear.

As someone who had relied on scents and sounds to navigate for most of her life, the silence in the village was deafening. The only noises came from Claire and her men as they walked further into the village and the soft flapping of Puck's wings overhead.

Claire kept her eyes peeled, for what, she wasn't actually sure. Some signs of why this happened here? According to Zack, this had been a massacre of the small Elven village. The Elves and the witches that lived here had been wiped out by the Flamell coven. That was the part that confused Claire the most. The Flamell coven had wiped out other witches too, bonded pairs of the Elves according to the journal.

And now, standing in the village center, looking around as the earth tried so desperately to swallow up the very existence of the village, Claire wondered why. Why attack this village? Why kill everyone here? Why abandon it afterwards? There was no monument, no flowers, nothing that signified that people died here.

Chills rose on Claire's arms and she rubbed them softly. Desmond frowned at her but she waved them off. Without speaking, Desmond and Malcolm broke off to search the ruins of the houses starting with the ones closest to the village center. The village elders would have lived in those if it was similar to Windshire or Brandlevine.

Everett stayed with her. Puck landed on what looked to be an old well. His padded feet, a soft thud on the mossy stone. He chirped softly, eyes locking with Claire and then inclined his head in the direction of one of the crumbling houses closer to the Forest.

Claire stepped in that direction and Puck leapt to the ground in front of her. He trotted, his plush tail waving as Claire and Everett followed. He stopped outside one of the ruins, a lone tree growing in its yard.

Claire had a flash of familiarity as she stared at the tree. Its energy was so familiar but she struggled to place it for a moment. Helene. This was a Dryad's tree. It looked as abandoned as the rest of the village was, it's old trunk split and dry.

No leaves hung from its bare branches that reached up like claws toward the sky.

What happened to the Dryad from the journal? She would have to ask Zack, but from the state of the tree, she knew the story probably didn't have a happy ending.

Puck chirped and the thread of magic that connected Claire to him inside of her jumped. She turned towards him but the thread settled. He was trying to tell her something. She dropped into her magic center slightly, focusing on his thread but nothing else happened. Then she realized what he was trying to tell her. Her magic was beating at the bindings softly, asking to be used.

Ignoring Everett's huff, she stepped into the yard, opening her magic and Energy Reading abilities up. Something here was trying to tell her something, possibly had the answers they were looking for. She tried not to let the excitement of a potential discovery rise as her magic did as she moved further into the abandoned yard.

The ruins of the house were dark and cold, the only energy coming from anywhere close was the moss that clung to the stones. And... *there*. The tree, despite its dead appearance, had a pocket of energy at the base of its trunk, where the dead wood disappeared into the earth. The tree should have deteriorated a long time ago if the lack of wood in the rest of the village was any indication, but somehow it still stood.

She knelt down at the base of the tree and allowed her magic to warm her palms as she pulled it up from her center. Taking a deep breath, she placed her palm at the base of the tree where the pocket of energy sat and pushed.

She was instantly thrown into a different scene, from the viewpoint of the tree she realized. Her eyes sliding shut as images assailed her mind from the Energy.

The crumbling village in front of her transformed into a bustling scene. No longer was the stone falling apart but instead clean, well-kept houses filled her vision. Smoke curled from the chimneys as children laughed and played. From where the tree stood, she could see into the village center.

Children and adults crowded around a woman with curly dark hair that matched Claire's own. For a second she wondered if this was the Dryad but then the woman in her vision brushed her hair behind her ears and Claire's breath caught. Her ears had a point to them. This woman was Elven. And important, if the attention paid to her was any indication.

The Elves and witches of the village crowded around her, hanging on her every word. All except for one. A witch who was too far away for Claire to make out any details of her face stood across the village center, arms folded with no apparent interest in joining the crowd. Who was she? Why was she unhappy?

Before Claire could puzzle on it any longer, the scene changed. Gone was the happy village of before. Now, screams filled the air.

Instead of chimney smoke, thick black smoke poured from the roofs of the houses that were on fire. Magic sparked in the air as the screams continued. Children and adults were running past Claire's tree towards the Elven Forest but Claire couldn't see if they made it or not. She let out a sob as a magic blast struck an Elven and witch couple, setting them on fire. They died holding each other and crying from the pain.

As quickly as the chaos of the scene started, it ended as the scene changed. The deafening silence that had greeted Claire and her men was back with a suffocating sorrow. The woman from the first vision, walked along the ruins of the village, black smoke still curling in the air. Her hand was covering her mouth and as she approached Claire's tree, Claire realized she was sobbing, tears streaking down her cheeks as she checked each body where it lay. Tears burned in Claire's eyes as each body she checked caused the woman to sob harder.

When she reached Claire's tree, the woman turned and faced

the devastation, hiding her face from Claire. Her hands glowed green as she lifted them in the air, chanting a language that was as unfamiliar to Claire as it was familiar. As Claire watched, the earth rumbled and the bodies melted into the land. Rain came pouring down from the clouds above, putting out the rest of the fire and settling the strong smell of ash in the air. Once the earth had absorbed the bodies, she turned and stepped towards the forest. Claire strained to see out of the corner of her, well the tree's, vision. The woman chanted again and magic sparked in her hands. She pushed out a wave of it towards the Forest but Claire couldn't see what the magic did. With one last look at the village, the woman walked towards the Forest and out of Claire's sight.

"Claire! Claire!" Her men's panicked shouts brought her back to the present. She was curled over on her knees, tears streaming over her face as a glow faded from around her body.

As soon as the glow faded, Everett was there, his forest scent chasing the ash smell from her nostrils as he yanked her into his arms. Malcolm and Desmond closed in on them, Malcolm's throat letting out a steady growl as he traced her arms with his hands and cupped her face. Claire shook in their arms for a few moments longer, gripping one of Desmond's hands with her own and burying her face in Everett's chest as she fought to catch her breath.

"What in the Realm was that?" Malcolm demanded, "You were supposed to keep her safe!" He shot at Everett.

"Don't fight, please," Claire's soft plea had Everett releasing the breath he had just taken to defend himself. She couldn't take any shouting right now as her senses struggled to acclimate back to this plane.

"Claire, little witch, what happened?" Claire turned her face from Everett's chest to meet Desmond's worried blue eyes.

"I think I saw what the tree saw. Like a vision." She was still struggling to put thoughts together as the images from the vision flashed through her mind.

"A vision," Desmond prompted gently, ignoring Malcolm's growl.

"There was this pocket of energy," Claire tried to organize her thoughts, "at the base of the tree. My magic guided me to it."

"I thought we talked about sending magic into things," Desmond tried to tease but his tone was still worried.

Claire huffed softly trying to smile, "We talked about not accepting strange magic from strange creatures and objects, nothing about sending it into trees."

Desmond rolled his eyes but his expression lightened slightly, "Let's just stop accepting or sending magic into strange anything, okay?"

Claire hummed but didn't agree outright. She knew better than to make a promise she couldn't keep. "When I touched the energy with my magic, I became the tree I think? Or was able to see its memories?"

"What did you see?" Everett asked, shifting to cradle her more comfortably in his arms. Claire sighed and relaxed into them, soaking up their comforting warmth to chase the lingering chill from the visions away.

"I saw the village. Before the attack. There was this woman with dark hair. An Elf. She looked important from the way the villagers were treating her. Then the scene changed and I saw the attack. There was fire and smoke everywhere. People were screaming." She stopped, overwhelmed at the memories and the emotions. The panic and sorrow.

Everett crooned at her and Claire looked up to see his gryphon in his eyes. Malcolm's growling turned softer as if he was also trying to comfort her but was struggling against his protective instincts. She decided to rip off the bandage so to speak and continued on.

"I saw people running past the tree towards the Forest..."

She paused and took a deep breath, "Not all of them made it. Afterwards, the scene shifted and the woman came back again. She... she buried the bodies and then the earth started reclaiming the village. She did something to the Forest as well but I couldn't see it." Claire frowned, closing her eyes as she tried to remember what the woman had done.

"Hey, it's okay." Desmond soothed as her forehead wrinkled from the strain of trying to remember. He lifted a hand and smoothed over her forehead, his magic sinking into Claire and settling her nerves.

She opened her eyes and gave him a small smile in thanks.

She shifted, trying to get to her feet. Everett growled softly but helped her up. Malcolm pulled her into his chest as she stood and Claire let him hug her for a few moments before she stepped back, looking towards the Forest.

"We need to know what she did," Claire said softly, stepping away.

Malcolm growled softly, catching her hand in his but not stopping her. They walked closer to the Forest's edge, the trees rising before them like massive, silent guardians.

"These trees remind me of the ones at the Academy," Claire frowned, placing a hand on one of the massive trunks, feeling the ancient energy humming beneath her palm. These trees were older, older than anything that walked the realm of that Claire was sure.

"The Elven Forest juts up to the Academy," Desmond said, "Although the true boundary of the Elven Forest is about a mile from the Academy's edge."

She let go of Malcolm's hand and stepped around the tree, trying to go deeper. A gentle force pushed her backwards. She frowned as Malcolm steadied her, growling into the Forest as if he could scare it into submission. "I think it's warded."

Desmond reached a hand out past her, to the spot where she

was pushed back. The wards were not as kind to him, pushing him back so forcefully he stumbled backwards.

"Desmond," She cried out, hurrying to him.

"I'm fine," Desmond waved a hand, "but that was odd."

"It wasn't nearly as forceful with Claire," Everett pointed out the obvious.

"Why?" Claire asked, taking Desmond's hand and running her eyes over his frame.

"Maybe it recognized you somehow?" Everett suggested but his face looked as confused as the rest of them were.

Claire frowned and let go of Desmond's hand to place hers on the trees again, ignoring Malcolm's protesting grumble. This time she placed both hands on the tree and leaned her forehead against it. "We need to go into the Forest." She whispered. "Will you let us pass?"

Her mind felt hazy as her magic sunk into the tree's ancient energy. The tree didn't respond in words, but a memory, or was it a vision, filled her mind. The clearing where Everett and her would picnic at the Academy. A specific path from it that led deeper into the Forest. Where the Felua had appeared from. A sense of urgency filled her from the tree's sluggish energy before throwing her out of the vision.

She stumbled backwards, Malcolm catching her yet again. This time his growl was directed at her, probably for sending magic into something. She smiled and patted his chest, ignoring the grumble.

"We have to go back to the Academy." Claire said, "The Forest is warded here. We have to enter through the Academy."

"Why is it warded here?" Malcolm asked, still frowning at the Forest like he could scowl it into submission.

"The woman in my vision warded it. At least, I think that's what she did," Claire frowned, her mind still a bit hazy as her magic separated from the tree's energy.

"But why?" Everett repeated Malcolm's earlier question.

"Maybe she didn't want what happened here to affect the Forest?" Desmond wondered.

"Maybe." Claire said, "Either way, we won't be able to enter here. We have to go back to the Academy."

Malcolm growled and Claire didn't blame him. They had left the Academy because of the danger. Now they had to head straight back into it.

CHAPTER 22

"I don't like this," Malcolm grumbled from the doorway causing Claire to pause in her packing.

Her dragon had a familiar scowl on his face and his arms were crossed over his broad chest. By the realm, he was handsome, and it seemed that her magic agreed as her bond with Malcolm flared warmer as she took him in.

"I know." She said simply, folding the shirt and placing it in the bag. She stopped packing and moved the bag over, taking a seat on the bed and patting the place next to her. Everett and Desmond were downstairs, filling in Desmond's parents. It was a discussion that had started over breakfast and had spilled over into the library afterwards. Claire had escaped upstairs to start packing when it became clear.

Malcolm crossed the space in a few strides and sat down next to her. Claire didn't have to wait long before he pulled her into his lap. Smiling, she looked up at him and placed a hand on his chest, stroking his soft shirt that was stretched across his broad chest. She smiled a little wider at his dragon's approving rumble.

"I don't think anyone likes it," Claire said, "but we will all be together at least."

"It feels too much like a trap. The only way through to the Forest is via the Academy that has seen the most sightings of aggressive beasts?"

"I think most of them would pale in comparison to your dragon," Claire said, not disagreeing but trying to make him feel better.

Malcolm huffed and she cupped his jaw, "I'm not trying to minimize your feelings or the risk," she said, staring into his golden eyes, "but I trust you to keep me safe so trust me to do the same for you?"

Malcolm huffed but tugged her closer, until her head was nestled under his chin, he buried his nose in her hair, practically vibrating and Claire realized that his dragon was probably riding him hard. He could use a distraction. They both could. She smiled wickedly as a thought occurred to her.

Ignoring his growl, she wiggled out from under his chin and stood up. Turning, she swung a leg over his lap and straddled him. His growl cut off as soon as she settled on his lap again.

She had an idea of how to distract him.

She had teased Malcolm enough over the last few weeks. Now, she wanted more from him. They didn't know what laid ahead of them but Claire knew what she wanted at this moment.

Malcolm seemed to pick up on where her thoughts were going quickly as his hands gripped her hips, thumbs stroking that sensitive skin where her thighs met her hips. "What are you doing, little treasure?"

"Hopefully seducing you." Claire teased, enjoying the way Malcolm's eyes widened.

She didn't really know what she was doing here but he always seemed to enjoy her teasing. She lifted one of her hands to grip his hair, in a way that her men often did to her when they went in for a kiss. She lowered her lips to his, placing soft kisses on his upper and bottom lips before Malcolm growled and dragged her closer. Her inner thighs stretched as he dragged her closer, her core coming into full contact with his. Claire wasn't completely unaware of biology, courtesy of an awkward lesson by Mary, the cook at the orphanage on a pig for all the girls living there, but she was unprepared for how big it felt against her.

Malcolm's kiss seared her lips and sent another blast of heat straight into her core, her magic lighting up the bond between them with an urgency that had Claire moving, twisting for something. She rocked her hips and gasped again as she rocked into Malcolm's hardness. The bolt of pleasure had her doing it again and Malcolm groaned. She smiled against his lips at the sound, enjoying the fact this was impacting him just as much. She did it again and Malcolm stood abruptly. She broke their kiss with a squeak as he turned and laid her down on the bed.

Malcolm hovered above her and Claire wondered what it would feel like for him to press his weight against her. He searched her eyes for something and Claire offered him a small smile as she lifted her hands to cup his face.

"Claire, do you know what you're asking?" He breathed, his voice worried as his eyes flashed.

"I want you." Claire said, "All of you. I think I've teased enough?" She smiled, arching an eyebrow at her.

Malcolm groaned and dropped his head to her chest for a few breaths. Claire fought not to squirm, a battle she quickly lost as Malcolm's hot breath brushed her breasts again.

Malcolm groaned again and lifted his head, "You'll tell me to stop if it gets too much?" His voice was hoarse as his golden eyes gleamed at her now. Claire guessed that his dragon was very invested in this moment.

Claire just smiled and nodded. She knew he wouldn't hurt her and she wanted all of him. Malcolm studied her for a few more moments, as if he could read her thoughts and was still unsure. She decided to help him out a bit. She dropped her hands from his face, running them down his back until she fisted his shirt in her hands and tugged upwards. Malcolm seemed to come to his decision and helped her pull his shirt off of him.

Claire nearly forgot her original plan to seduce him as she took in his broad golden chest. Her brain seemed to blank and she could only feel as her hands reached up and smoothed across his golden skin. Malcolm held rock-still like he was scared of spooking her. Claire grinned internally, that wouldn't do. She wanted a willing participant in this experience. She rose up to a sitting position and lowered her head to his chest, brushing a soft line of kisses across his chest like Desmond had done to her. His skin was warm and slightly salty and his smell of cinnamon and smoke filled her nostrils.

Malcolm groaned and fisted a hand in her hair but didn't make a move to pull her away so Claire continued.

As she trailed kisses across his chest, she let her hands wander, over his chest, down his arms, then back over his chest to trail down his stomach. When her lips found his nipple and sucked it into her mouth, her hands dipped into his pants, tracing the bare skin she found there, her fingers tentative but curious. She enjoyed his soft groans and rumbles as he tried to keep still for her exploration. Every groan she pulled out of him felt like a victory. She dipped her tongue out to taste his skin.

That was apparently Malcolm's limit as he grabbed both wrists causing her to lift her head to look up at him. His eyes were glowing, jaw clenched and a strange sense of satisfaction filled Claire at the sight of him so close to the edge. "What do you want, little treasure?" He gritted out.

"I want to make you feel good," Claire said. She wanted to drive him as crazy as he drove her. She was intrigued with the idea of pushing her growly dragon until he snapped.

Malcolm groaned and lifted his eyes to the ceiling, as if that would give him patience. Claire gently pulled her wrists from his grasp and reached for the buckle on his pants. Malcolm let out a hiss but didn't stop her as she loosened the buckle. With a growl, he batted her hands away and pushed his pants down fully.

Claire blinked. She hadn't expected to be so… big? It was much different than the crude drawing in the lessons Mary had taught, or rather described to Claire.

Claire was overwhelmed with the desire to touch it. To make Malcolm feel good. Would it be like when Desmond had touched her? Was it just as sensitive? Claire wrapped a tentative hand around it, stroking the skin there that felt like velvet and heat.

And that was when Malcolm broke.

In a flash, Claire was lying back on the bed, her growly dragon pinning her arms above her head and pressing his body length against her. His cock pressing against her stomach. Claire went to speak but Malcolm kissed the words away. He lifted his head and stared down at her. "My turn, little treasure."

Claire gasped as he transferred her wrists to one hand, his hold gentle but firm and his thumb stroked over his pulse point. His other hand traced down her arm, over her jaw, and down her front. His thumb stroked over the hollow of her throat before his hand dragged down her chest until it reached the hem of her shirt. All the while, his glowing eyes locked on hers.

"Malcolm, please," Claire shifted upwards. Malcolm growled and lowered his weight onto her hips more, pinning her in place to stop her movement. Claire managed to shift her legs open and they both groaned when their cores met.

"Please what?" Malcolm asked, lowering his head to trace his lips along her jawline, licking and nipping the sensitive skin underneath her ear.

"Touch me," Claire begged. She needed more. More kisses,

more sensation. Desmond had given her a taste but now she wanted more from her growly dragon. The bond between them seemed to flare stronger with every flash of Malcolm's dragon and her dancing magic.

Her dragon must be riding the edge more than she thought because he quickly yanked her shirt over her head. He released her wrists but pressed them into the bed. "Keep them there." He ordered in a growly voice that sent heat shooting straight to her core, soaking her underwear.

His eyes flared and he took in a long breath, biting his lip as he did so. Claire had an urge to bite it instead but before she could act on the urge, his mouth was on her breasts and she lost the ability to think.

She might have cried out his name, she wasn't sure. Unlike Desmond's soft, teasing touches, Malcolm sucked her nipple straight into his mouth and lashed it with his tongue. Just as quickly as he did that, he released it and blew cool air on it, causing her nipple to tighten into a hard bead. The dual sensation had her head thrashing back and forth as she arched her back.

When he turned his attention to her other breast, Claire forgot to keep her hands where they were, threading them into his hair to the sound of his growl. She wasn't sure if she wanted to pull him closer or push him away, the sensation almost too intense to bear.

As if he heard her thoughts, he released her other aching nipple and waited till her eyes met his, stroking a thumb over her nipples. "Is this okay?" He asked, his tone surprisingly soft.

Claire nodded, "I want more. I want you. I want to touch you."

"If you touch me, little treasure, I'll lose control."

"What if that's the point?" Claire bucked her hips. She wanted him as crazy as she felt right now.

Malcolm smirked and pressed a sweet kiss to the center of

her chest above her heart and then dragged his lips lower. Claire squirmed as his lips traced the line of skin above her pants. She lifted her hips, desperate to feel his skin against hers.

Malcolm growled and tugged her pants down. When she laid exposed to him, Claire was struck with a sudden bout of shyness. His glowing eyes traced over her and Claire fought not to squirm. What was he thinking about? Was she enough?

That thought struck her. It had been a while since she had questioned her place with her Triad. But here, now, literally bare to one of her men, Claire couldn't help but wonder if she was enough.

As soon as she thought that though, Malcolm moved, tracing his warm palms from her ankles up her legs, pushing them gently apart. "Beautiful." He murmured, dragging his eyes up to hers, "Absolutely beautiful, little treasure."

Claire blushed, unable to help it but her entire body sagged with relief. The motion caused her legs to fall open farther and when Malcolm lowered his head to her center, she wondered if he could see her entire body blush.

He took a deep breath and growled as he lowered his head. The vibration from his growl that close to her center caused it to weep and Claire squirmed again. Mary definitely didn't cover that.

That was the last thought she had before Malcolm lowered his head and licked her there. He licked once, twice, and on the third time focused on a bundle of nerves that had Claire seeing stars and the breath stuttering from her chest.

He focused his attention on that bundle of nerves with an intensity that had Claire squirming as it felt like pressure built in her body and her magic danced restlessly in her center. When he slid one hand up to his mouth and pressed a single finger inside her, Claire felt like she hurtling towards the edge of the cliff and was helpless to stop it.

She opened her mouth to say something but all that came

out was a high-pitched moan when his tongue curled around her bundle of nerves and *sucked.*

She shattered, blasting straight over the edge of that cliff and falling, pleasure causing her every muscle to tense and then go boneless. When she came to, Malcolm was still gently pushing his finger in and out of her, glowing eyes on hers. Claire's bond with him felt so strong in that moment that she could feel his satisfaction. But there was still something missing. And Mary did cover this in the birds and bees part of her lesson.

"Malcolm." His name a breathless whisper on her tongue when she could get her brain to work, "I want you."

"You have me," Malcolm whispered his own answer, rising up and catching her in a gentle kiss.

Claire pulled back so she could cup his face. "No, I want all of you. I want you inside of me," She said the last part with a blush.

Malcolm's chest rumbled as he stared down at her, gauging her seriousness. Claire pushed all of her feelings of rightness down the bond towards him.

He brushed a gentle kiss across her lips and for a brief second Claire worried he was going to deny her this. Then his hand skimmed down her side, stroking her hip, to the back of her leg. He cupped it and pulled her leg over his hip, opening her for him. His cock brushed against Claire's sensitive entrance and she whimpered, bucking her hips upwards to try and get more friction.

"Easy, little treasure," Malcolm murmured softly, his hand stroking her there and causing the pleasure to build again, "We have to take this slow so I don't hurt you."

"You could never hurt me," Claire said, letting out a moan when his finger pressed inside her, sliding in easily with how wet she was.

He pulled out his finger and pressed a second one in, his eyes on Claire's face for any kind of discomfort. His fingers stretched but there was no burn and Claire bucked her hips again.

"Please, Malcolm, I'm ready. I want you."

Malcolm groaned and lowered his head to her neck, kissing and licking the sensitive skin there until Claire was squirming. He withdrew his fingers to cup her breast as his cock brushed her entrance again and began pressing in.

Claire's eyes widened at the feeling. His cock was much larger than his fingers and the stretch was immediate. Malcolm sucked one of her nipples into his mouth and the bolt of pleasure echoed at her core. She bucked her hips and he slid further in. They both let out a groan when his hips finally bumped Claire's

Claire fought not to move, to relax and let her body adjust. He was just so big. She squirmed slightly and Malcolm groaned.

He kissed her deeply as he pulled out a bit and then rocked forward. Claire groaned into the kiss. That. She wanted more of that.

When she broke the kiss to whisper that in his ear, Malcolm lost a bit of his control. He pulled back and snapped his hips forward harder. Claire clutched at his shoulders and lifted her hips to meet his next thrust.

That same feeling of hurtling towards the cliff's edge filled her. Pleasure seemed to radiate out from where they joined and fill every inch on her body, from her head to the tips of her toes. Malcolm moved faster, driving the pleasure to new heights and Claire shattered again.

Malcolm let out a long groan and thrust his hips two more times before warmth splashed inside Claire and he pressed his weight down onto her.

Panting softly, Claire caught her breath and enjoyed the Malcolm-sized blanket on top of her. As he caught his breath, he lifted his head.

"Are you okay, little treasure?"

Claire smiled up at him. "I'm wonderful."

He arched an eyebrow, a grin breaking out on his handsome face, the golden glow in his eyes dimmed as if his dragon had been sated. "Wonderful?"

Claire blushed but stood by her words. "Wonderful."

Malcolm gently lifted himself off of her and Claire frowned when something leaked out of her down there. Malcolm looked down and cursed softly. "Don't worry, Claire," his use of her name conveyed his seriousness, "we'll have Desmond do a birth control spell."

Claire stilled and wanted to shake herself. That had been the one thing that Mary had harped on the girls over and over again was that sex led to pregnancy. Claire hadn't expected sex to feel that good and had completely forgotten that part.

Malcolm mistook her stillness for something else and was quick to reassure her again. Claire held a hand up to his mouth, rolling her eyes when he placed a gentle kiss on her palm.

"I wasn't thinking about that." She admitted, "It's not that I don't want kids one day…" She had honestly thought she would never get the chance to. That no one would want a blind, orphaned witch.

"It just isn't the right time," Malcolm finished her sentence in a way that Claire agreed with.

She nodded, "Not yet. Not till we find answers and know what being a Champion requires."

Malcolm frowned and Claire wanted to shake herself again for causing the dark expression to settle on his face. Before she could say anything else though, he scooped her into his arms.

She let out a squeak as he carried her to the bathroom and rolled her eyes at his laughter. "Come, little treasure, let's get you all cleaned up and then we'll find the others."

CHAPTER 23

Claire blushed hard as she met Desmond's amused eyes as she and Malcolm descended the stairs.

Desmond laughed softly at her embarrassment and snaked an arm around her waist and tugged her into him. "Did you have a nice time?" His amused voice whispered in her ear.

Claire blushed hotter but answered him. "A very wonderful time." She corrected and Malcolm chuckled behind her.

"She needs a birth control spell," Malcolm said bluntly. Claire groaned and blushed again, turning her face into Desmond's chest.

Desmond leaned down to whisper in her ear, "It's nothing to be embarrassed of, little witch. I am happy to take care of you."

Desmond placed a hand on her stomach lightly and Claire felt the cooling brush of his healing magic settled into her core, chasing away the aches of never-before-used muscles. She kissed his cheeks in thanks as the front doors to the manor opened, letting Holly and Zack in with Everett right behind them.

Holly pulled her away from Desmond, hugging Claire tight.

"We can come with you," Holly offered, whispering into her ear.

"We've got this," Claire refused gently. She didn't want to risk anymore of her new family on this unknown. Her chest panged as she let go of Holly. Even though she didn't want to risk them, leaving her friends wasn't easy.

"Promise me you'll be careful," Holly stepped back but gripped her hands.

"I promise. Promise me you will do the same?"

"We will," Zack stepped up next to them and threw an arm around Holly's shoulders. "We will let Bethany and Cody know too."

Claire winced slightly, her fiery best friend was not going to be thrilled that they had left without them. But Bethany would have not taken no for an answer and Cody would have followed wherever Bethany went.

"Are you ready, Claire?" Andy asked. Claire turned to see Andy and Helene standing with her men, Frederick and Ilena behind them.

Andy and Helene returning with them was the compromise that Desmond's parents offered. Because they had to be light on the details, Desmond and Everett had only mentioned that the things they found at the village were leading back to the Academy. Andy and Helene would go back with them to help 'protect' the group according to Frederick and Ilena.

In reality, they would actually be helping to protect the group but they would serve as an anchor point at the Academy when she and her men ventured into the Forest.

Claire gave Holly and Zack one last tight hug each, unable to say goodbye again. The fierceness in which they both hugged her back told her they understood what she was trying to say. The Elven Forest was a dangerous place for unwanted visitors before the Great War, now it was even more so. But it was the only place that held the answers they were searching for.

Claire's stomach seemed like a pit of nerves and even Desmond squeezing her hand couldn't settle them as they walked towards the portal.

* * *

THE LAST TIME Claire had come through the portal, she hadn't had a chance to take it in with the aftermath of the Felua attack so prominent in all of their minds. The stone archway that held the portal sat right outside the boundary of Brandlevine's coven lands. It didn't exist inside the coven lands for security reasons, even though the portal only went to the neutral Academy. Each territory had one so their students could travel back and forth.

Maybe the Academy wasn't as neutral as it seemed, Claire thought. With sending Claire an invitation and then calling her to be a Champion of the Realm, those didn't seem like neutral moves of a semi-sentient Academy.

The Champion of the Realm topic was one that hadn't gotten a lot of attention in the last few months. Other more pressing issues had stayed at the forefront but Claire knew it was only a matter of time until the Champion issue reared its head.

As the stone archway loomed closer, Puck chirped above them and Claire looked up to see him descending lazily towards her. She extended her arms and caught him with a soft 'oof'.

"The portal won't hurt Puck?" She asked worriedly, the thought just occurring to her.

"It shouldn't," Andy said, "it's designed for all magical creatures."

'It shouldn't' didn't sound as definitive as 'Absolutely not' and Claire frowned.

"It'll be fine, little witch," Desmond murmured in her ear, "Elves and Fae used to use these portals all the time. I looked it up last night."

Claire smiled up at him, warmth filling her at his thoughtfulness.

She waited patiently beside Malcolm as Desmond and Andy activated the portal. Malcolm pulled her to his chest, and Claire leaned back against him. The bond thrumming between them felt even more vibrant than it had before and Claire blushed, wondering if their newfound closeness had anything to do with it.

Despite Desmond's reassurances, she still held tightly to Puck as they stepped through. When they stepped out onto the otherside, Puck let out a purr in her arms pushing a wave of warmth down their bond. Claire let out a small sigh of relief. She really needed to start working more on her bond with her familiar and utilizing his magic with hers.

Everett wrapped his arm around her and guided her away from the portal entrance so the others could step through. Gwen, the Headmaster's secretary, greeted them when they were all gathered.

"Welcome back!" She smiled warmly. "The Headmaster is expecting you."

Everett kept his arm wrapped around her as the group walked into the Headmaster's office. She barely kept her squeak of surprise in when he pulled her down onto his lap in one of the chairs, the move one she would expect from Malcolm not Everett. She looked up at him and frowned softly at the lines of strain around his eyes. Coming back here was causing him more stress than he was letting on. She snuggled into his chest, adjusting Puck in her arms and ignoring the rest of the room. If it made her silent, steady protector feel better to hold her, then she would gladly let him.

The Headmaster cleared his throat and Claire lifted her head so she could see him.

"Is that a Notus?" He asked, indicating towards Puck.

Claire nodded.

The Headmaster dipped his chin in acknowledgement, eyes burning with questions. Instead, he turned to look at Desmond. "I take it your request to come back isn't actually to spend time at the Academy before the school year begins?"

Desmond shook his head, "That's the only reason I felt comfortable giving over paper. We've made discoveries that lead us to believe our next answers lie in the Elven Forest."

The Headmaster's eyebrows shot up at that statement. "You are going into the Elven Forest?"

Desmond nodded and briefly outlined the last few weeks at Brandlevine with Puck's appearance and their trip to the abandoned Elven village. When he was done, the Headmaster leaned heavily back in his chair.

"Technically, I'm not supposed to offer assistance as the Academy is meant to be neutral but is there anything you are hoping to find at the Academy before you go into the Forest?"

Claire appreciated his play on words. Technically, he wasn't offering assistance outright but instead asking if they were searching for something.

Desmond looked at Claire who shook her head. She didn't need anything here. And her magic was telling her to get to the Forest as soon as possible.

Helene spoke up, "I have one thing for Claire before they head in. I can give that to her this evening."

Desmond nodded, "We'll leave in the morning then."

Claire's stomach tightened and Puck shifted on it. This was the right thing to do but dread still filled her all the same. What kind of answers were waiting for them?

She was shaken from her thoughts by Everett standing and helping her to her feet. "Come, Claire," Helene held out a hand towards her, "I can show you this while Andy helps your Triad pack."

Claire was still feeling a bit jittery from her feelings of dread so leaving her Triad was harder than it had been in the past. She placed Puck on the ground so he could follow them and accepted Helene's hand. She looked back over her shoulder a few times at her Triad.

After the third time, she caught Helene's eyes. Helene gave her a gentle smile, "Your bond is growing stronger, it's natural to miss their presence."

Claire blushed as she thought about how her bond grew with Malcolm earlier this afternoon.

Helene led her the familiar path past the Class Buildings and a right turn towards the garden. She held the gate open for Claire and led her past the garden plots and towards Helene's tree. Helene placed a hand on her tree, a soft smile on her face, and Claire felt like she was intruding on a private moment.

After a few breaths, Helene dropped her hand and turned to Claire. "This is what I wanted to show you."

Claire felt confused. "What do you mean?"

Helene gestured towards her tree in a graceful movement that reminded Claire of a branch waving in the wind. "My tree. I think that you can learn the signature of its energy and then use that to communicate with Andy and I while you are in the Forest."

Claire's eyebrows shot straight up. That seemed a little out of Claire's skillset, even with how her magic had been progressing.

Helene smiled at her expression. "You can do this." She assured her.

"How are you so sure?" Claire didn't even know where to begin. I mean sure, she could read energies and tap into a tree's energy but to be able to memorize one tree's individual energy signature and send messages along it? That seemed like a bit of a stretch.

Before Helene could answer that question, Claire asked another one, "And what kind of messages? Like words?" She couldn't even do that with her Triad yet.

"Well feelings would probably work too and are easiest to push but yes, I believe you could send messages with words too. You are stronger and more powerful than you allow yourself to think. I think when you fully recognize your power, there's very little you won't be able to do."

Claire furrowed her brow. She didn't quite believe she would ever get that powerful but that was a thought for a different day. "How do I connect to your tree's energy?"

Helene walked her through the process. It was very similar to how Claire connected with plants in general but to connect and memorize this tree's specific signature, she had to dive deeper, reaching the heart of the tree that felt a lot like Helene. It felt soft, musical almost, with a steady energy that reminded her of the professor.

Claire opened her eyes and grinned at Helene, "I did it!"

Helene smiled back at her as Puck batted at a butterfly next to them. "You did! I could feel you there. Now try to send a message to me."

Claire thought for a moment and then sent the feeling of safety she got when she was around her Triad members. They found out that Claire could send feelings to Helene via the tree but Helene couldn't send them back to her. Whatever communication they were going to have in the Forest was going to be one-sided.

Waving goodbye to Helene, Claire led Puck out of the garden and headed towards their rooms. The Academy was weirdly silent even without its students. As if the whole of campus was holding its breath.

Claire paused in the middle of the courtyard and took in the large grassy lawn with the trees lining each side. She smiled when she focused on the tree that she and her friends had spent many an afternoon under. One that Everett had first found her at and sat with her. The imposing administrative building rose in front of her with the Combat Arena at her back.

So many memories here. Known memories. She turned a half circle, looking towards the woods on the other side of the Combat Arena. The woods were dark with the falling daylight. Quiet. Unknown.

Puck pressed against her legs, his soft fur tickling as he rubbed against her. She smiled and bent to pet him. "Come on, Puck, let's go see if they scrounged you up some turkey."

Puck chirped happily and started trotting in the direction of their building. Claire wondered if he knew where to go because he felt her own bonds tugging her in that direction. Her entire world had been Windshire and then this Academy but really her world was in the building she just entered.

She would do anything to protect her world. To protect them. They would make it back here, she would make sure of it.

CHAPTER 24

The next morning, Andy and Helene saw them off. When Claire had gotten up to the suite last night, her men had acquired three large packs they were filling. Claire had asked where hers was and had enjoyed the way her men scrambled to tell her that they were being a bit overprotective at the moment and that she didn't actually have a pack to carry

She couldn't blame them. She knew that she was going to do whatever possible to make sure all four of them left the Forest so maybe it was better if her hands were free to carry her daggers instead. She had buckled the sheath on this morning and now as they stood on the entrance to the path to the clearing, she took comfort in the familiar weights hanging on either side.

Tuning back into her surroundings, Andy was speaking.

"I don't think I have to warn you about the Felua. They are solitary creatures but are fiercely territorial and who knows how many you will encounter. Be especially careful of the colonies of Vespertilios. They hunt in packs and nest in caves. They are small but their strength is in numbers. Also be careful of the plantlife. Look before you bed down for the night."

Helene placed an arm around Andy's waist and broke in, "My love, they know this. They've been trained for this."

"But Claire..."

"Claire will be fine." Helene said firmly.

Andy let out a breath and worried her bottom lip, "I know, I'm just..."

"Worried." Helene smiled gently at her. "We all are. But they are going to be fine."

If Claire wasn't feeling so anxious to get into the forest, she would have smiled at the way that Helene kept finishing Andy's sentences.

"Alright then." Andy said, "Communicate down Helene's tree if you need us."

"We will." Desmond agreed, shaking Andy's hand, "We'll check-in regularly."

Claire accepted Helene and Andy's hugs before returning to Malcolm's side. Her growly dragon had been in a cranky mood all morning and had barely let her out of his sight. Puck floated lazily above them, playing with the sparrows that had nested on top of the Combat Arena.

Waving goodbye to her professors one last time, Claire slipped a hand around Malcolm's arm and flashed him a reassuring smile. "It'll be fun." She teased, "Just think of it as an adventure."

He shot her an unimpressed look and Claire giggled as they made their way deeper into the woods, heading toward her and Everett's spot.

Too soon, they stood in the clearing. Claire smiled at the tree that she and Everett had shared their first picnic, and her first kiss under. She stepped up to the tree and leaned her forehead against it, silently thanking it for the good memories.

The tree's energy was warm and ancient but it surged forward to interact with her magic as soon as it felt her presence. The tree's energy pushed into her forcefully, trying to tell her something. Claire accepted it, trying to keep her face blank so she wouldn't get another lecture from Desmond and lose the message.

The energy lingered in her magic center before flowing right through her causing a tugging on her center. One that directed her towards the Elven Forest border. Claire tried to follow it with her magic but all she could get a sense from the pull was that the location was deep inside the Forest. A thought occurred to her.

"Where was the Elven Capital?" Claire asked.

"The Elves were secretive about its exact location but deep in the Elven Forest. Due north if I remember right." Everett said, coming to stand next to her.

"I think we need to go there."

"Why do you say that, little witch?"

"Just a feeling." With how on edge her Triad was, if she admitted that the tree pushed magic and gave her the feeling, she had her own feeling that the Triad would call it all off.

“A feeling?” Desmond was already suspicious.

“A feeling from the trees,” Claire admitted.

Malcolm growled, “I don't like this. We haven't even started and they are trying to lure her in.”

“What if it's not the same ‘they’?” Everett wondered, her silent strategist had wheels turning in his head.

Claire grabbed his hand, squeezing softly. “What do you mean?”

“What if the pull you feel to the forest and the vision you had from the Dryad's tree are separate from the creatures attacking?”

“So there's two unknown parties that want Claire in the Forest?” Desmond asked.

Everett shook his head, “I think there is one party that wants her in the Forest and the other party is trying to keep her out by making us think the Elves are behind the attacks.”

"Great," Malcolm grumbled and her growly dragon looked so put out that Claire couldn't help but laugh.

"That's good news then," Claire said, "we have one ally at least."

"I wouldn't go that far." Everett retorted, "We still don't know why they want you in the Forest. Their intentions might not be as innocent as you think."

"The trees wouldn't lie. They can't. They're trees." Claire pointed out, "They can carry messages and they can transmit Energies. And nothing about this Energy feels malicious."

Desmond barked out a short laugh at her explanation but shrugged, "She's right. We should head in. We're losing daylight."

Claire frowned and looked up. The morning sun was still low on the horizon but Desmond had a point. The thick canopy of the trees was already filtering out the sun.

Malcolm grumbled but took point, leading them on a faint path towards the Elven Forest boundary. The pull in Claire's center eased as they started moving forward. Desmond took her hand in his, letting Everett take up the back. The alert gryphon's eyes constantly swiveled across their surroundings, searching the shadows of the trees for anything out of place.

As they got closer to the boundary, Claire's stomach tightened and danced with nerves. Her palms started to sweat lightly and Claire withdrew her hand from Desmond's to wipe it on her pants. The forest was quiet, the batting of Puck's wings above them the only breeze. A lump of nerves seemed to lodge in Claire's throat and she swallowed thickly.

Desmond stole her hand back into his, frowning when he caught sight of her face. "Are you okay?" His bond thrummed with worry.

For a second, Claire wanted to lie in case her men wanted to turn back but she swallowed it down. They were as committed to this as she was, even if they didn't like it. "Nervous." She whispered.

Desmond squeezed her hand, "Me too."

Claire stared at him in shock and Desmond laughed quietly at her. "I can get nervous too. It's natural when we are heading into an unknown situation. Use your nerves to stay sharp, but don't let them overwhelm you."

Claire didn't know any of her men could get nervous but her stomach settled at Desmond's words. She could use her nerves to keep them all safe too. She looked up at Puck, jumping from tree branch to tree branch, and tugged on her bond with him lightly. Puck paused on the tree branch he was holding onto, and then using his claws, held on as he hung upside down, blinking at her with his large cat-like eyes.

Claire laughed and Desmond rolled his eyes. Puck waited until Claire was underneath the branch and then released it, dropping gently to curl around the back of her neck and hang on to her shoulders.

His furry cheek brushed against Claire's as he let out a soft purr and thrummed a question down their bond. Claire nuzzled back into him, lifting a hand to stroke his soft head and tried to form a picture with her thoughts. *How far were they from the boundary line?*

Puck chirped softly in her ear and Claire felt his muscles tense before he launched himself from her shoulders and flew over Malcolm's head, disappearing into the thickening trees. Malcolm turned around and arched an eyebrow at Claire.

"He's going to check how far we are from the boundary line," Claire said.

Malcolm nodded and kept moving. Desmond caught her elbow and helped her over a particularly large root. The faint path they had been following was nonexistent to Claire's untrained eyes right now but Malcolm seemed sure of himself.

"We make it a point to patrol this area," Everett said from

behind her, as if reading her thoughts or maybe their bond, "Malcolm knows where we are."

Claire shot him a smile over her shoulder and he returned her grin before going back to analyzing their surroundings.

"This gate used to be used by the Elven students coming to the Academy," Desmond explained further, "this area is still patrolled regularly but usually not this close to the gate per an agreement with the Elves."

"An agreement?" Claire questioned.

Desmond nodded. "We will have to ask Headmaster Dorian the specifics, but remember, the Elves were secretive."

Claire nodded. That made sense with everything she knew about the Elves. What if someone accidentally crossed the gate?

"You're getting better at communicating with Puck," Desmond said, changing the subject..

Claire nodded, "It's getting easier. I wish we had more time to practice together though. I feel like there's a lot I don't know about a familiar bond."

Desmond frowned, "I didn't get a chance to read too much about it, unfortunately. Other than that they are supposed to help you control and utilize large amounts of magic."

Claire frowned. That seemed an incredibly limited definition compared to what Claire felt with Puck. He almost felt like an extension of her thoughts at times. One more question to add to the endless list Claire kept hunting for answers for.

Speaking of Puck, the bond was getting stronger like he was coming back. A small dark shadow flitted ahead of them, getting lighter the closer he did and causing her men to let out a breath when they recognized him. Claire let a smile dance around her lips and let go of Desmond's hand to catch Puck to her chest. The group paused as Claire focused on her bond with the Notus. An image pushed down through their bond. *A clearing up ahead thick with the scent of magic. A tree that had been split into an archway.*

How far, Claire asked Puck.

Puck pushed the image of Everett and her clearing at her three times. *Three times the length of that clearing.* They were close.

"We're close," Claire announced, "Maybe one hundred paces?"

Malcolm nodded. "We're closer than we ever patrolled before. The magic is thick here. Usually it would be pushing us to turn back now."

"It's probably because Claire is with us," Desmond exchanged frowns with Malcolm.

"That's a good thing then," Claire said, "it means we are in the right place."

Everett stepped up behind her and ran his hands over her shoulders and down her arms, rubbing her upper arms gently. He buried his nose against her neck and Claire fought not to shiver. "Yes, but allow us to be grumpy over it. You're our mate and there's a serious unknown up ahead."

"You're allowed to be grumpy," Claire addressed all of them, "I think we can agree that no one will take any unnecessary risks. But we don't have to do this." She offered one last out even though her magic was tugging her farther ahead now.

There was a moment of silence before Desmond spoke. "We need the answers. We can't be stumbling along blindly anymore. We need to know."

Claire nodded. "Then let's go." No one had to like it. That was life. But they could get through it. Together.

Malcolm took point again but the group stayed tighter together now. When they reached the clearing, Claire knew.

The magic here was thick, like a heavy blanket. Desmond grimaced and Claire frowned. "It's fine, little witch." He assured her, "It's not that bad. It's not exactly welcoming but it's not hostile either."

Claire bit her lip. The magic didn't feel hostile to her at all.

Heavy. There was a ton of it saturating the clearing. But it felt warm, welcoming. The archway that Puck had shown her was across the clearing from them. It looked like originally it was two trees that had been entangled together when they were young. Now, each trunk was larger than probably all her men's arms wrapped around it. They joined together at the height of Everett's gryphon and Claire wondered who all had passed through this gate. Did her parents?

"What now?" Desmond asked.

Malcolm frowned and checked a time piece. "It's only been two hours. We should have plenty of daylight."

Claire read the doubt in his voice easily. Here, this close to the Elven Forest, the trees were thick, the leafy branches casting a never-ending shadow. When daylight fell, it would only get much darker. That might be the first time Claire would ever have an advantage.

"We should try and enter." Everett decided, "We don't know how long that'll take. We can always camp on just the other side of the gate."

Malcolm grumbled but agreed. Cautiously, they approached the gate. Puck landed on Claire's shoulder again, his weight a comforting presence. Desmond stepped up to the gate first, cautiously putting a hand out between the trees. He frowned when he didn't encounter anything.

He stepped through and Claire's heart skipped a beat for a second. He turned around and looked at them and then walked around one of the trunks to join them in the front again.

He rubbed a hand across his face. "It's definitely a gate but it's inactive. My guess is that the Forest behind it is an illusion."

"Your guess?" Malcolm asked.

"I don't think it would be wise to get lost in the illusion." Desmond bantered. "Can't go leaving you all by yourselves now. Who knows where the illusion leads."

Claire frowned. The gate was inactive? How were they

supposed to get through? Was this all in vain? No, it couldn't be. There had to be a way to activate the gate. She pushed the thought down to Puck who pushed confusion back towards her. Her familiar didn't know either.

Claire took a step back from the gate, away from her men who were discussing options. She studied the trunks on either side, tracing over where they joined at the top and the empty space between them. They were missing something. She was missing something.

She looked over the trunks again, her eyes straining to see any differences, anything that seemed out of place. Nothing. The strain caused her to close her eyes briefly to rest them. When she closed her eyes, instead of blackness, the trees remained, glowing green. Claire's eyes snapped back open, but the trees looked normal. She closed them again. The trees were there, framing the gate and glowing a faint green. She opened her eyes again, looking at her men who were listening to Desmond as he gestured towards the gate.

She closed her eyes while looking at them and she could see their faint outlines glowing as well. Desmond's blue, Everett's green, and Malcolm's red.

This had never happened before so why was it happening now. What was different? Claire looked around the clearing and then it dawned on her. The most obvious thing and she wanted to smack herself like Bethany smacked Cody when he realized the obvious. The magic. The whole clearing was covered in a heavy weight of magic and somehow that was causing Claire to 'see' even with her eyes closed.

Magic was the difference. Would the addition of more magic change anything? Claire turned back to the gate and closed her eyes. This time, she called her own magic up, asking it to fill her eyes. The faint glow of the gate shone brighter as she fed her own magic into her 'eyesight'.

With this brighter glow, Claire could see glowing white

symbols on the trunks of the trees on either side of the gate. They were runes of some sort. Her hands itched to trace them but she paused. Puck shifted on her shoulder again and pressed his cheek against hers. He would help.

Everything else died away as Claire let her magic out from her center, letting it fill her eyes and her hands until her palms and fingers were tingling from the pressure. Eyes still closed, she traced the symbols on the gates with her hands, sending magic into each one until the five glowing symbols hung in the air in front of her.

Claire opened her eyes, catching her Triad standing next to her out of her peripheral vision but she didn't move her focus from the symbols. Calling more magic from her center, she pushed the symbols into the gate. When the first symbol touched the gate, it was sucked in immediately. As the fifth symbol was absorbed, the gate began to glow and the space between the two trunks glimmered.

She had done it. She had activated it. By herself. A sense of pride and confidence filled her. Maybe she could do this and her magic would be enough to protect her men from whatever lied ahead.

Puck shifted on her shoulder claws digging in lightly as he grounded her back to the here and now. She needed to pull her magic back in. It fought at first, enjoying its freedom but Puck's magic in her center tugged insistently and her magic responded to the call.

She allowed her focus to break from the gate to look at her Triad. Desmond reacted first, a proud smile on his face as he scooped her into his arms. "We're over here trying to figure it out and you're over here being a little badass."

"Desmond," Claire complained, "if you put 'little' before 'badass' it takes away from the effect."

Even Malcolm barked out a laugh at her joke. He pressed a kiss on her head as Desmond released her. Everett squeezed her gently before letting her go.

"We should go," he reminded everyone gently, "not that I don't trust Claire's abilities but I would rather not test to see how long the gate will hold."

Claire nodded. She had a feeling the gate would hold until she said otherwise but she didn't push it. She took Everett's offered hand and stepped up in front of the gate with him. Even though her magic was telling her everything would work, she still felt a pang of unease.

She looked over her shoulder, "Stay close, please," She pleaded with Malcolm and Desmond. They took a step closer, Desmond taking her other hand and Malcolm placing a hand on her back. Together, they stepped through the gate.

CHAPTER 25

If the magic was heavy in the clearing, it was nothing like the magic through the gate. It felt like they were walking through thick mud, every step a struggle. Thankfully, only five steps into the gate, they were on the other side.

Claire's eyes widened. It simultaneously looked but didn't look like the same forest at all. Everything was... brighter here? Despite the thick canopy of trees, the shadows were brighter, the air seemed crisper. Everything felt more alive. The trees were still massive but some of them looked like no tree Claire had ever seen. Their trunks were a multitude of colors, every shade of brown, purple, red, and gold wove in an endless stretch around them. Thick green, gold, and blue leaves in every shade, size and shape rustled above their heads, their canopy so thick you couldn't see a hint of the sky above.

Claire looked around her in wonderment, spinning in a circle and trying to take in every detail. She caught Desmond giving her a soft smile. "What?"

"Just looking at you glow, little witch,"

Claire looked down at her hands and frowned. Her arms

were tanned from the long hours in the sun, but she didn't think she was glowing.

"Your smile, little witch." Desmond said, stepping closer and cupping her face, "And your eyes." He pressed a soft kiss to her lips and she stood up on her tiptoes to deepen it. Puck let out a squawk and jumped to the ground off her shoulders in annoyance.

Desmond groaned and tugged her closer until he flinched, breaking the kiss. He turned to look at the ground and scooped up the pinecone that Malcolm had just pegged him with. "No canoodling." Malcolm said in a deadpan voice and Claire lost it. Holding onto Desmond, she covered her stomach with one arm as she bent over from the laughter.

"That's never going away, is it?" Desmond said with his own smile.

"Never," Claire said breathlessly, straightening and stepping away from Desmond, rolling her eyes at the betrayed look he shot her.

She turned around to study the gate they had exited from. The air between the trunks still shimmered. "Should I try to close it?" She wondered out loud.

Everett stepped up next to her. "If you can, it's probably best. We don't need anyone else coming through."

Claire pursed her lips. She agreed that they shouldn't leave it open for anyone else to stumble through but it would also cut them off from anyone trying to help. "You can open it back again if we need?" Everett said, his voice lifting at the end in a question.

Claire nodded, she remembered the runes. They came to her easily, as if they had always been inside of her. A memory maybe? Or instinct? Puck wove through her legs as she stood, offering her support.

She reached down and picked him up, placing him on her shoulder as she closed her eyes and called up on her magic. The gate looked the same from this side, although the runes were in the opposite pattern as they were on the Academy side. She studied the runes but she also studied the tree trunks that made the gate, trying to commit their magical signature to memory so she could find her way back.

Puck pressed his cheek against hers as she began to trace the runes, her magic jumping to her call with a ferocity that startled her momentarily. It felt much more intense on this side of the gate and Claire pushed away those questions as she focused on not overloading the runes. Puck's magic in her center helped rein in some of the ferocity of hers and Claire took a breath as she pushed the runes towards the gate.

After the glow faded from the gate, she opened her eyes. Everett stood next to her, his eyes scanning the Forest with a worried look on his face. She shifted to see Malcolm and Desmond also staring at the Forest with similar expressions on their faces.

"What is it?" She asked, her magic dancing in her center as if responding to the worry that was rising in her.

"When you started closing the gate, it felt like someone was watching us," Everett answered her, his voice barely above a whisper but Claire heard him loud and clear.

Her eyes scanned their surroundings. On the surface, the Forest looked the same as it had before she closed her eyes. "Is it still there?" She asked, her voice no louder than Everett's.

Everett shook his head, "It's gone now. It disappeared as soon as you finished." The frown on his face told Claire he wasn't thrilled about that either.

Desmond and Malcolm moved closer to them. "The plan was originally to camp on this side of the gate because of the daylight fading but that doesn't seem to be a problem here." Desmond said, looking up at the trees with a familiar wrinkle in his brow. Her wizard was trying to sort through all the new information that had been presented to them. She could practically see his brain working.

"Can you still check-in with Helene's tree?" Everett asked Claire.

Claire hadn't even thought about it. They had assumed they could just walk through the Elven Forest boundary and it would be the same forest that backed up to the Academy but Claire knew that wasn't the case. "Let me try," She said, toeing off her shoes and dropping to her knees.

She should just be able to connect to the tree without connecting to the earth first but Claire had a feeling that she was going to need the extra grounding. Her men gathered around her, one eye on her and one eye on the Forest and Claire took a deep breath, centering herself. She called her memories of Helene forward in her mind. Her musical voice, her quiet steadiness and warmth. Those memories folded into her memory of the tree's signature with ease. Once that memory was clear in her mind, she called up a strand of her magic and focused on the tree's Energy.

The signature was faint, fainter than it had ever been, but Claire was able to grab hold of it. She sent a feeling of safety down the signature with more force than she had ever sent something down the bond. She wasn't sure if Helene would even get the message as the signature was so faint but she tried one more time before opening her eyes.

"I think it went through." She said, opening her eyes, "The signature was faint, fainter than it's ever been."

"It went through." Malcolm's quiet confidence in her that echoed in their bond had her entire body warming in appreciation.

She took his hand and accepted the help to her feet. Everett was frowning at the Forest again. Claire touched his arm and he answered her without removing his gaze from the trees.

"I felt it again, briefly as you used your magic to reach

Helene's tree. I think whatever it is, is attracted to you when you use magic."

Claire frowned, knowing what his next question was going to be. Desmond caught her frown. "It's not for forever, little witch, but maybe keep your magic-use on the downlow for a bit."

Claire swallowed her protest and nodded. Thankfully, her men didn't ask for the verbal promise she couldn't give them. If it came down to protecting them, she would use magic in a heartbeat.

"Are we going farther in?" Claire asked instead.

"Do you still feel that pull or did it stop with the gate?" Everett asked.

"I still feel it," Claire said, "I thought it would stop with the gate. It's not as strong, but it's still there."

"Then we follow that," Everett said and Malcolm growled. Everett faced Malcolm, "Do you have a better idea?"

Malcolm growled at Everett's challenging statement and Claire placed a hand on his chest. He jerked his head in a no and Everett nodded. "Then we follow Claire."

"I'd follow you to the ends of the Realm, little witch." Desmond teased to lighten the mood.

Claire cracked a smile but Everett and Malcolm didn't. She sighed internally but chose to ignore them. They probably wouldn't relax until they were all out of the Forest again and Claire didn't have the energy right now to try and make them. Her foot caught and she blushed as she thought about how she could make them relax.

Desmond caught the look on her face and grinned wickedly, he opened his mouth to say something and Claire slapped a hand on it. "No canoodling." She told him sternly, fighting her blush and her smile.

Desmond rolled his eyes and tucked her hand into his arm but didn't say anything. The pull from trees was guiding her towards the left side of the clearing so she stepped in that direction. Malcolm's pack filled her gaze as he cut in front of them and Claire frowned.

He looked back over his shoulder at her. "You can tell me if I'm off course but you are not going first," He growled.

Claire arched an eyebrow but didn't argue. They fell into the same pattern as earlier, Malcolm in front, Desmond next to her, and Everett taking up the rear. Desmond helped guide her over the unfamiliar terrain which was good because Claire was having trouble tearing her gaze away from the Forest around her.

The trees with their different colored trunks and leaves were not the only new plants in the Forest. Multi-colored flowers sprung from the ground or from the trees themselves. Some gave off a sweet odor while others gave off a strong musky odor. Claire's nose wrinkled as they passed a particularly strong one and she sneezed. Everett chuckled at her and then it was his turn to sneeze when the smell reached him.

Although the plants were beautiful, Andy's warning remained strong in her mind so she held back from touching any of them. Some she didn't want to touch at all but others she was drawn to. Claire wondered if that was her magic's instinctual way of telling her which ones were safe or if the ones that she was drawn to were actually the poisonous ones.

It was probably much better not to touch anything.

They had been walking for at least another hour when Malcolm stopped.

"What is it?" Desmond asked, looking around them. They were in a small clearing, less than half the size of the clearing the gate was in.

"Nothing. Claire's hungry," Malcolm said.

Everett and Desmond turned to look at Claire as her stomach rumbled. She held up her hands, "Don't look at me. I didn't realize it until just now."

"It must be the bond." Everett said to Desmond. "It's growing stronger."

Desmond nodded, "When I focus on it just enough, I can feel what Malcolm must have felt."

They looked at her again and Claire blushed at the realization about why her bond was stronger with Malcolm. Claire bit her lip, worried her other two men were going to be jealous. Everett only smiled at her blush while Desmond laughed out loud. Everett took her hand and led her to a tree root that was protruding from the ground at the perfect height to sit.

"Relax," Everett murmured in her ear, "we aren't jealous. But that doesn't mean I'm not going to be anxiously awaiting my turn."

Claire's face felt like it was on fire now and this time Everett did let out an amused huff at her expense. Malcolm grinned as he handed her a sandwich out of his pack and Claire rolled her eyes at all of them.

Claire wasn't getting a bad feeling from their current spot but her men weren't sharing the same calmness apparently as they ate quickly. She was still working on the last half of her sandwich when Everett started patrolling the outskirts of the clearing, staring into the Forest as if he could force it to reveal its shadowy secrets.

Claire fed the rest of her sandwich to Puck and took Desmond's offered water. Wiping a bead of water from her lips and ignoring Desmond's heated look, she had blushed enough for the day thank you, she focused on the direction the pull was guiding them towards.

The trees were so thick here, that you could barely see more than ten yards in any direction before the view was blocked out by the trunks. They would have no way of knowing what was ahead of them at this current rate.

Claire looked down at Puck, curled up at her feet and cleaning his face. Using their bond, Claire asked Puck to go ahead and scout. He ignored her and Claire asked again, pushing images of him flying ahead at him in case she wasn't clear. He got to his feet and shook out his feathers. He sat back down at his feet and Claire felt the stubbornness from him. He didn't want to leave her and Claire wasn't sure that was a good or bad sign.

Despite Puck's stubbornness, they walked for the next few hours with no interruptions. They didn't run into a single creature during that time and Claire didn't know if that meant that the creatures here were few and far between or if something else had scared them off.

The Forest was darkening now, indicating that wherever the sun was, it was fading. They made camp in the hollow of an old tree, the thick trunk and protruding roots providing enough protection for Malcolm to relax slightly. They didn't risk building a fire and as the darkness fell, her men shifted uneasily as the blackness descended. Claire didn't mind it though. It felt like her whole life in darkness and shadows had prepared her for this trip.

CHAPTER 26

Claire blinked awake, her magic dancing in her gut. Something was happening.

As her eyesight came into focus, she saw Everett's sleeping face just inches from her own. Cinnamon and smoke danced in her nostrils from behind her. Malcolm's golden arm thrown across her stomach, securing her to his chest as if someone would steal her away in their sleep.

She searched for Desmond through her bonds and felt him just on the other side of Everett. The bond was quiet, as if he was still asleep. Claire took a deep breath and relaxed back into Malcolm's hold slightly. It was still dark, only the slightest lightening of shadows indicated that it was close to dawn. What had woken her again?

She didn't want to shift and wake her men if it was nothing. But something had woken her, or woken her magic. She kept her body still and relaxed but cast her magic outwards into the clearing, sinking into the Energies that surrounded them.

The trees were steady and strong in their Energies, the plants around them had a lighter, almost whispery feeling to their Energies. She steadily worked her way outwards, touching each living being gently as she did so. Her magic ran across two Energy readings that were not like the surrounding plants and trees. These Energies were from living, breathing creatures and matched. They were similar beings and large from the size of their Energies. Yet they moved almost soundlessly across the floor. Claire focused her magic on them, trying to gather as much information as she could from their Energies and wishing she could *see*.

An image flashed in her mind as soon as she expressed her wish. An all-too-familiar creature that stood six feet tall with jagged horns and large teeth. It's tawny striped body faded into the shadows of the trees as it stood with its mate, their eyes fixed forward as they hunted. Hunted them.

Claire's muscles tensed and Everett's eyes flashed open as Malcolm's forearm went rigid. "Two Feluas, heading this way. They know we're here." Claire gasped out in a whisper.

Everett's eyes darkened and he rolled over instantly, waking Desmond with a rough shake and a hand over his mouth to muffle his protest at the sudden wake up call.

Malcolm released Claire and she scrambled to her feet, reaching under the blanket to grab her dagger belt and securing it around her waist.

When she turned, Malcolm was drawing his sword out of his sheath. Claire kicked the blankets into a ball and then stuffed them into the nearest pack in case they had to leave quickly.

"Stay or leave?" Malcolm asked Everett.

Everett frowned, "We might have stumbled into their territory by accident. If we leave now, they might leave us alone. But if they are locked onto the hunt then this is a better defensible spot then the open where they have the territory advantage."

Malcolm turned to Claire, "Are they hunting?"

"They're hunting. They know we are here."

Malcolm nodded, accepting her words as fact. Claire's

insides warmed that he was including her instead of shoving her behind him to protect her.

"How far out are they?" Desmond asked.

The answering roar spoke before Claire did. Clearly, the Felua didn't care about the element of surprise. With large jagged horns and teeth the size of Claire's hand, they were confident in their hunt. The pair slunk through the shadows, muscles rippling as they entered the small clearing before them. Malcolm stepped in front of Claire and she refrained from rolling her eyes, clearly including her only went so far.

The Feluas split up, the larger male one walking to the left as the smaller female went right. Claire wondered if they had babies near here.

"Dark magic?" Everett asked, his voice low as if not to provoke them. He tracked the male while Malcolm turned slowly to track the female. Luckily, the tree behind them rose tall, providing cover at their back. Unluckily, the roots protruded on either side making a pocket that left Claire and her men with limited movement.

"No, their eyes aren't red." Desmond said, magic dancing visibly at his fingertips.

"Just territorial then," Everett said.

"They might have babies." Claire offered.

Desmond huffed, "That would be our luck, to walk by a Felua den."

"Focus," Malcolm growled as the female lowered herself into a crouch.

"Can't you just shift?" Desmond hissed at him.

"Not without squishing you all," Malcolm growled back. "We'll have to hit them both hard quickly and get them down."

"If I can get clear a little ways, I can shift." Everett said, not moving his gaze from his Felua.

Claire frowned. They were in the wrong here having passed onto the Feluas territories. If the pair had babies, they were just defending them. Claire didn't have any more time to go down that trail of thought as the male Felua growled and lunged at Everett, head lowered and his horns flashing dangerously.

Claire stifled a cry as Everett used his own sword to deflect the Felua's horns and then land a slicing blow on his shoulder. The Felua roared in pain and retreated which caused the female Felua to attack, pissed at the injury to her mate. She jumped, prepared to land on top of Malcolm. Desmond threw an air blast at her which caused her to land short. Malcolm sliced his sword through the air and the Felua swiped at him, catching him in the side with her claws.

It was Claire's turn to cry out as Desmond stepped in front of Malcolm, forcing the Felua back with air and fire blasts. The male Felua, apparently recovered, attacked as well, Everett dancing with it, avoiding its swipes as he tried to keep it away from Claire and Malcolm.

Malcolm staggered backwards a few steps and Claire caught his arm, lifting it and wincing at the deep gashes on his side. Everett's grunt drew her attention away from Malcolm's darkening shirt and she saw him limp for a few strides before shaking it off. This was too much and someone was going to get seriously hurt soon. Claire would rather it not be her men either but she couldn't fault the Feluas either. What could she do?

Puck chirped in the tree above her, dive-bombing Desmond's Felua from behind. An idea sprung to her mind. What if she stunned the Feluas the same way she stunned Puck at their first meeting?

Claire withdrew her daggers, the pommels a familiar weight in her hands as she called her magic up and formed the intention. Stun, not kill. She called more magic than she did for Puck, the Feluas more than ten times the size of her little familiar. The magic came easily to her call but she kept a tight hold on her intention for the spell and pulled magic until the daggers glowed brightly, lightening the early morning shadows around them..

With Puck, she had been very close when she delivered the spell, but she would not be able to get that close to the Feluas. Her men were likely to have a fit if she even suggested it but she was going to have to direct the spell somehow. The daggers glowed brighter in her hands and Claire wondered if she could use them to direct the spell. She wouldn't get more than one chance to figure it out. She plucked her bonds with Desmond and Everett lightly, not wanting to distract them but enough to get their attention.

Holding the daggers in front of her, she aimed them to the middle of both fighting Feluas and envisioned the stunning spell going out in both directions towards both Felua. 3, 2, 1...

"Drop!" She shouted at Everett and Desmond, who dropped to the ground without hesitation, their trust in her absolute. Puck shot up into the air as Claire slammed the two daggers together in front of her in an x movement and let go of the magic. It shot out of the daggers in a wave, flying over Desmond and Everett to slam into the Feluas who were thrown backwards from the force of the magic. Their bodies skidded to a stop a few feet from the edge of the clearing, motionless.

Claire held her breath, watching their bodies to make sure they weren't moving. Desmond and Everett climbed to their feet, their eyes also on the Feluas, spells and swords still at the ready. When neither creature moved after a minute, they dropped their stances backing towards Claire and Malcolm.

"I don't know how long they are going to be out," Claire said frantically, the adrenaline still coursing through her veins. She wasn't sure that was going to work.

"Then we better get moving." Desmond said, his hands lighting up with pale blue healing magic. He placed a hand on Everett's leg for a moment and then moved to Malcolm's side. He frowned when he lifted Malcolm's shirt. He placed a hand over the gashes, ignoring Malcolm's growl. After just a few moments, he pulled back, still frowning. "That'll have to do for now until we get to a safer place."

Malcolm lowered his shirt and sheathed his sword. "I'll be fine. Let's move."

Desmond grabbed both packs before Malcolm could grab his, the move telling Claire that he was more worried about her growly dragon then he let on. When Malcolm growled but didn't protest, Claire's own frown deepened. Everett took the lead this time, starting in the direction Claire pointed towards. She had no idea if the direction would take them further into the Felua's territory or out of it but Claire was hesitant to waver off their only known path.

Desmond took up the rear behind them, magic still sparking at his fingertips as he cast wary glances behind them in case the Feluas woke up. They moved quickly. At least as quickly as they could with Desmond carrying two packs, Everett's slight limp and Malcolm clutching his side. Puck flew circles around them, weaving in and out of trees and making sure nothing surprised them.

When every other step Everett took made him limp more and Malcolm turned paler at her side, Claire called it.

"We have to stop." She said.

"I'm fine," Malcolm avoided her eyes.

"You're not. We need to take another look at your side."

"But the Feluas," Malcolm's golden skin was pale as he turned to look behind them.

"If they come back, I'll just stun them again." Claire said, shaking her head. She would do it a thousand times over if it meant keeping them safe and with the boost in her magic from being in the Elven Forest she would be able to follow through on that.

She turned to Desmond and helped him take off the two

packs. She snagged a water canteen off one of them and held it out to Malcolm. "Drink." She ordered.

Malcolm let out a soft growl but took the water canteen. "Bossy," Everett teased and Claire turned to him next.

"You too. Take your pack off and sit. Let Desmond look at your leg."

As Everett took his pack off, Desmond hesitated and frowned, "I'm a little drained. I can't heal both of you or I won't have enough magic to hold off another attack."

"Heal Everett." Malcolm said, sitting down on a tree root heavily. "That way we have two fighters in case something happens."

Claire frowned and pulled a blanket out of the pack shaking it out and laying it on the ground. "Come lie down." She told Malcolm, "We can at least clean your gashes."

Malcolm heaved himself off of the tree root and took careful steps to the blanket. Claire helped him down, frowning because Malcolm's easy compliance meant he was hurting more than he let on. She cradled his head on her lap, brushing his hair off his sweaty brow. She tried not to let the panic whispering in her gut overwhelm her at the sight of her normally strong mate in pain.

Desmond finished with Everett and came to kneel at Malcolm's side. Claire gasped when Desmond lifted up Malcolm's shirt. The gashes were deeper than she thought, bright red fresh blood oozed out of them mixed with darker clotted blood along the edges. Four deep gashes, one for each of the Felua's claws.

Desmond's mouth tightened as he tore a strip off the blanket and dumped some water from the canteen on it. Malcolm grumbled as Desmond began dabbing at the cuts, trying to clear away the blood so they could get a better look. Desmond's face looked torn as his brow tightened. Claire was sure he was debating internally what to do.

"Show me how to heal him," Claire said quietly, meeting Desmond's surprised look. Her mate needed her. It was time that Claire started believing in her magic and its power. Time that she finally shook off all of the old memories and hateful words of her 'limited' abilities. She needed to step up, for her Triad. If what Helene had said was true, Claire was more powerful than she could imagine. Healing was surely something within that power.

Claire shifted from Malcolm's head to settle next to Desmond at his side. "Healing magic requires an affinity," Desmond explained as if trying to warn Claire why it might not work, "for my magic, it's a softer, cooler touch and comes naturally. I don't weave as much intention around it. For you though, weave the intention around it. You want to heal the gashes on Malcolm's side. Imagine the flesh knitting together."

Claire took a deep breath and nodded. She placed her hands lightly over Malcolm's side, hovering but not touching, and called her magic. It came slowly, as if it was hesitant. Claire took another breath. *I can do this,* she reassured herself and her magic. A cool blue glow similar to Desmond's filled her hands and Claire focused on the image of Malcolm's wounds knitting themselves together and healing.

When the intention was clear in her mind, she lowered her hands to Malcolm's side, ignoring his hiss. As the magic sunk into his side, his wounds started closing quickly and Malcolm groaned in pain. Claire darted her eyes to his face, panic curdling in her gut that she was hurting him and causing her magic to retreat slightly.

"It's okay." Desmond said softly, placing a gentle hand on her forearm. "Just go slower, let the flesh come back together naturally, don't force it."

His quiet instruction and gentle touch settled Claire and she focused on feeding magic into Malcolm's side in smaller, slower amounts. The wounds closed slowly, Bright pink flesh appearing underneath the blood now.

"Let me wipe off the blood and we can see what they look like," Desmond murmured, giving her arm a gentle squeeze.

Claire called back her magic and lifted her hands, looking up at Malcolm's face. He had thrown an arm over his face to hide his expression after his first groan but his color looked like it was improving.

Desmond wiped away the blood and grime and Claire nearly melted to the Forest floor in relief at the sight of the bright pink closed gashes.

"That's good." Desmond said, "If you can do a little more, we can take away some of the pain."

Claire nodded eagerly and Desmond walked her through forming her intention to ease his pain and at the end the new flesh didn't look quite as angry, fading to a softer pink.

"Good job, little witch!" Desmond said proudly, placing an arm around Claire's side and tugging her into him. Claire relaxed into his side gratefully, "If he gets a chance to shift into his dragon, he'll be good as new but if we can't find a clearing large enough for his mangy beast then he'll be fine in a few days."

The loud growl that Malcolm let out at Desmond's name calling had Claire diving onto his chest. Her dragon was back. He let out a soft oof but locked his arms around her when she tried to get up. He rolled them over to his good side and cuddled Claire in close. She buried her face in his chest, her body finally feeling like it could take a breath.

"Oh no, it's fine." Desmond said from behind Malcolm, "You two take a nap, I'll keep watch."

Malcolm simply grumbled his response and the sound combined with her body's sudden relaxation as the adrenaline finally wore off had her drifting off to sleep.

CHAPTER 27

It felt like Claire had just closed her eyes when Everett was shaking them awake. "Time to go." He said softly.

Claire scrambled to her feet, ignoring Malcolm's growl and looking around them for trouble. Everett squeezed her arm, "Everything's fine, but I want to put some more distance between us before we camp for the night."

Claire nodded, the adrenaline leaving her body making her sway on her feet slightly. Everett observed her with a frown and Claire gave him a reassuring smile. She was fine, a little tired, but that was just the effects of the adrenaline.

They set out again, walking at a much brisker pace than before. They walked for only a few more hours before Puck squawked a warning. A few seconds later, an enraged roar cut through the trees, bouncing off the trunks.

"Not this pair again," Desmond groaned at the familiar sound.

A dark feeling pushed at Claire and she didn't wait to draw her daggers. "It's different this time. Something's wrong."

Her men followed her lead, dumping the packs instantly and

drawing their own weapons. There was no tree at their backs this time, just the forest around them. Her Triad shifted their backs to each other, trying to keep Claire and their packs in the center.

When the Feluas pushed through the trees, Desmond and Malcolm cursed. It was the same pair as before but instead of golden eyes, those eyes now gleamed red.

"They weren't red before." Malcolm stated the obvious, his own sword gripped tightly in his hand. Claire darted a look to his side, knowing that it was healed but worrying just the same, "What changed?"

"Someone must have gotten to them when they were stunned," Everett murmured quietly, giving Claire a sideways glance.

Claire felt terrible. She had knocked them out and made them defenceless and someone had taken advantage of that. Puck brushed his cheek against hers. "I can knock them out again?" She offered.

Desmond frowned, "If they are truly under a dark magic spell, they won't rest until the spell is complete. You could knock them out, but we would just be dealing with them after they woke up."

Claire frowned, not liking the idea of being hunted the rest of the way to the Elven Capital. She would have to dismantle the spell like she did for Puck.

Desmond realized it the same time as she did, both exchanging a grim look. "What do you need to get it done?" He asked.

"Just to focus," Claire murmured, palming her daggers, "I'll try to be quick."

"Don't worry about being quick, just worry about doing it." Malcolm said, "We'll give you the time."

The Feluas split up in front of them, navigating the Forest with a grace that Claire would admire if they weren't trying to kill them. Claire focused on the female, her tawny body almost disappeared into the shadows. She slipped her Fae dagger back into its sheath, keeping the Elven one tight in her left hand. She called up her magic and pushed it towards the Felua, focusing on its Energy.

Unlike Puck, its tainted Energy resisted fiercely and Claire had to fight to slip into it. She was vaguely aware of Malcolm slipping in front of her as she sank into the Energy, her vision going hazy until the only clear focal point was the female Felua who lunged towards Claire, as if sensing her presence. Malcolm headed the Felua off and Claire sank deeper into the Energy, finding the dark magic the feeling of it like a black sludge that overwhelmed the Felua's natural Energy.

Claire focused her intention and began drawing the black sludge out. Like before, it manifested in a black mass of swirling magic in front of Claire. It flickered towards Malcolm, as if looking for a new host and Claire yanked on it hard. Absolutely not.

She kept pulling on the dark magic and it kept coming, the writhing mass growing larger and larger in front of her. Whoever set the spell this time, wasn't taking any chances of her drawing it out. Her muscles strained from the effort but she kept pulling until the dark magic was contained in front of her in a mass that was as tall as Claire was. The female Felua staggered and slumped to the ground. Her partner roared his rage and Malcolm joined Everett and Desmond as her Triad focused its efforts on driving him back, away from Claire.

Drawing the fire rune in the air, she shifted her magic from the Felua's Energy into the rune, the flames growing and dancing around the dark magic. The dark magic fought back this time against the fire, pushing it back towards Claire. She would need help.

"Desmond," she cried out.

The move Everett and Desmond executed was seamless as

Everett stepped in front of Desmond, drawing the attention of the male Felua. Desmond's fire joined Claire's as together they burned the swirling mass of dark magic. It fought them, thrashing like a wild creature and Desmond's air magic joined Claire in keeping it contained. The swirling black ball of dark magic grew smaller and smaller before it disappeared completely.

Claire caught Desmond's eyes, both breathing heavily. One down.

The male Felua was fighting furiously now. Its protective instinct over its fallen mate compounded with the dark magic spell driving it wild. Claire called her magic again, it rose to her call slower, exhausted from the strain of the day. Claire ignored the ache in her muscles and yanked on it again. They had to do this *now*.

"Claire," Desmond caught her attention, drawing it away from the angry male Felua.

Claire turned slightly towards him, a ball of fire in his palm. "Take the Energy," Desmond said, reading her exhaustion through their bond.

Claire looked at Everett and Malcolm holding off the male Felua and wrinkled her nose. Was there time?

"Do it now," Desmond instructed, "I can feel your exhaustion and you're going to need it to end this."

Claire cupped the ball of fire, sinking into the Energy easily. Bypassing the first fiery hot layer, she sunk into the second layer of pure Energy and yanked hard. She had never tried this in a large amount before and the effect was exhilarating as the Energy flowed through her, lighting up every nerve ending before settling in her center.

She smiled at Desmond gratefully before turning back to the Felua. With the excess Energy flowing through her, she sank easily into its Energy, finding the black sludge almost instantly and yanking on it. The Felua's cry of pain broke her concentration and she glanced at it. It was backing away from Malcolm and Everett but there were no visible marks on it. She must have caused the pain when she yanked on the dark magic. Claire returned to pulling the dark magic out, slower this time but in a steady pull. That weakened the Felua, causing it to stagger until it collapsed next to its mate.

Claire didn't have time to be worried about it as the dark magic lashed out towards her and Desmond. Her Elven dagger lifted almost instinctively, a shielding spell bursting from it with just a thought from Claire. The dark magic ricocheted off of the shield, back into the swirling mass. Anger swirled in Claire's gut as her muscles tensed. Whoever was behind was growing bolder in their attacks on her and her family. Anger directed her magic and she sent a large force of it through the fire rune she drew, burning the dark magic away with no help from Desmond. Muscles trembling, she stared at the space the dark magic once occupied.

Forest and spice filled her nostrils as Everett stepped up behind her, drawing her back into him. "Are you okay?" He asked softly.

Claire was torn. "Physically, yes. But I'm angry. Who is this person and how did they get to the Feluas? Why do they keep attacking us? Why can't we just be safe?"

"They must have followed us through the gate." Desmond said, answering one of her questions..

"Or were already waiting here." Everett countered, "Claire closed the gate after we went through."

"Maybe they knew how to open the gate?" Desmond frowned. "So are we dealing with an Elf or someone else?"

"Can you trace them?" Everett asked Claire, "Trace their energy?"

"I don't know," Claire said, surely she would have sensed them by now.

"Use your magic," Malcolm growled, "find who's following us."

Claire's eyebrows shot up and the look Desmond shot Malcolm was glacial, "Ease up, Malcolm."

Malcolm rubbed his hand across his face. "I'm sorry, little treasure."

Claire squeezed Malcolm's arm. "I'll try," She promised. Her magic was subdued, exhausted, but Claire sank into it, coaxing it out as she sank to the ground and buried her hand in the earth to ground her. Pulling as much magic as she dared, she cast a wide net out around their surroundings, sinking into the trees and looking for anything out of place.

Her magic flowed through the trees and plants and over the two sleeping Felua but nothing else popped out at her. Frowning, she opened her eyes and got to her feet, muscles trembling.

"Nothing." She said frustrated. "Nothing's out of place."

"Is it possible whoever it is is cloaking from her?" Everett asked Desmond.

Desmond rubbed his face, "It's possible. That means that this person is very powerful though. Not many people can cloak even from an Energy Reader."

Malcolm grumbled and scowled at the Forest around them, as if he could find the person from his scowl alone.

"We'll have to take extra care," Everett said.

Claire nodded, "What about the Feluas? We can't leave them here in case the person does it again."

Desmond frowned, "She has a point."

"If we are out of their territory and they wake up, they might go back to it." Claire suggested.

"The key question there is are we out of their territory," Everett said, "I don't fancy waking them to ask."

"What about Puck?" Claire asked, an idea coming to her. Puck coasted down from a nearby branch he had taken shelter on during the fight. "Can you tell where their territory line is?" She asked the furry Notus.

Puck chirped and took off in the direction that the Felua had come from. Claire relaxed slightly. Before, Puck had not wanted to leave her at all. They must not be in any immediate danger now if he was willing to go find the Feluas' territory line.

Claire kept a careful eye on the sleeping Feluas as they waited for Puck. Her men kept looking between the Felua and their surroundings, as if they could catch a glimpse of whoever was behind the dark magic attacks. Claire had a feeling whoever it was was probably nearby but not close. This was a person who didn't like to get their own hands dirty, instead using innocent creatures to carry out their agenda. If they had a problem with Claire, they should just confront her themselves instead of hiding.

Her face twisted into a scowl at the thought. What had she ever done to them anyways? She had lived a quiet life at Windshire before the Academy. Other than Vivienne and her friends, Claire didn't have any enemies and even then, those girls were minor annoyances in the scheme of things. Was this Vivienne's doing? Did she want Claire's Triad so desperately that she was trying to get Claire out of the way? She didn't seem like she had the power level to command the dark magic it would take to control these creatures but maybe they should look further into her. Claire glanced at her men, they were going to love that.

Claire felt Puck coming back before she saw him. He landed softly on her shoulder and rubbed his cheek against hers as he pushed an image through the bond. They weren't far from the Feluas' territory line at all. But most importantly, past the territory line was a hollowed out tree with sleeping Felua babies hidden inside. That's why the Feluas had been so aggressive the first time.

Claire relayed the message to her men and Desmond rubbed his face, "Well that's good news, we *are* out of their territory.

The next key question is how do we wake them up and convince them to go back to their babies instead of attacking us again."

"I have an idea for that too," Claire said.

"Why do I have a feeling we are not going to like this idea?" Desmond arched an eyebrow at her.

Claire smiled and shrugged, "Because you probably won't like it? I'm open to other suggestions though."

When her men just stared at her, Claire rolled her eyes. "Exactly. We don't have a lot of options here."

"Alright, little mate," Everett said, "let's hear it."

"I think I can sink into their Energies and wake them up and then ask them to go back to their territory."

"You think?" Malcolm grumbled.

Claire rolled her eyes again, "I think we can all agree we are operating on a lot of unknowns here. We are standing in the Elven Forest for the Realm's sake."

She paused and looked away towards the trees. She was nervous yes, but more than that a steady determination filled her. She had to start owning her abilities. She let out a sigh before speaking, "Before we left, Helene told me that she thinks my magic is only constrained by my limitations of what I believe. I believe I can do this. This is the safest way to ensure that no one else gets hurt. Not you, not the Felua. No one."

She kept her eyes on the Forest in the silence that followed her words. Cinnamon and smoke filled her nose before Malcolm stepped up behind her and placed his hands on her shoulders. "You're right. We are just…"

Claire turned, "Protective, I know. But can you understand that I'm protective over you too?"

Malcolm grumbled and Claire waited him out. "Yes." He admitted, "But I would argue that we are more so."

Claire smiled and shook her head at him. "Agree to disagree on this one?"

Desmond broke in. "I'll agree to that. If you both start an argument now about who's more protective, we'll be here all day." He teased.

"What do you need from us?" Everett asked, drawing her attention.

Claire shrugged, "I'm not sure."

"Maybe you should shift?" Desmond told Everett. "We don't have room for Malcolm to shift but it might be better if you did at least."

Everett nodded and started stripping out of his clothes. Claire couldn't look away from the bronze skin he revealed, that place in her center heating as he stripped down to his underwear. Lifting his eyes to catch hers, he gave her a wicked grin before exploding into his gryphon, his white feathers gleaming even in the shadows of the Forest. He lowered his head and bumped her stomach lightly, careful not to touch her with his razor sharp beak. Claire reached out to rub the soft feathers on his head and he purred at her touch.

"You know he doesn't have to take off his clothes to shift. I gave him an amulet that lets him shift with them on," Desmond pointed out, a mischievous smile on his face.

Everett's gryphon snapped his teeth in Desmond's direction before bumping Claire's stomach for pets again.

Claire's body shook with laughter as she obliged the gryphon. "I don't mind you taking your clothes off to shift." She told him. She hadn't had a chance to be alone with her gryphon since the day of the first Felua attack. She missed him and his kisses.

Malcolm barked out a laugh as Desmond shook his head with a smile. "Alright, enough canoodling with the gryphon, little witch. We need him to look menacing, not like an overgrown house cat."

Everett snapped his beak at Desmond again, who sidestepped out of the way gracefully.

"Before you wake them, little witch," Desmond continued on, ignoring the cranky gryphon, "you need to pull on more Energy. I would rather you be at full strength before we wake them up."

It was a good idea, but the dark circles under Desmond's eyes had her hesitating. She didn't want to take any more magic from him if he was exhausted. Claire looked around her at all of the trees and wondered why she hadn't thought of it sooner.

"Yes, but let me try something else besides your fire," She said.

"What are you thinking, little treasure?" Malcolm asked.

"That I'm surrounded by Energy," Claire said, smiling at him. She stepped a few paces away from Everett's gryphon and sank to her knees. She pressed her palms into the cool grass, fingers splayed out as she felt the gentle give of the Forest floor beneath them. The grass tickled the back of her hands. Without even connecting her magic to the earth, she immediately felt more grounded. It almost felt like... home.

She called up her magic and opened herself to the Forest's Energy. It was like an endless well at her fingertips as the Energy of every tree, plant, and flower flared open at her presence. She pulled gently, aware of the vastness, and it felt like every nerve ending inside of her lit up.

The hairs on her arms raised as she pulled Energy from the Forest in a slow steady thrum. When it felt like she couldn't contain anymore inside her body, she shut the connection off and sat back on her heels. She opened her eyes, unaware of when she had closed them. Even living with her sight, Claire had been so used to the darkness she often found her eyes closing when she wasn't thinking about it.

A soft glow as she opened her eyes drew her attention. Her hands and forearm glowed with a soft white light that faded as she watched it. She raised her eyes to where her men were standing. Everett's gryphon stood behind Malcolm and

Desmond, its piercing gaze locked on hers. Desmond and Malcolm's eyes were softer, but almost cautious as they looked at her.

"What is it?" Claire asked, getting to her feet.

"You glowed," Malcolm said shortly.

"It was a pretty glow," Desmond reassured her quickly, "I just don't think we expected it."

Claire laughed, "I thought you expected the unexpected now?" She teased Desmond.

"I mean, you always exceed my expectations." Desmond said, snaking an arm around her back and tugging her softly into his chest.

She stood up on her tiptoes and pressed her lips to his softly. "Wouldn't want you to get bored thinking you figured it all out."

He caught her lips again, kissing her deeper, "Never, little witch, never. I have a feeling you will keep us on our toes for the rest of our lives."

"Not to break up the canoodling," Malcolm said, "but maybe let's save it till after we wake up the sleeping Feluas." The soft smile he threw Claire told her that he wasn't actually mad but he did have a good point.

"Okay." She said, stepping back from Desmond and turning towards the Feluas, "Let's do this!"

"I like her enthusiasm." Desmond told Malcolm, "It's like we are going to get sweet buns instead of waking two very dangerous creatures."

"That's because I'm more dangerous!" Claire threw back over her shoulder as she walked towards the Feluas, Everett on her heels.

"That you are, little witch, that you are."

Pausing twenty feet away from the Feluas, Claire studied their sleeping forms. They looked much less dangerous while sleeping, almost like the overgrown house cats that Desmond had compared Everett too earlier. Overgrown house cats with massive horns and teeth that is.

How to wake them, Claire wondered. It would have to be gentle. If she woke them suddenly, then they were more likely to react aggressively. She would have to coax them awake. Then to keep them from attacking, send them back towards their territory line. Maybe she could use their sleeping babies as motivation to go back?

Everett's gryphon nudged her back softly, either telling her he had her back or telling her to get on with it. Without looking, Claire knew that Desmond and Malcolm stood next to him, ready in case the Feluas woke up swinging or growling in their case.

Claire didn't put it off any longer. She wanted to draw her daggers but refrained in case the Feluas viewed it as an aggressive action. She lifted her hands instead, still feeling the excess Energy from the Forest coursing through her. She called her magic up, and then sent it out, finding the Feluas Energies easily. She sank into them, the action easier since she had just been in their Energies.

Once connected, she sent a small pulse of magic through both connections at the same time. *Wake up,* she thought as she sent a second pulse of magic.

Their golden eyes blinked open slowly, unfocused at first before awareness sharpened their gaze. The male found his feet first, nuzzling the female until she also stood. He stood protectively in front of her, letting out a growl as he faced Claire and her men. Everett's gryphon puffed out his wings and she felt his muscles tense, ready to jump over her and engage the Feluas.

She sent a soothing feeling down her bond with Everett and turned her attention back to her connections with the Feluas. She pushed the image Puck had shown her of the Feluas' babies sleeping in the tree down the connections. Both Feluas roared and crouched as if they were ready to pounce. Claire took a step back. Okay, clearly that triggered their protective instincts but to attack not to go back to their babies. Everett tensed behind her and let out his own roar.

Claire thought quickly, she didn't want another fight, her men were already exhausted. She just wanted the Feluas to go home. The Feluas stopped roaring, and the female stood tall. Everett paused as well. What had changed? Claire wanted to smack herself when she realized. She had pushed the thought of going home to the Feluas through the still open connections.

She tried it again. *Go home.* She pushed down the connections. The Feluas paused, still unsure. She pushed again, harder and more forceful this time. She pushed more magic down the connection when she pushed the thought again, *Go home.*

As soon as she pushed it she held her breath, Everett was still tense behind her and she could feel Desmond and Malcolm's tension as well. The Feluas took a step backwards, eyes locked on Claire's. She sent reassuring feelings down her connections with them with the repeated message to go home. The female dipped her head to Claire slightly, turning to disappear into the Forest. The male Felua hesitated until the female had disappeared before following her. He never turned his back on them, instead backing away easily over the roots.

As soon as they disappeared, Claire let out a heavy breath of relief, her body sagging back against Everett's feathery side before she straightened. "It worked!" She spun to Desmond and Malcolm.

"Never any doubt, little witch." Desmond's grin matched her own. He swept her up in his arms, placing a kiss on her forehead before passing her to Malcolm. He folded her into his arms, pressing his own kiss on her hairline.

The air changed as Everett shifted back behind her. Claire turned around and to her disappointment, he was already clothed. He chuckled at her pout and Malcolm pinched her side lightly.

"You are a distraction, little treasure." Malcolm rumbled in her ear.

"The best kind though," Everett said, stepping up and pinning her between them. Their warmth pressed into her but Claire's body heated in a different way as naughty thoughts about her time with Malcolm ran through her brain. Everett's eyes darkened in response to whatever was on her face.

She squeaked as he darted down and captured her lips. She sank into his kiss, leaning forward while she simultaneously wanted to press backwards into Malcolm. Everett must have heard her unspoken ask and he stepped forward, crowding her backwards into Malcolm, who steadied her with hands on her hips that began stroking up her sides as soon as she steadied.

Claire grabbed onto Everett's shirt, twisting it in her fingers as he tilted her head, deepening the kiss and causing the fire in her center to flame hotter. Malcolm's fingers grazed the side of her breasts and Claire gasped into Everett's mouth when he did it again.

"As hot as this is," Desmond's voice drawled next to them, "we really shouldn't linger."

Malcolm muttered something that sounded like 'cock block' under his breath but Claire's usually keen hearing was hazy from Everett's kiss. Everett leaned back, breaking the kiss and smiling softly at Claire's dazed look. She smiled up at him, rolling her eyes as she took in his pleased grin.

"As much of a pain in the ass as he is," Malcolm said, ignoring Desmond's protest, "he's right. We should get farther away from here in case whoever spelled the Feluas is close by."

Claire frowned but agreed. Whoever it was, was probably not letting up anytime soon. Malcolm and Everett grabbed their packs. Desmond already had his own and reached a hand out to Claire. She accepted it and squeezed lightly, sending warmth and love down her bond with Desmond.

They started moving further into the trees following the pull that was a steady thrum in Claire's center. She kept a hold of Desmond's hand as they walked, looking behind them for the Feluas or any sign someone was following them. They moved slower than before, the exhaustion evident in her men but Claire felt fantastic from the Energy she had pulled from the Forest. They would need to find somewhere to rest soon and hopefully tomorrow wouldn't be as eventful.

CHAPTER 28

Claire couldn't sleep. Next to her, the flickering firelight caught Everett and Desmond's sleeping faces. The strains of exhaustion showing on their faces even in sleep. Behind her, Malcolm's warm scales rose and fell in a steady pattern, indicating his own exhaustion. She was just as exhausted but sleep eluded her.

Malcolm had insisted on shifting into his dragon form for the night, forcing them to continue walking until they found a clearing large enough for his dragon form. Puck had helped with that, scouting in circles around them until he found a clearing large enough to fit all of them. Even then it was a tight squeeze. Malcolm shifted into his dragon first, his head grazing the tree branches. He couldn't spread his wings out all the way and his dragon let out a grumble before settling into a half circle. Desmond and Everett unpacked the blankets, creating a small pile next to Malcolm's belly, the heat emanating from him warded off the evening chill.

Claire drank in the sight and feelings of her men greedily. She had almost lost them today. Despite their reassurances, she knew today was tough. Tougher than she had ever imagined.

And they were only two days into this journey and no closer to finding the Elven Capital and answers than they were before. All they had found was more problems and more danger.

Claire looked at the edge of the clearing towards the direction the gate was. Should they just turn around and go back? They had no idea what was ahead of them but Claire knew what was behind her. Her friends, her men, the family she had created that she had so desperately been searching for her entire life. Was she willing to risk it all? Were the answers they were seeking worth the reward?

Desmond seemed to think that finding the answers was the only way to protect them but Claire wasn't as sure. Someone or multiple someones was going to a lot of trouble to make sure the answers stayed hidden. Maybe there was a good reason behind that?

A yawn nearly split her cheeks. She wanted to close her eyes but every time she tried she kept seeing Malcolm's wounds. She shifted against Malcolm again. It was a testament to how tired he was when Malcolm's dragon didn't open his eyes. A glinting green light caught her eyes though, Everett's eyes flickering in the firelight met hers.

Wordlessly, he raised his arm and Claire slipped away from Malcolm's side to curl up against Everett's chest. "You should be sleeping." He observed quietly.

"Can't," Claire's body betrayed her when another yawn split her cheeks.

Everett brushed her curls back from her forehead, his hand leaving warm tingles across her skin. She hummed and Everett repeated the movement, stroking her hair.

"Talk to me?" He suggested.

"Too many thoughts," Claire whispered, staring at his shirt.

"About today?" Everett prompted, hand still stroking her hair.

"Today, all of this." Claire struggled to find the words. She didn't want to diminish her men's feelings or sacrifices. "How much danger is acceptable before it's too much?"

Everett sighed, pondering her words, "You're scared?"

Claire shrugged, "Not really? Maybe? For you three? Yes."

"Why are you scared for us?" Everett asked.

"Because you three will always throw yourselves in front of me when any danger arises and I don't want to lose you." Claire confessed. "It would kill me if anything happened to any of you because of me." She kept her eyes firmly on his shirt but Everett didn't let her get away with that. He lifted her chin with his fingers gently until her eyes met his.

"Just like how you never dismiss our feelings, I won't dismiss yours." He said softly, his green eyes warm, "I can offer you reassurances that we are all highly trained but you are right, we are facing unknowns that we have never faced before. But we are stronger together and I believe that as long as we are together we will make it through anything this Forest could throw at us. But not only are we stronger together, you are stronger than you can imagine. There is no one in the Realm that can use magic like you can. And your magic is still partially bound. We are going to get through this. Can you believe that?"

Claire wanted to, so desperately, but doubts still whispered in her mind. What if she wasn't enough to save them.

Everett smiled softly, reading her face, "How about this, do you trust me? Do you trust us to keep you safe?"

Claire nodded without hesitation and Everett's smile grew a little. "Good. I trust you to do the same. Can you believe in that for now?"

Claire's lips twisted in a wry smile as she realized where he was going with this. Desmond wasn't the only brilliant one in her Triad. She nodded again.

"Your words," Everett prompted gently.

"I believe in that," Claire said.

"Good, then let's go to sleep, little mate. Tomorrow's another day."

"I can't," Claire whispered softly.

"Do you want help?"

Claire arched an eyebrow at his question and looked up at his face. His green eyes glinted in the soft firelight, the heat behind his gaze causing a different type of burning.

"Oh."

He gave her that half-smile she so adored. "Yes, *oh*." He teased softly.

"But the others…" She peeked over his shoulder to see the soft rise and fall of Desmond's back.

"You'll just have to be quiet." His grin was a little wicked. His hand moved from her back to her side, finding the hem of her shirt and teasing the skin there with his thumb. He didn't move any further though, his eyes holding onto the question from before. He wouldn't do anything further without her permission.

Claire worried her lip with her teeth as she thought. She didn't want to wake Desmond and Malcolm up but a small voice whispered that they would probably just join in. She thought of the delicious feeling of being sandwiched between Everett and Malcolm after her first flight on Malcolm's dragon and shivered softly. Them joining in wouldn't necessarily be a bad thing but she wasn't sure if she was ready for that intensity.

"I don't know if I can stay quiet." She whispered her confession.

"I'll help you," Everett said, "but I need your words before we go further."

"Yes, Everett. I want you."

They weren't the words he was expecting but the warmth in his eyes and down their bond told her he didn't care. His hand slipped from her side under her shirt and stroked up and down her back in slow motions as he lowered his head to hers, brushing his lips against her forehead, her cheeks, the tip of her nose.

"Everett..." She complained softly.

"Shh," he hushed her, "wouldn't want to wake them." His hand slipped from her back around to her front. He ran a thumb under her waistband and she arched her back trying to get him to dip it lower.

His hand deftly unbuttoned her pants and Claire let out a soft moan when he cupped her center. He held still for a few moments and Claire squirmed at the light pressure and the heat building inside her. Her magic lashed restless at her bindings as if pushing her further and faster and Claire lifted her hand to run through his platinum hair.

"Everett." She whined.

He let out a soft, evil chuckle and then silenced her with his lips. She made a noise of protest that turned into a groan when he finally started moving his fingers, coating them with the moisture that was leaking out of her.

He kept his strokes light and Claire shifted her legs, trying to pin his hand in between them. He immediately stopped and broke the kiss. "Put your leg on my hip." He ordered softly, his lips a breath from hers as he gave the command, "And don't move it."

"Everett."

"For someone who was so scared of waking them, you sure are doing a lot of complaining."

Claire rolled her eyes and stifled a squeal as he leaned forward and drew her bottom lip into his mouth, biting down on it gently. He released it and then arched an eyebrow at her. What was she supposed to be doing? Oh right, her leg.

She shifted her leg, moving her knee over his hip. The motion tightened her pants and Claire nearly groaned at the increased pressure. Everett captured her lips with his again as his fingers started moving faster against her core. He easily found the bundle of nerves that seemed to hold the greatest amount of pleasure. Instead of stroking it, however, he did quick circles around it until Claire wanted to beg.

She kissed him harder instead, trying to convey the need to fall over that ledge of pleasure she was standing on. He teased her for a few moments longer before his thumb caught that bundle of nerves and rubbed hard. Once, twice, and on the third time, Claire fell, her body jerking against Everett who caught her close and held her through it.

As the pleasure eased, sleep tugged her away and she let her eyes fall shut. Everett buttoned her pants back up and then brushed a kiss against her forehead, shifting them so her head rested on his arm. With her last wave of consciousness she pushed warmth and love down their bond that was now singing contentment.

* * *

"CLAIRE, CLAIRE," a familiar voice called her out of a deep sleep.

Claire blinked her eyes open, squinting at the light that filled them. She still wasn't used to waking up to the light, even months after getting her sight. She blinked until the light wasn't burning her eyes and then focused them on the figure before her. Desmond crouched in front of her, a soft smile on his face. The absence of the heat around them meant that Malcolm must have already shifted back. Forest and spice surrounded her still and Everett's warmth at her back helped ward off the slight morning chill.

"Good morning, sleepyhead." Desmond teased softly, "We let you sleep as long as we could but we should get going."

Claire raised her head off Everett's arm and saw that they had already packed up everything minus the blanket Everett and her were laying on or the one covering them. Everett placed a soft kiss at the back of her neck and Claire let out a small sigh.

Desmond held a hand out to her and Claire took it, shivering slightly as Everett threw the blanket off of them. Desmond helped her to her feet and Claire stepped into his warm embrace gratefully. Desmond let her snuggle in his arms for a few minutes while Everett packed their blankets away. He pressed a kiss on her head and stepped back, smiling at her soft pout.

"Did you not sleep enough?" He asked, forehead creasing softly.

Claire shrugged, "I'll be okay."

Malcolm stepped up behind her and Claire leaned into his chest. His hand reached around and pressed a small cloth bag into her hands. Claire opened it and the smell of warm nuts had her smiling. She munched on them as they set off, sharing them with Puck when he landed on her shoulder. Hopefully, today was less exciting than yesterday.

They stopped for a brief lunch next to a small stream and refilled their water canteens after Claire confirmed the water was clean. Throughout the day, Claire felt the watchful eyes of the Forest creatures on them but they all seemed curious and not harmful. She pointed it out to her men anyways with the observation that maybe they were getting closer as the Forest seemed more alive than it had closer to the gate.

They chatted occasionally but kept a comfortable silence for most of the time. They were enjoying that comfortable silence when Claire felt it. They were not alone. She dropped Desmond's hand, drawing her daggers and throwing a shield spell up around them just in time to catch four arrows. The arrows hovered in the air, each on a straight path towards the center of their chests.

Her men reacted instantly, drawing Claire into the middle of them and drawing their weapons. Puck stayed up tall in the trees and disappeared out of sight. Moments later, an image pushed down her bond with Puck, five men who blended in with the Forest easily. Sharp features and pointed ears. Elves.

Claire pushed that same image down her bonds with her Triad, Everett's slight nod telling her that they received the message.

"We mean you no harm," Desmond called out, "we are just looking for someone!"

One moment there was no one in the clearing with them and the next it was like the Elven patrol melted from the trees surrounding them. Her Triad shuffled back closer, blocking Claire from view and she swallowed down her frustration. Again, she understood the protective instincts but hadn't she proved she was a badass as well?

"Trespassing in our Forest is a death wish even before the Great War, wizard." A deep voice, reminding Claire of the trees around them, answered Desmond.

"We know. We would not have done so unless it was urgent." Desmond said, his tone respectful.

"I hope it was worth losing your life over." The voice answered.

Everett shifted slightly and Claire took a small side step to see the speaker. All of the Elven men were clearly warriors, their bows an extension of them as they held notched arrows at the ready. Two men flanked another, whom she guessed was the speaker and clearly the leader of this group. His features were sharp and angular, similar to most Elves. A scar cut across his left cheekbone from the corner of his eyebrow to his chin. His eyes were a deep brown and his brown hair was peppered with grey, hinting that even with his lifespan, he had lived a long life. She shifted to get a better view and he caught sight of her. His already light skin paled until he looked paper white. He lowered his bow and the other Elves shot him confused looks.

"Princess?" His whispered words had everyone freezing.

Claire took another small step out from behind Everett.

Malcolm growled and she sent soothing feelings down their bond, softening the growl. She studied the Elf as he studied her in turn.

"Do you know who I am?" Claire asked when no one broke the silence.

"You..." the Elf started then trailed off, "you look like your mother." He cut a sharp look to the other Elves who dropped their own bows. Claire decided to follow the offered gesture and released the shield spell, the arrows dropping to the Forest floor.

"You knew my mother?" She asked softly.

The Elf nodded again, still seemingly in shock at Claire's appearance.

"What's your name?" Claire asked when he didn't add any details to his nod.

"I'm Toan." The Elf said, pressing a fist to his chest in what must be a gesture of respect.

"I'm Claire." She said, repeating the gesture. "This is my Triad, Desmond, Everett, and Malcolm,"

Toan barely glanced at her men, keeping his eyes on her as if he was afraid she would disappear. Claire looked at Desmond, wondering what they should do now.

"We've been searching for answers about Claire's parents," Desmond said, "you knew her mother?"

Toan nodded again, "I was part of her guard when she was a child."

"You called her 'Princess'," Malcolm broke in.

Toan finally broke his stare from Claire, looking around. "We shouldn't talk about this out in the open. Come with us."

Malcolm looked like he was going to protest and Claire sheathed her daggers, placing a gentle hand on his side. He looked down at her and sighed when he read her face. Claire looked at Desmond and Everett. Desmond gave her a smile and Everett gave her a nod. They would follow her lead.

Claire nodded at Toan and she fell in behind him as he turned and began to cut through the Forest. She felt her men fall in behind her, tension still thrumming down their bonds to her. They would follow her lead, but they weren't about to relax anytime soon. Toan cut through the Forest with a grace that reminded Claire of the Feluas. She wondered if that was from years of living in the Forest.

The other Elven warriors didn't speak as they surrounded the small group. Claire couldn't tell if it was meant to be a protective effort or a containment effort but she tried not to worry about it. Toan didn't seem like he harbored any ill feelings towards them and he knew her mother.

Puck followed them in the trees above Claire but didn't show himself. Claire didn't draw any attention to Puck. Her familiar probably had a good reason for staying hidden and would reveal himself whenever he wanted to anyways.

They ran into a bubbling stream and Toan turned to follow along its banks. They walked only for a short while when the trees thinned out and a large clearing opened up. The bubbling stream came from a small spring that opened from the Forest's floor and was as wide as Malcolm's dragon from nose to tail. It felt like the trees here were older. They were larger here than in any other part of the Forest they had been through. Everett's gryphon could easily fit inside one of their trunks and spread out his wings comfortably.

Toan cut around the spring and headed towards the largest center tree. He laid a hand on the massive trunk and spoke words in a language that was so familiar to Claire she frowned before her eyes widened. It was the same language the woman in her vision spoke. An ancient Elven language. The ground rumbled underneath their feet softly and Everett caught her elbow to keep her steady. She flashed a smile at him before her attention was caught by the tree's massive trunk splitting open at the base to reveal a doorway.

It was a brilliant defense if only Elves could open it and Claire caught Malcolm's slightly impressed look before he reverted to his familiar scowl. Toan turned back to the group, mouth opening to usher them inside and that's when Puck made his appearance.

Claire felt him coming long before she saw the grey blur diving in from the sky. One of the Elves lifted his bow and Everett released Claire's elbow to knock it away. A scowl twisted the Elf's face and he swung his bow towards Everett, notching an arrow. Claire froze and her magic reacted to her terror, blasting out of her and weaving around her Triad, sending the Elves and Toan flying backwards, landing heavily on their backs.

Horrified at her loss of control over her magic, Claire tried to rein it back but her lingering fear for Everett made it hard. Puck landed heavily on her shoulder, grounding her out of the last of her terror as her bond with him in her center sparked and began helping her rein in her reactive magic. By the time they were done and Claire's magic was back inside her, she and Puck were panting slightly. Claire looked up from where she dropped to her knees trying to control her magic. Her men were surrounding her, their backs to her and their weapons drawn. Magic sparked at Desmond's fingertips as he stared down the Elves who had gotten to their feet.

Toan was watching Claire when he realized she was back. He held a hand out to his men who dropped their bows. "I'm sorry." He said. "My warrior reacted to a threat. He did not realize the Notus was your familiar."

"I thought Notuses were viewed as friendly creatures by the Elves?" Desmond said, magic still at the ready.

Toan looked back at his warriors, exchanging a glance with whom Claire guessed must be his second. "The Forest has not been quiet since the Great War. Many truths we thought to be absolute are changing."

Claire got to her feet to defuse the situation when Toan's answer didn't seem to satisfy Desmond. "It's okay. I'm sorry too. I'm still learning to control my magic and I reacted instinctively to a threat on my mate."

"Your mate?" Toan looked contemplative, "You said your Triad earlier."

"Triad and mates." Claire corrected.

"All three of them?"

Claire nodded and Toan returned the gesture, "That makes more sense now. With your magic unbinding in preparation for your coming of age it will be more volatile."

Claire had so many questions from his statement and he must have read it on her face. "Please, come inside." He gestured towards the tree. "We will get you settled and I will answer what I know."

Desmond released his magic and Everett and Malcolm sheathed their weapons at Claire's nod. Toan slowly walked back over to the tree, one eye on Claire as if her magic would spook just by moving closer to her Triad. She wanted to roll her eyes but she also appreciated the respect he was showing. Claire followed him to the tree, Puck still on her shoulder and her men pressed in behind her.

When Claire stepped through the doorway in the tree, the tree's Energy surrounded her, pressing into her in a… playful way? Claire touched the tree's Energy with her magic in acknowledgment and then pulled it away, still hesitant to use her magic so soon after her explosion. The tree's Energy retreated slightly but Claire could still feel it saturating the air. Looking around at the expressions on her men and the Elves' faces, she wondered if she was the only one who could feel it.

They stepped into a large room, the tree's trunk did not look this large from the outside and the soft touches of magic around the room meant the size had been magically enhanced.

"Our people have always taken comfort in living in the

trees," Toan shared, "The entire Capital is in the trees. Most of the ground floor rooms are gathering places as they are the largest. As we climb, there will be different rooms both inside the trunks and in the branches."

He gestured at narrow steps built into the trunk that spiraled upwards to a small platform about thirty feet up. His men went first and when Claire went to follow Toan, Everett caught her elbow and Malcolm stepped ahead of her so she was sandwiched between Malcolm and Everett.

A slight draft of wind teased her hair in front of her face and Claire brushed it aside to see Desmond grinning at her from the rear. She understood the plan now. If anyone fell, Desmond would catch them with his air magic. Apparently her men weren't trusting Toan nearly as much as Claire was. She frowned at Malcolm's back as she thought. Was she being too trusting? Too naive? She checked on her magic again, she wasn't getting a bad feeling about any of this but was her magic reliable right now?

Before Claire could think much more on it, they arrived at the platform. The Elves ahead of them stepped through another door that wasn't visible from the ground floor. Toan followed them through and Malcolm only hesitated briefly before disappearing through the door after him.

Claire followed without hesitation, even her nerves and worry couldn't temper the kernel of excitement that filled her. Her mother was from here. Maybe she still was or Toan knew where she was?

The platform they stepped out onto was much larger than the one inside the tree, fitting the large group comfortably. Vines and branches formed bridges to other platforms as Claire realized they were quite literally 'in the trees'. The other Elven warriors disappeared down one of the bridges to another platform in a different tree. Two of them stayed there while the other two continued on to the next platform, the network of bridges between platforms stretching as far as Claire's eyes could see in a large circular pattern surrounding one massive tree in the center about four platforms away.

It was this tree that Toan began leading them towards. He stepped out onto the swaying bridge confidently. Malcolm grumbled but followed him. Claire stepped out onto the bridge after him and focused on where her feet were stepping. Luckily, her 'depth of vision' as Zack called it had gotten substantially better in the last month or so and she was able to place her feet carefully from branch to branch.

Thinking of Zack made her think of the rest of her friends. She wondered what they were doing right now. The Academy would be starting in a month and she would get to see them all together soon. That is, if everything in the Elven Forest went well. Frowning, she realized she hadn't checked in with Helene's tree since they had entered the Forest. With all of the excitement of the Feluas, she had completely forgotten. She paused on the bridge and Everett placed a gentle hand on her back, a question strumming down their bond. She sent him a picture back of Helene's tree.

The word *Later* thrummed down their bond back at her and Claire almost stumbled. She had 'heard' a word. Usually they could only communicate in pictures or feelings not words. Her bonds were growing stronger. Everett arched an eyebrow at the wide grin she threw over her shoulder but returned her smile. He gave her a gentle push to remind her that she was still on the bridge and Claire focused on crossing it. Malcolm had already reached the next platform and was looking back at them, arms crossed and a familiar scowl on his face.

Claire reached him shortly and held out her hand for one of his. He took it without hesitation, tucking it into his elbow as they followed Toan around the platform to the opposite side of the tree. They were only one platform away from the massive central tree now. Now that they were closer, Claire could appreciate the size of the tree more. She peered over the edge of the platform they were on and saw a large lower platform on the central tree that connected to the other trees. Multiple smaller platforms dotted the trunk of the tree all the way up its trunk and into its leafy branches at the top.

"That is the Royal Tree." Toan explained, "For millennia, our Royal Family lived in that tree here at the Capital. The lower platforms are the receiving chambers and the family's residence begins in the upper platforms."

"You said lived, past tense." Desmond pointed out.

Toan took a breath and let out a sigh, emotion cracking on his face the first time since Claire had seen him. "Most of the Royal Family fell during the Great War protecting their people. We suffered great losses and the tree has remained empty till now."

"Till now?" Claire asked.

Toan nodded, "Your mother was a Royal. The Princess in fact."

Claire's wide eyes met Desmonds. A princess? Wait. Was?

"Was?" Claire whispered her question but Toan heard her perfectly. Toan gestured behind them and Claire and her Triad turned to the tree at their backs. Small canvas portraits dotted the vast trunk. Some were single portraits and others had entire families in it.

"These are the portraits of all we lost during the Great War." Toan said, gesturing towards the portraits that were hanging from various branches or sitting in the grooves of the tree's trunks. "We honor their memory by never forgetting them."

Claire's eyes traced over the portraits, starting at the bottom and gasping when her eyes caught one in the middle. She took a step backwards, legs unsteady.

Malcolm caught her, "What is it?" He growled, still on edge and leveling a glare at the tree as if he could glare it into submission.

"That's the woman from the village. The one I saw through the Dryad tree."

"The border village on witch territory?" Toan demanded.

Malcolm growled at his tone but Claire nodded her head.

Toan's expression turned sad as he looked towards the portrait again. He heaved a sigh that was so full of sorrow, "That is a picture of your mother."

Claire froze. Her mother? The woman she saw in that vision was her mother?

"Your mother had just visited that village. She loved it because Elves and witches lived together, finding true bonds in each other. As a Royal, she traveled often, making sure her people were happy. She had visited that village right after the deaths of our people by the hands of the Council. Someone must have reported her visit because the next time she came back it was massacred. She returned to the Capital immediately with the news and we prepared for war. Then a few years later, we lost her."

It was like Claire heard Toan's words in a fog. But that last sentence was crystal clear. Claire didn't make the connection until Toan said that last line. She knew having that hope was dangerous but she thought...

She thought her mother might have still been alive.

Toan must have read her face, a skill he was apparently very good at.

"I'm so sorry, Claire. She moved often, protecting you, but someone must have caught up with her. We found her body in a clearing near the witches' territory and you were gone. We feared the worst."

Claire had always wondered what her parents could be like. She had never allowed herself to hope they were good people, because who abandons a child? But Claire had been wrong. Her mother was a good person, a princess. And she had been protecting Claire. But someone killed her for it. Who? Why?

As if sensing her spiraling, Everett gathered her close into his chest. "I think that's enough for the night." Desmond said firmly.

Toan watched Claire sadly although she didn't acknowledge it. Instead she turned her face and pressed it into Everett's chest, trying to let the scent of her mate drown out the deep sadness and grief that seemed to weigh down her bones like rocks at the bottom of a stream.

"Of course," Toan said, "I'll show you where you can rest."

Everett scooped her up and Claire felt Desmond stroke her hair with a comforting hand but Claire couldn't seem to find the energy to acknowledge him.

Claire didn't pay any attention to where they were going. Instead, trying to breathe in Everett's scent to stave off the tears that burned her eyes and the back of her throat. When the door clicked behind them and it was only her mates and her, Claire let herself break.

CHAPTER 29

Claire didn't want to open her eyes the next morning. For a brief moment when she woke up, she had forgotten the events of yesterday. That moment lasted all of a single breath before the reality of the day before came crashing in.

Claire didn't know why it was affecting her so badly. It's not like they didn't think coming into all of this that her parents might be dead. For the Realm's sake, Claire had never expected to have a reunion with her mother or father most of her life, assuming they had abandoned her. But now, knowing that her mother not only loved her but gave her life to protect her? Guilt and grief warred inside of Claire. Guilt for ever thinking her mother had abandoned her. Grief over a woman Claire had no memory of other than a portrait on a tree.

Spearmint filled her nostrils as Desmond shifted closer in front of her. Everett was at her back and Claire's feet were on Malcolm's chest. She knew all of this without opening her eyes, letting the familiar darkness be her comfort measure today. Desmond's smooth fingers traced the furrowed crease on her brow and down her temple. He repeated the gesture until Claire's face relaxed and the crease disappeared.

"Are we staying in bed all day?" Desmond whispered softly.

At first, Claire thought he was asking Everett but when Everett didn't answer, Claire sighed. She wanted to but that wasn't fair. They had come for answers and she imagined Toan had questions also. The forehead crease came back as she thought about his sorrowful expression when he gave Claire the news. Who was Toan to her mother? Was he Claire's father?

Claire's muscles tensed at the last thought. She had been so consumed with her grief yesterday at her mother that she didn't consider Toan might be her father.

Desmond's warm hand cupped her cheek. "Hey," he said softly, "we can stay in bed all day if it's too much."

Claire sighed and opened her eyes, the heavy lids blinking open slowly until she could focus on Desmond's blue eyes just inches from her own. "No," she said softly, "we came for answers."

"Doesn't mean we need them all at once," Malcolm grumbled, the vibration of his chest tickling the bottom of Claire's feet. She went to shift them away but his warm hands kept them captive. He began rubbing them through her socks and Claire felt her muscles relax. From the pleased look on his face that was the point.

With Desmond cupping her face, Malcolm rubbing her feet, and Everett's hand splayed across her stomach, Claire soaked up every bit of comfort her Triad was offering her. Another half hour must have passed before Claire forced her eyes to open again. She could wallow later. They needed answers so they could figure out who was threatening her and her family. Avoiding the answers wouldn't make them any less true.

Claire took a deep breath and then let out a soft sigh, opening her eyes and propping herself up on one elbow. Desmond smiled up at her, lying on his back next to her. He reached out and took Claire's free hand, interlacing her fingers with his. The warmth from his palm was a solid point of comfort. Claire leaned down and brushed a kiss across his lips before squeezing his hand and sitting up.

"Are we getting up?" Everett's voice was gravely from sleep, sending a shiver down Claire's spine.

"Yes." Claire answered, "We are getting up."

She looked around the room, taking it in for the first time. They were still clearly inside a tree, the room smaller and cozier with the bed taking up most of the space. Their packs were stacked next to the door hewn into the trunk. A wooden divider cut off a section of the room and Claire could see a basin sticking out from behind it. Clearly, the Elves were not huge on materialistic comforts other than the basic but it was simple and cozy. It was just missing one thing.

"Where's Puck?" She frowned.

"He was nesting in a branch outside," Everett informed her, "we asked if he wanted inside but he ignored us."

Claire shook her head but smiled. Her familiar could be stubborn at the best of times.

Claire crawled forward, trying to get over Malcolm at the end of the bed. She let out a soft 'oomph' as Malcolm tugged her down. She landed softly on his chest and rolled her eyes at her smiling dragon.

"Good morning, my dragon." She greeted.

"Good morning, little treasure." Malcolm said, his palm cupping the back of her head and tugging her down for a kiss. His lips were warm and soft as he teased her, keeping the kiss light.

All too soon, he let her go and Claire's eyes blinked back open, taking in his smug grin. She rolled her eyes at him and pushed off of his chest. Malcolm let her go and Claire escaped behind the divider to splash some water in the basin over her heated face.

When she came out, Everett was removing a change of clothes for her from one of the packs. He gave them to her with a soft kiss to her forehead before ducking behind the divider himself. Desmond and Malcolm were still in the room but weren't looking her way. Claire felt ridiculous for being self-conscious but she couldn't help it. She turned her back to the room and stripped down quickly, changing into the trousers and tunic-style green shirt quickly.

She turned around and her face flamed hot as she saw she had her men's undivided attention. Claire bit her lip and looked down. She heard Desmond approach, the scent of spearmint growing stronger. He took her extra clothes from her, dropping them on the bed and backing her up against the wall.

"Don't be embarrassed, little witch." He said before kissing her deeply. Claire's lips parted on a gasp and Desmond's tongue immediately reached out to tangle with hers. He pressed her harder against the wall, one hand cradling her head and Claire felt just how much she affected him. She let out a soft moan and rocked her hips against his as the heat built in her core.

Desmond groaned at her actions and reached down, breaking the kiss as he grabbed the back of Claire's legs and lifted her. Claire let out a squeak that turned into a moan as he covered her lips with his again.

Claire suddenly realized that Everett and Malcolm were still in the room and her body tensed slightly. Desmond felt the change immediately and broke the kiss. She blushed again as he stared into her eyes. A soft smile crept over his face as he looked at her, eyes tracing over her pink cheeks. She felt their bond intimately in that moment, as if Desmond was right there in her mind as his blue eyes stared into hers.

"It's okay, little witch." He said, "I can promise they don't mind."

Claire blushed and let her head fall forward. Trust Desmond to make it uncomfortably awkward with his honesty. She felt

Everett approach and shyly turned her head on Desmond's shoulder to look at him.

"You're gorgeous." He said softly, his green eyes vibrant. His hand lifted and he rubbed his thumb across her swollen bottom lip. "Desmond's right, as per usual, we don't mind watching each other with you."

Claire's eyes drifted past Everett to Malcolm. Her dragon stood with his arms crossed and a grumpy expression on his face but when Claire met his eyes, he sent a surge of love down their bond that was so strong, Claire's knees would have gone out had Desmond not still have her in his arms.

The moment was broken by Claire's stomach rumbling and her cheeks heated again as she dropped her forehead back to Desmond's shoulder and groaned. Her men chuckled and Desmond let go of her legs, steadying her on her feet.

"Let's go get you fed," Desmond teased.

Claire smiled and shook her head but accepted his hand. Everett scooped up her other one and Malcolm opened the door for them.

Bright sunlight and fresh air greeted them as they stepped outside. The crisp breeze teased Claire's cheeks and chased away her lingering blush. The Capital was alive and buzzing this morning. Elves called out to each other and engaged in conversation on the platforms below them. From what Claire could tell, they were on one of the higher platforms, a set of stairs off to her right.

Toan's head appeared on the stairs. "Oh, you're awake!" He said, "I was coming to take you to breakfast."

"Great," Desmond smiled warmly, "Claire's starving."

Claire elbowed Desmond in the side and wrinkled her nose at him. He just laughed at her and tucked her closer as they followed Toan down the stairs.

Toan guided them down another two sets of stairs and across one branch bridge to the next tree over. They walked around the tree as the platform widened out and revealed a table and chairs that looked like they were carved from the platform they sat on. Various bowls sat on the table filled with fruits and bread. Some of the fruits were familiar to Claire but others were not. A familiar creature curled up on one of the chairs, head lifting when they approached.

"Good morning, Puck." Claire lifted him from the chair, burying her nose in his furry feathers. He purred in her arms sending a comforting warmth through their bond that chased some of the bone-deep ache inside her away.

"Smart familiar you have there." Toan remarked as they all took their seats. "Appeared down here about ten minutes ago so I took that as a sign you were awake."

Claire nodded as she placed Puck on her lap after she sat. "He's very smart."

Toan passed a bowl of bread around. "If you don't mind me asking, how did you find him? Notus typically don't stray from the Elven Forest."

"He found me actually." Claire said, accepting a bread roll from Everett. "He was under a dark magic spell and appeared at Brandlevine, Desmond's coven. He transported me out of the coven manor house but I was able to break the dark magic spell. When I did, he bonded with me."

Toan just stared at her. "Dark magic?"

Claire nodded. "That's one of the things we wanted to ask you about actually." She briefly recounted the Felua attack, stumbling over the part where she killed it. She quickly recounted the other creature sightings.

When she finished, Toan's face was carefully blank but his eyes were stormy. "What you say is very troubling indeed. All the Elves and even the Elven creatures retreated to the capital after the Great War started. For someone to reach them here, it means they have access to our gates."

"Could it be another Elf?" Everett asked.

Toan shook his head, "Absolutely not. We would never betray our own like that. Besides, I can account for every Elf and their movements. We were already small in numbers before the Great War but afterwards, everyone moved into the capital."

Everett's frown indicated he didn't necessarily believe Toan but he didn't press him either.

"The other Elven creature sightings were closer to the Academy grounds," Desmond mused, "only Puck ventured out to Brandlevine."

Toan looked thoughtful, "If he was always meant to be Claire's familiar than her magic's bindings unraveling would have attracted him to her faster. It's possible he was already outside the Forest, called by her magic when this person happened upon him and ensnared him with a dark magic spell."

Claire frowned as she stroked Puck's back with one hand. She popped a piece of fruit into her mouth and thought while she chewed. She didn't like that Puck was in danger because of her but it had all worked out. Puck let out a soft purr, as if sensing her thoughts and Claire let the feeling relax her.

"Speaking of her magic's binding," Malcolm frowned, "is it normal for Elven magic bindings to cause your children to lose their sight?" His tone was accusatory.

Toan's eyes snapped to Claire's as if he thought she was still blind and Claire shook her head. She had her sight now.

"Before your mother left with you, you had your sight." Toan said, frowning. "And a normal magic binding."

"Then the binding must have happened afterwards." Desmond mused. "Why would her mother bind her magic at the cost of her sight?"

Toan sighed, "I have a theory. It's true, your magic was bound when you were a toddler. We should have expected it given how powerful your mother was but when you were a toddler, you tried to grow a whole new forest so your mother and grandparents performed a magic binding ceremony on you.

In a normal childhood, your magic would have stayed bound with the bindings loosening until your coming of age ceremony at your twenty-fifth year. You would have attended the Academy as well as specialized summer classes here at the capital."

"What is your theory?" Desmond pressed when Toan paused.

"Even after your magic was bound, you were still leaking it. But we could usually contain it here at the capital. Towards the end of the Great War, there was an attack close to the Capital. Dark magic actually. Winona fled with Claire as we were worried whoever it was was after the Royal Family. If Winona thought Claire's life was in danger from her magic, she would have bound it no matter the cost."

"Winona..." Claire whispered, "That was my mother's name?"

The table quieted at her whisper and Everett grabbed her hand, squeezing it softly as she gripped Puck's fur with her other one. She hadn't even known her mother's name. She hadn't even thought to ask earlier. The guilt and grief from this morning rose up and threatened to swallow her. She would have been a terrible daughter. Was Toan her father? Claire almost didn't want to ask that question. What if he wasn't? What if he was? She kept her eyes on Puck and blurted it out.

"Are you my father?" Lifting her eyes up at the silence.

Toan's brown eyes held the same sadness they had yesterday as he shook his head. "I'm not your father. I know who he was though. I was a part of Winona, your mother's guard. Technically I'm a distant cousin of hers so sort of like an uncle for you."

"If you were in her mother's guard, why did you not go with her when she fled the capital with Claire?" Everett pressed.

Toan let out a wry smile. "I would have if Winona had told anyone that was her plan. She disappeared in the night with Claire and left a note explaining why she did so, to protect you,

Claire. She didn't tell anyone where she was going but I assumed she went to Erick."

"Erick?" Desmond asked.

Toan looked at Claire before answering. "Erick was your father. It was not widely known among the general Realm though. The Council knew. They threw a fit over it because separately your mother and father were powerful but together… they could level mountains if they ever chose to."

"Do you know if he's still… alive?" Claire hesitated on the question.

Toan shook his head, "I don't know actually. Erick was a Fae prince. When the Great War escalated, he returned to his people to lead the Fae warriors."

"You really are royalty." Desmond said softly to Claire with a smile.

Claire returned it but it felt hollow. These were exactly the answers she was supposed to be looking for but for some reason hearing them filled her with an emptiness that felt suspiciously like grief.

Desmond's smile dropped and his lips twisted in a soft frown. His hand reached for her leg under the table and gave it a soft squeeze.

"What can you tell us about the Great War and how it started?" He asked Toan, changing the subject.

Claire covered his hand with her own briefly and squeezed it, grateful for the subject change.

Toan arched an eyebrow but played a long, "We keep impeccable records in the Great Tree. Are you looking for something specific?"

Desmond shrugged, "Nothing specific but a general overview of the Great War from the Elves' perspective would be helpful. As I'm sure you can imagine, the Unitam Council has a version of events they have shared."

Toan looked thoughtful for a moment, hands steeple under

his chin. "I can give you some books in our archives, journals from Elves at the time. I can't share more than a few without permission from the Elders. I will talk to them while you review the first journals. I can take you now, if you're finished."

Malcolm frowned at Claire's mostly full plate but she had lost her appetite when they started talking about her parents. "That would be great." She answered Toan before Malcolm could say anything. She could eat later, if her appetite came back.

CHAPTER 30

They followed Toan back to the tree they had spent the night in, the Great Tree according to Toan. Puck perched on Claire's shoulders as they walked. Toan turned back to look at her and smiled.

"What is it?" She asked.

"Your mother's Notus used to sit on her shoulders the same way." He said. "I'm sorry, it's just when I catch you out of the corner of my eye, you look just like her."

"You were close?" Claire asked, sensing the sadness emanating from him.

"I was already into my third decade when your mother was born. She captivated everyone even as a baby and I spent the next decade training to be in her guard. I watched her grow up, fall in love, and have you."

As much as Claire wanted to hear more about her mother, her chest was tight and her brain felt like it was spinning a bit from trying to process everything. Toan gave her a gentle smile. "I can tell you more later." He said, "We have time."

Claire nodded and smiled gratefully at him while feeling a

bit silly. These were the answers she wanted. Why was she so scared of hearing it?

Instead of going back up the stairs to the level they slept on, Toan headed down two staircases to a different door with books carved into it. He pushed it open to reveal a large room filled with books. "This is our archives available to all. We keep sacred books and scrolls in the Elder Library but you should find some of what you are looking for here."

Claire and her men spread out into the room. Low tables and couches were interspersed with book shelves that rose from the floor. Shelves were also built into the trunk of the tree but they weren't the orderly straight rows of Brandlevine's library. The shelves grooved with the grain of the tree's wood. Three books were lying on their sides, stacked on top of each other in one groove and right next to it a collection of five books stood on its end. It was chaotic and charming and Claire spun in a circle trying to take it all in.

Desmond looked less thrilled with the disorder as he perused a shelf off to Claire's right, his forehead creased.

Toan walked over and pulled a few books out of a groove in the tree. He walked a few paces away and pulled out a single book to add to the small pile.

"I would start here." He offered them to Claire. "These are our heritage books. They'll tell you about the history of the Elves and our family lines."

Claire took them from him gingerly. The books looked old but felt solid underneath her grasp.

"I will have to leave you here. I need to talk to the Elders and our evening patrols and make sure all is well."

Claire looked at Everett and thought about their silent follower. Everett nodded at her look.

"On our way in," Everett said, "we stumbled into a Felua's territory by accident. After we got away, they came back under a dark magic spell. If all your Elves are accounted for, there's someone else in the woods."

Toan's face darkened and hardened until he was all warrior and none of the sorrowful man from earlier. "We will take care of it." He said shortly. He left the room.

Claire carefully set the books Toan had handed her down on one of the tables. Desmond sat next to her and stole one of them off of the pile, his touch just as careful with them as Claire's was.

He cracked it open, spreading it out on the low table in front of them. "The Elven Family Lines…" He read aloud. His eyes traced over the page, his face impressed. "This has every family line, it looks like going back millenia."

"Really?" Claire asked, leaning closer, her eyes tracing over a literal tree sketched out onto the page.

Desmond flipped the page, reading out loud, "The Elven Royal Lines." His eyes traced over the page. "It looks like there are three original Royal Lines, the Mayfaires, the Oakfawns, and the Birchwoods."

"Which one is Claire?" Everett asked.

Desmond's finger traced up the three main branches to the far corner of the page, "It looks like Claire is a Mayfaire."

Claire leaned closer, pressing her shoulder to Desmond's as she followed where his finger was pointing. The sketch of the tree was done in vibrant colors of green, gold, and blue. Claire's side of the tree was sketched in golds but some of the names were darkened out. "Why are some of them darkened out?" she mused out loud.

Desmond hesitated, "I think that signifies the Elves who are no longer here."

Oh. Claire's stomach clenched, what little breakfast she had eaten sat like a brick in her stomach. Malcolm growled softly at Desmond as Claire tugged the book closer to her. Her fingers traced her mother's darkened name. She noticed her father's name was unlisted but Claire's name was. *Arielle Clarissa Mayfaire.*

She didn't know how to feel, looking at her name. If Toan hadn't told them her mother's name, she wouldn't even have known it was hers. And now that it was...

Claire felt like a twisted mass of thorny vines. She wasn't able to pick out any one emotion as they all seemed to fold into each other. Sadness, guilt, anger. Sadness at losing out on a childhood and a mother she would never get a chance to know. Guilt that she thought this realm had abandoned her. Anger at herself. Why hadn't she tried harder to find out more answers about who she was and where she was from?

"Claire," Desmond's voice made her realize he had been trying to get her attention for a while now.

"Yes?" She asked as she shoved down the swirling emotions inside of her. Puck rubbed her legs from where he was laying across her feet but the motion didn't bring the usual comfort.

"Do you want to talk about it?" Desmond asked.

Claire bit her bottom lip. Not really. She wasn't even sure how she would talk about it. How could she express all these feelings and thoughts when she couldn't even figure them out herself?

She chose the ignorance route. "Talk about what?" She aimed for nonchalance but the soft look that Desmond gave her meant she didn't achieve it. She wanted to roll her eyes when she realized they were probably feeling it anyway through the bonds.

"Whatever has you so twisted up inside?" Desmond pressed her further and Claire sighed, sitting back on the couch. Desmond followed her back, placing an arm around her shoulders and settling her on his chest. Malcolm and Everett stopped their search through the shelves. Everett took a seat facing Claire on the table, carefully sliding the book over as he did so.

Malcolm remained standing next to Everett, arms folded in his classic pose.

Claire frowned, staring down at her fingers as she tried to figure out where to start. Her men were patient, waiting. Claire figured her earlier twisted thorny vine analogy might work.

"I feel a lot." She said, wincing at how lame that must sound. "I mean, these are supposed to be the answers I've waited my entire life for but now that we're here and I'm hearing them… I don't want to." Claire frowned again. Did that make her seem like a child?

"It has been a lot," Desmond said, "more than I think anyone was expecting."

Claire nodded. "Yes, and I think a bit all at once. I don't know. I just…"

"Is it possible that the answers you are getting are not the answers you want to hear?" Everett asked quietly.

Trust her quiet gryphon to have the exact words Claire was looking for.

She bit her lip, throat suddenly tight. "I always knew there was a possibility that they weren't alive." Her voice was barely a whisper but rang out clearly anyways in the silent library.

"It was either that or they truly didn't have a thought or care about abandoning a child. I told myself it was the latter growing up I think as a way to protect myself. There was something wrong with them versus there being something wrong with me. But there wasn't. Something wrong with them I mean. They did want me and I never knew that."

She had to stop or the tears threatening to spill would never stop. She bit her lip again, the slight pain grounding her slightly. Desmond pressed a soft kiss to her temple and Claire swallowed tightly.

"I never knew but maybe I should have. Maybe I should have searched harder instead of accepting what the Windshire coven told me. Because now, hearing the answers, I don't want to 'cause it hurts. It's like my very bones ache and are weighed down. This is supposed to be everything I ever wanted to learn but instead it just hurts"

"That's grief," Everett said when she paused, "what you're describing is grief."

Now Claire felt worse because she forgot Everett also lost his parents. He smiled gently at her as if hearing her thoughts.

"Grief is not a competition, little mate. Don't feel bad. That weight in your bones though, it does get lighter. You find people who help you carry it. You keep their memories close, and yes it'll hurt. It'll hurt for a while and sometimes it'll be unexpected and it'll catch you off guard but eventually the weight won't be that much to carry. You'll still feel it but you'll carry it easier."

"Why does it have to hurt so much though?" Claire whispered, losing the battle of trying to keep her tears at bay.

"It hurts because the opposite of grief is love," Everett matched her whisper. Malcolm placed a hand on Everett's shoulder and squeezed. Everett looked up at him briefly with a tight smile and turned back to Claire reaching out and grabbing one of her hands with his.

"The opposite of grief is love and it hurts us because we've lost that love. The harder we've loved someone the harder it is to lose them. Our grief is a reminder of that love and that's why the hurt will get easier because even when we grieve we are reminded of that love."

"We'll help you carry it, little witch." Desmond said softly in her ear, "When it's hard to carry, we'll help you carry it."

That's when Claire allowed herself to break a little bit. Desmond gathered her close and Malcolm wedged himself in next to her. The love they pushed down the bonds towards her made her cry harder but after the tears ran out, Claire did indeed feel a little bit lighter.

CHAPTER 31

"Why don't we come back to this book later?" Desmond suggested, once Claire had righted herself. She was sitting on Malcolm's lap, her grumbly dragon doing remarkably well at her tears.

Claire felt a bit exasperated with herself and her reaction but didn't protest as Desmond closed the Elven family lines book and placed it at the bottom of the pile. He picked up another smaller book and opened the front cover, scanning it quickly. "Oh, this one might be interesting."

"What is it?" Everett asked, still sitting on the table in front of them.

"It's a journal by an Elder Elf who sat on the Council up to the start of the Great War.

Claire sat up straighter, ignoring Malcolm's groan. "That sounds exactly like what we've been looking for."

"Read it to us," Malcolm grumbled, holding Claire tighter.

Desmond flipped through a few pages and then started summarizing. "It looks like the first few journal entries are normal, discussing regular meetings with the Council although…" A smile spread across Desmond's face, "I think we all would have really loved this Elder. She doesn't sugarcoat her words at all nor does she hide her feelings about the witch representative."

"What do you mean?" Claire asked.

"She calls the witch ambitious but in much ruder terms." Desmond chuckled as he flipped through the pages, eyes scanning over each quickly. "She calls the Witches resentful and ambitious, the Shifters quick to anger and reactive, and the Dragons proud and stubborn."

Claire looked up at Malcolm who shrugged. "We tend to be." He said.

"Oh, hello," Desmond murmured, drawing Claire's attention back to him. From his tone, it sounded like he found something good.

"I know you can speed read," Malcolm threatened, "but you need to start speed talking as well."

Desmond rolled his eyes but started speaking. "This journal entry outlines a conversation she had with the Fae representative. A conversation where the Fae representative told her about dark magic found in the Fae lands, or at least the taint of it, like it lingered after a spell."

"Dark magic?" Claire frowned. There was dark magic even then? Was it the same person?

"Dark magic." Desmond confirmed. "The Elven representative, Lorna, asked if it could be the Taos, the Fae representative's, people but Taos swears none of his people were involved. Lorna doesn't tell Taos this but she writes in her journal that this screams of witch involvement, specifically the 'trouble faction'."

"The trouble faction?" Everett asked, "Does she mention any more details about them?"

Desmond frowned and flipped through the pages, "She doesn't say anymore on them in the next few pages other than telling Taos he should bring it up to the Council."

"Maybe she described them in an earlier journal?" Claire wondered. "We could ask Toan for Lorna's earlier journals."

Desmond nodded, "Let's do that for sure."

Claire asked the other question on her mind, "I thought dark magic was illegal but it's popping up now and then. What if the two events are connected?"

"You mean like if it was the same person or group?" Everett asked.

Claire shrugged, "Yes? It just seems odd that it occurred before the Great War and it's occurring now. I thought the Council was strict against people who used it."

Everett and Malcolm shared a look that Desmond and Claire caught. "Care to share with the class?" Desmond arched an eyebrow, looking mildly annoyed that he was out of the loop.

Malcolm sighed, his chest rising and falling against Claire's shoulder, "It's probably not talked about at Brandlevine but growing up, the perspective in the Dragon Mountains was that the witches received leniency from the more unsavory punishments."

"The Council played favorites?" Claire questioned, not understanding the political speak.

Thankfully, Everett took pity on her confusion. "The Council will turn a blind eye towards anything a witch does if it serves in their interests. Or any of their favorites. What would garner a death sentence for anyone else who tried it would get a slap on the wrist if you were in the Council's favor."

Claire looked at Desmond who frowned but didn't disagree. They had discussed the Council being corrupt or lying about events but knowingly pardoning people who broke the most severe laws in the Realm?

For a few moments there was silence as they all processed the implications. The only sound was Desmond flipping through the pages of Lorna's journal with a ferocity that made Claire wonder if he was trying to find information that confirmed or denied Everett and Malcolm's words. This had to be harder on him than the others with his father as a Councilmember. When his expression grew tighter, Claire knew whatever he was reading confirmed it.

"What is it?" She asked, rubbing her foot against his leg trying to provide a measure of comfort.

"Lorna doesn't know why the witches would be involved in dark magic against the Fae but she does recount times that the Council has been lenient with 'errant' witches. The Council was always split on the decisions but the shifters always sided with the witches and the dragons did more often than not. Lorna wonders what has changed in the last 100 years that the shifters would side with the witches. Especially with stuff like this. Listen to this story."

He adjusted the book on his lap as he spoke. "There was a case they tried where the witch basically bullied a group of teenage shifters and forced them to shift which is illegal to influence with magic. The punishment is your magical powers bound for five years and the witch got off with a warning because she was 'young and didn't know' as the witch representative said in her statement."

Malcolm growled. Forcing a shift was a barbaric violation of someone's magic. Even growing up a witch, Claire understood that although she rarely if ever interacted with shifters growing up. Other than the occasional merchant trader or two.

"Does Lorna say in that journal if Taos brought the dark magic use up to the Council?" Claire asked.

Desmond flipped through the book, face twisting into a grimace. "Yes. But the Council dismissed it." He paused in his reading, eyes flaring wide as his eyebrows practically met his hairline.

"What is it?" Malcolm demanded.

"They dismissed it but three weeks later, dark magic was

used in the Market attack. A witch used dark magic on an Elven Trader who refused to sell her a certain herb."

Malcolm's eyebrows also shot up and Claire frowned. Dark magic hadn't been mentioned in previous descriptions of that attack.

"Seriously?" Everett questioned, his own tone one of disbelief. Claire didn't blame him, a dark magic attack on a fellow citizen of the Realm was close to unheard of. Especially not with the current laws. Whoever broke them was supposed to be made an example of to prevent others from using such dangerous magic.

"Does she say anything about why the attack happened?" Claire asked, wondering if the story that had been told was true. "The witch died as well didn't she?"

Desmond shook his head, "Nothing about why the attack happened. Lorna is particularly critical of witches and all she focuses on is the audacity of the witch to attack."

He flips through a few more pages, shaking his head, "Nothing here on the witches fate... except, hello?"

Malcolm growled, "I know you have the flair for dramatics but I swear by the Realm if you don't spit it out right now..."

"Okay, okay!" Desmond said, "You're getting testy. Are you hungry?"

Claire hid a giggle at Malcolm's answering growl, but nudged Desmond with her foot to get him talking.

Desmond winked at her but continued before Malcolm could growl at him again. "Okay, so you would think that if the witch was actually put to death like the law would dictate, that Lorna would mention it. But she doesn't. And in this sentence when she's ranting about it, she uses present tense to describe the witch."

"Okay..." Malcolm glared at him and Desmond rolled his eyes.

"Okay so present tense means the witch was alive. Probably."

"Probably?" Everett arched an eyebrow as he leaned forward.

Desmond threw his hands up in the air. "Yes. Probably. I don't know. She doesn't say for certain but she doesn't seem like the type that would use the wrong tense when writing."

"What does she say then?" Claire broke in before Everett or Malcolm could spin Desmond up more.

Desmond frowned as he flipped through the next few pages. "Her last journal entry just says that she and Taos plan to talk to the Council about the attack and try to come up with a new trade accords. This is dated right before the official record says the Elven and Fae representative walked out."

"I wonder if she kept journals afterwards too?" Claire wondered. "Maybe that would tell us what happened after?"

Desmond thumbed through the other books that Toan had given them and frowned. "These look like more heritage or early history books. If she does have other journals, I doubt they would be in here." He looked around at the library.

"Why do you say that?" Claire asked.

"Most Elders keep their journals in their own personal libraries," Malcolm said, his voice soft in her ear.

"But why was Lorna's in here?" Claire questioned.

Desmond frowned. "That's an excellent question, little witch. We'll have to ask Toan."

"Why do you call me that?" Claire asked without thinking about it. "I mean still. Little witch."

Desmond looked thoughtful. "Do you not like it?"

Claire smiled to show she was teasing, "I mean the little part could go from all of your nicknames."

Her men laughed and Malcolm squeezed her tighter. "I like all of your nicknames," Claire said, "I just... I mean I guess I'm not a witch though."

Desmond nodded, hand under his chin and elbow on his crossed knee as he looked at her. "I know that. And I suspected it for a while. I guess when I call you that I think of meeting you at Windshire Coven that fateful day. Everett was grumpy from the long trip." Everett growled at Desmond who brushed it off with a smirk, "And here you were, this adorable little witch out to change our worlds."

Claire smiled and blushed as she thought about that day and how nervous she was about the Academy but also how much they had affected her.

"I can change it if you want?" Desmond offered, "If you would rather leave that part behind you?"

"I like it," Claire said slowly, "but I like it because you're calling me it." She searched for the words she was trying to say. She didn't want Desmond to feel bad about it but it almost felt...like she was betraying her heritage, her mother and father.

She looked at Desmond and the soft smile on his face as his eyes read hers had him smiling. "I'll change it, little pumpkin."

Everett snorted. "Little pumpkin. Are you calling our Fourth short, round and orange?"

The look of horror on Desmond's face as he realized what he said had Claire busting out in laughter. Her brilliant mate was a little dim sometimes.

"We'll work on it." She assured him after she had caught her breath.

Desmond smiled at her and then shot a dirty look at Everett who was still chuckling under his breath. "Okay." He said, clapping his hands together. "Let's go find Toan and see if we can get some answers from him on where Lorna's journals might be. He clearly doesn't mind us reading them if he gave us this one."

CHAPTER 32

Ever the planner, Desmond kept talking as they exited the library, Puck on Claire's shoulders as Malcolm shut the door behind them.

"We need to ask Toan more about your father. If the Fae found dark magic in their lands and that was one of the things that started the Great War, then your father and his people might know more information that could help us solve what's happening here and now."

Claire's lips twisted but she nodded as they walked around the platform to the next bridge. She hadn't asked Toan much about her father. Especially after learning her mother was gone. What if he was too? Claire barely felt like she was able to carry this grief. What if she had to add to it?

Everett picked up her hand and squeezed it. She looked up to his soft smile and took a breath. Whatever the news, her men would help her carry it.

"Excuse us?" Desmond called to an Elf on the next tree over. The male Elf was dressed casually, a basket of leafy herbs was in his arms. As he turned towards them, Claire saw that he had gold eyes but not the gold like Malcolm's, more a pale yellow gold. Claire looked at that basket and frowned as something bothered her.

"What is it?" Everett asked softly, his green eyes glinting in the sunlight that fell through the trees.

"I don't know. I feel like I am supposed to remember something important."

She frowned as she tried to remember it and Everett swiped his thumb over her cheek. She smiled at him and pushed it out of her head. If it was important, she would remember it later.

"We are looking for Toan. Do you know where he is?" Desmond asked.

"I believe I saw him head the lower platform of that tree." The Elf pointed to a tree about three over from where Claire and her men stood, "If you go down the stairs there, and cross that bridge," he pointed to a longer bridge that connected two branches together, "you'll make it to the next set of stairs that should take you to the platform."

"Thank you," Desmond called and waved at the Elf.

The Elf waved back and disappeared around the tree with his basket.

"Come on, little mate." Everett said, letting go of Claire's hand and placing his on the small of her back, guiding her to the stairs the Elf indicated. As they went down the stairs, Claire wondered if this is why the Elves were so tall and lean all the time. They went up and down stairs all the time.

Even though Claire was in good shape, her leg muscles burned slightly going as she walked. Puck's weight was no help and Claire gently nudged him off her shoulder with a thought. He squawked softly but leapt off her shoulders and flapped his wings over the bridge till he was on the railing of the other platform.

Claire's magic swirled in her gut and she frowned, unsure if her stomach was restless with nerves about answers from her father or if it was restless due to something else. Malcolm stepped out onto the bridge first, taking the lead like normal. Claire stepped after him with Desmond right behind her and Everett following. The bridge was narrow like the other bridges and Claire avoided looking down. She wasn't scared of heights but she didn't like to remind herself of how far up she was either.

Puck gave her the first sign of danger, pausing in his grooming and golden eyes narrowing at all four of them now at the middle of the bridge. Claire felt the dark magic next. The Energy was faint, but the slick, oily feeling flagged her magic. These two warning signs happened in a matter of moments. And then...

The bridge broke.

Claire's stomach rose to her throat as her world literally dropped out from underneath her. Panic clawed her throat and she couldn't scream if she wanted to. Her men shouted and that's what cleared Claire's mind. Her eyes darted to Malcolm who was yelling at Desmond and gesturing at Claire. His magic couldn't save all of them and Claire had no doubt Desmond would save her at the expense of themselves. Claire didn't think she just pulled hard at her magic, harder than she ever had and sent it out of her with one thought, *Save them.*

It exploded out of her in a blinding white light, shooting into her Triad hard. Claire panicked then, trying to pull it back. What if she was hurting them but her magic resisted, and Claire almost felt like it was asking her to trust it. Heart in her throat, she let go of her magic, watching it encase her men in a white bubble that was barely translucent, the sheer amount of magic creating the bubble shimmering in a swirling mass as it halted her Triad's fall.

Claire kept falling as her only instruction to her magic had been to save them. A grey blur plummeted towards her, shooting past her men. Puck. His magic danced in her center and yanked some of hers back as the ground got closer. Her magic returned to her just in time to soften the blow of her landing. Claire still gasped when she landed hard on her back, the air pushing out of her lungs forcefully from the impact.

She took a second, laying on her back to look up. Her men still encased in her protective bubble of magic, their protective shouts muffled. Puck landed heavily next to her, chittering angrily. It was like the sounds were slowly returning to her ears. Elves rushed out of the trees and Claire caught Toan's worried voice as he pushed through the crowds until his face entered her vision. She frowned softly when he blocked her view of her men. The world felt like it was moving in slow motion as compared to the panicked rush of the last few seconds.

Toan knelt over her, his mouth moving quickly and Claire fought through her brain fog until she could focus on his words.

"Claire, Claire, are you alright? Claire." Her uncle said, worry seeping into every word. He hovered his hands over her shoulders, as if scared to touch her but wanting to make sure she was okay.

Claire forced her head to nod, wincing when the movement sent pain jarring down her spine. "Dark magic." She croaked out.

Toan frowned deeper at her words. He turned and barked out orders at his men before turning back to her. "Don't move. We're getting a healer. Can you bring your men down though before they try to bring the Forest down with their shouts? Only if you can though. Don't strain yourself. They'll be fine where they are if you can't."

Claire cracked a small smile at that and her uncle's face slackened with relief although his eyes stayed worried. Now that her ears seemed to be working again, she could hear her men's shouts more easily. Puck chittered at her side where he pressed into it and Claire closed her eyes, focusing on her magic. It was hard to convince her magic to let her men go, it seemed to think they were safer in the bubble and Claire didn't necessarily disagree with it but she knew they were probably beyond angry. She coaxed her magic back, the shimmering bubbles becoming more translucent and lowering her men to the floor where the Elves made room for them to land.

As soon as they were safely on their feet, the bubbles shimmered then released her angry Triad.

"Claire," Desmond cried out, falling to his knees next to her. Toan backed away as Malcolm and Everett took his place but stayed close, his eyes still worried.

"I'm okay." She croaked as air filled her lungs, "Just had the breath knocked out of me."

Now released from its protective hold on her men, her magic filled her center again providing a soothing coolness to Claire's body. She closed her eyes and relished the feeling for a breath before trying to sit up.

"Stop, Claire!" Everett's hands joined Desmond in keeping her lying flat. "Hold on, wait for the healer."

Their use of her name indicated how panicked they still were. Claire looked at Malcolm who's glowing eyes and rigid stance told her he was only a few seconds away from exploding into his dragon. "I'm okay." She soothed. "My magic caught me in time. I just had the breath knocked out of me."

"Move aside, move aside." An old voice rasped out from behind the crowd. The Elves parted to reveal an old Elven woman, her thin body hunched over with age as she leaned heavily on a walking stick. The wrinkles in her skin reminded Claire of the grooves in the tree trunks around them.

Although her body was old, her eyes seemed young as her grey ones met Claire's blues. She paused in her descent, her eyes cutting to Toan. "Winona?" She asked him sharply.

"Claire." Desmond snapped at her with more force than Claire had ever heard from him.

The old woman ignored Desmond, eyes still on Toan who sighed and rubbed his face. "Winona's daughter."

Gasps rang out from the gathered crowd but the woman just nodded and dropped to her knees besides Claire. Her walking stick fell from her grasp and hit Desmond in the shoulder, narrowly missing his head. The look he shot her could have melted ice but she just ignored him. A twinkle in her eyes as she met Claire's gaze gave Claire a feeling that she knew she was provoking her mate. Claire tried to narrow her gaze but couldn't find it in herself to put any intensity behind it.

"I'm Greta, young Princess." The woman introduced herself. "You've caused quite the excitement here. Let's take a look at you."

Her gnarled hands like a tree's uppermost branches stretched over Claire, a green glow filling them as she scanned Claire's body.

"She's fine." Greta said after her exam, "Just the wind knocked out of her."

Claire wanted to roll her eyes but refrained. Her mates' panic still resonated down their bonds echoing in the back of Claire's mind.

Greta got to her feet, leaning on Desmond's shoulder to do so. Desmond's mouth twisted but Claire reached a hand out to him, silently asking her for help in sitting up. She successfully distracted him but as soon as she was sitting, Malcolm was there, pulling her into his lap. Claire went to move and realized his muscles were practically vibrating with tension from controlling his shift. Claire settled but still reached her hands out to Everett and Desmond who shuffled on their knees closer until they crowded around her.

"I'm okay." She whispered. "I'm okay. Are you okay?"

"We're fine. Someone saved us without thinking about herself." Desmond scolded lightly.

"Don't do that to us ever again, little treasure!" Malcolm's arms were like steel around her. "We wouldn't survive losing you."

"And I wouldn't be able to live with myself if something happened to you." Claire argued, the adrenaline wearing off and causing her eyelids to droop though, softening the blow.

"Let's talk about it later." Everett soothed. "We're all okay. That's what matters."

Claire nodded slightly, pressing her face into Malcolm's chest. They were all okay but they had come very close to *not* being that way. A shudder worked through her body and Malcolm's grip tightened. She took a deep breath of his cinnamon and smoke scent as she willed her body to relax and gather its energy.

Around them, the sounds softened as Toan and Greta shooed the crowd away. A shadow crossed Claire's face and she opened her eyes to see Toan standing above them.

"How are you feeling?" He asked.

"Tired, a bit sore." Claire admitted.

"That's understandable. You should not have been able to use that level of magic until your coming of age. The bindings should have prevented that."

"They've been loosening," Claire admitted to him, watching his face.

His eyebrows furrowed and his mouth tightened before he rubbed his hand along his jaw, letting out a heavy breath. He nodded once, a short sharp movement as he processed that information.

"Where were you heading before the bridge fell?" Toan asked.

When her men still appeared to be speechless in their lingering panic and worry, Claire answered, "To find you actually. The Elf with the golden eyes said that you were down on a lower platform."

Toan froze and the magic inside Claire's center reacted restlessly. The restless feeling danced down her bonds with her

Triad and they all looked up at Toan. "You said an Elf with gold eyes told you where to find me?" Toan demanded.

Claire frowned at his tone, unsure of his reaction but knowing something must be wrong. "Yes. He gave us the directions to go down the stairs and across the bridge."

"What is it?" Malcolm growled, the vibration pushing through Claire and easing the restless feeling slightly.

"Golden eyes are not a trait in the Elves." Toan said, "Golden eyes are a shifter trait and we have no shifters here."

The growl that Malcolm let out was loud and threatening and carried across the clearing causing the lingering Elves to vanish. Claire tugged her hand out of Desmond's to cup Malcolm's face and tug it down to hers. If she didn't calm him down quickly, they would be dealing with a very large, very cranky dragon on top of everything.

"It's okay," she crooned, "I'm safe. We're safe."

Malcolm's gold eyes flashed brighter as his dragon fought a battle for control and Claire kept repeating her words, thumb stroking over his cheekbone until his eyes dimmed slightly and he dropped his head heavily to her shoulder.

Claire ignored the pleasurable sensations drifting over her shoulder of his exhale on her skin. She moved her hand to the back of his neck and played with the hair at the nape while she waited for him to gather his control back.

"Are you sure?" Desmond questioned Toan.

"I'm sure. I have to talk to the Elders about this." Toan turned to leave.

"Wait!" Claire called, halting him, "The information we read. We had some questions for you about it. Lorna's journal said there was dark magic found on the Fae lands before the war, do you know anything about that?"

Toan's eyebrows creased as he thought and then shook his head. "I don't."

"Would my father know?" Claire asked.

Toan's face fell slightly but he nodded. "If he is still alive, your father would probably be aware of anything like that."

He looked like he wanted to stay and ask more questions but his eyes glanced away, torn between staying and his duty to inform the Elders.

"Go," Claire said softly, "we can talk later."

Toan nodded, "Let me show you to one of the common rooms before I go. I'll post my men outside of it. I have others checking the remaining bridges and staircases in case there is dark magic on others."

Malcolm stood, scooping Claire into his arms and Claire didn't protest. Puck jumped up onto Everett's shoulder and the group followed Toan to one of the ground level rooms. It was a large but cozy space, soft blankets thrown across low chairs. Clearly, a meeting place of some sort but currently it was empty. Toan left them there with a promise to be back before the hour with news.

As soon as the door closed behind him, Malcolm exploded. "We can't stay here. Clearly, it's unsafe and they can't maintain their own Capital borders."

Claire soothed him with a hand on his arm and he halted his tirade. Claire felt tired all of a sudden, a bone-deep weariness as she thought about their options. "Where would we go?" She asked, "Whoever it is has proven their reach."

"We could go to the Dragon Mountains," Malcolm said firmly as if there was no doubt.

Desmond and Everett hesitated and exchanged looks. "What is it?" Claire asked before Malcolm could growl at them.

"I think we need to go to the Fae lands," Everett said, his intelligent green eyes on Claire as he knelt before her and Malcolm.

Malcolm growled but Everett ignored it. "If the dark magic started there then it might also be where it is still originating and we can cut it off at its source. And if it isn't, we can still speak to the Fae royalty. We need more information and I think we can all agree that going to the Council is not an option. Not until we learn the extent of their involvement."

Malcolm tensed underneath Claire and she spoke before he could. "What if we did both? We could go to the Dragon Mountains first and then to the Fae lands." She twisted slightly to look up at Malcolm. "Didn't you say my Fae dagger came from a Fae your father showed mercy to? What if that wasn't a coincidence?"

The tension on Malcolm's face softened from anger to thoughtfulness as he took in her words and nodded. "We'll go to my father then. And then to the Fae lands if we can."

"What do you mean if we can?" Claire frowned. Surely he wasn't saying that Malcolm's father would keep them in the mountains.

"Like the Elven Forest, no one has been able to enter the Fae lands since the Great War." Desmond explained, taking a seat across from them, "But instead of a Forest that everyone can see, the Fae lands look like an open plain. It's an illusion. You'll walk forever inside of it and can get turned around easily. Very few who ever tried returned and when they did… their minds were fractured."

Claire frowned. That landscape reminded her of where Puck had teleported her to on their first meeting when he was still under the dark magic influence. She voiced that and Malcolm growled. "Where I found you was close to Fae land."

"Then that's more evidence that whoever is doing this is connected to the Fae land in some way." Everett pointed out.

Malcolm growled and Claire sighed. It looked like they were going to the Fae. Claire sank deeper into Malcolm's arms as her men started talking and planning. She just wanted a few moments of peace and to enjoy her newfound family. Was that so much to ask?

CHAPTER 33

It felt like ages since Toan had left them in the room but Claire knew it hadn't been that long. Her men had fallen silent, each lost in their own thoughts as they thought about the next steps forward.

Whoever was behind this, was getting closer and more brazen but to what end? Claire dead? Her Triad dead? What purpose would Claire's death serve? It had to serve some purpose because Claire for the life of her couldn't think of any other reason someone would want her dead. The only people she had 'offended' in her life were the cruel children of Windshire and Vivienne and she just couldn't see them as capable of doing this. No, this extended to before Claire. Maybe it was an enemy of her parents? As her mother's guard, Toan should know if her mother had any specific enemies.

As if her thoughts conjured him, Toan opened the door. His eyes scanned over the group as if making sure no other misfortune had fallen on them since he had left. He relaxed when he saw all four of them were still there. Well, five with Puck.

"Good news." He said.

"You found the Elf with gold eyes?" Desmond asked, standing up.

Toan frowned, "Unfortunately not that. No, the good news is that the Elders voted to share access to all information with Claire after witnessing the strength of her magic even before her coming of age ceremony. This information will include access to the Elders' personal libraries and private tutors for Claire."

Claire exchanged a look with Everett, how could she tell her uncle thanks but no thanks. Desmond, ever the polite charmer, took the lead. "Actually we were just discussing heading to the Dragon Mountains for Claire's safety."

Toan immediately shook his head, "You can't do that. Not with Claire's magic bindings unraveling like they are. Without proper training, her magic could manifest violently."

"I'm sure we can take care of it." Desmond said, not backing down.

"You don't understand," Toan was firm, "I told you that Winona was powerful, Erick equally so. Individually they were powerful but together, they could level mountains. Claire is part of both of them and from all accounts has inherited their combined powers. She could destroy even the Dragon Mountains without proper training."

"I would never do that," Claire said, a soft hurt blooming inside her that her uncle could even think that.

Toan softened when he looked at her, "Not intentionally, of that I have no doubt. But unintentionally, your magic reacts instinctively right now and if your men are threatened again..."

He trailed off but Claire had to concede that he had a point. If her men were threatened, she would do anything to protect them.

Desmond wasn't as convinced. "Who's to say she won't level the Forest here?" He shot an apologetic look at Claire.

"Our trees here are actually designed to absorb our excess

magic. The Royal Tree especially will serve as a grounding point for Claire with her bloodlines."

Desmond was quiet as he came up with a counterargument and Claire slipped out of Malcolm's arms to stand next to Desmond. She placed a hand on his arm and faced Toan. "What if we compromised? We'll stay here for a few weeks and I'll learn as much as I can. By that time the Academy session should be ready to start. If we aren't attending school, the Council will expect my Triad to work for them so we should probably show our faces there but on the first break we can go to the Dragon Mountains and then the Fae lands."

Claire knew there was a lot up in the air with her plan, lots of holes that they would need to fill but hopefully it was enough of a starting point that they could agree on.

"You're going to the Fae lands?" Toan asked sharply. Oops, guess that part of the plan had slipped out.

Claire squared her shoulders. "We are. I need answers about my father and in her journal Lorna said that the dark magic use started there before the Great War." Her tone was gentle but firm. She would not back down on this.

Toan rubbed a hand over his face. "The Elves and Fae were allies before the Great War only due to Winona and Erick's relationship. With Winona gone and Erick's whereabouts unknown, you might not receive the welcome you are expecting."

"To be fair," Everett pointed out, "we weren't expecting a warm welcome here either." He said, reminding the group of how Toan and his men had found them.

Toan nodded his head as if conceding the point to Everett. "What's the cost of not knowing, Uncle?" Claire said softly, drawing his eyes back to hers. "All of this confusion, the multiple sides of the stories, the false stories. There's too much we don't know, that the citizens of the Realm don't know. We need to know."

"What's the cost of knowing?" Toan countered.

Claire paused as he threw one of her worst fears at her but Everett stepped up next to her. "Whatever it is, we'll face it together. We need to know."

Toan rubbed a hand over his face and sighed. He looked at them, as if judging how much convincing it would take them to stay and not go.

"We'll stay for now." Claire repeated, "And I'll learn how to not only not level a mountain but also how to level one if I need to." She didn't want to unintentionally hurt someone with her magic but she did want to learn how to protect her Triad and her friends if needed. Her Triad especially would take risks if they thought Claire was in danger and she didn't trust them not to sacrifice themselves for her.

She smiled at Toan's look and Desmond laughed, sliding an arm around her waist and tugging her close. "She packs quite a punch when she wants to. Just ask Malcolm."

Malcolm growled at him but it had a lighter, playful note in it.

"We can help with patrols if needed," Everett said, "we all have experience."

Toan nodded slowly, "That might work. At the very least, it will get my people used to outsiders again. As you can imagine, there is a bad taste in their mouths from the Great War."

He leveled a strong look at her Triad. "I am going to ask you not to use your magic or shift unless absolutely necessary. The Elves that fled to the Capital fled from the horrors inflicted by your kinds during the war. There have already been rumblings about allowing you safe passage and lodging, it's only their curiosity about the princess that has kept the rumblings from turning into something more."

"I thought you talked to the Elders?" Claire asked.

"The Elders were doing some of the rumblings." Toan said back. "They will see with time what I do, a Triad that adores our

Princess but right now they see a Triad whose reputation precedes them even into the Forest. Tread lightly and it will all blow over."

Malcolm looked like he wanted to argue but Desmond spoke, "We can do that. For Claire." He said with a look towards Malcolm who nodded.

"Good. Come. I'll take you back to your quarters. My men have cleared a safe passage to the Royal Tree."

"Could we maybe avoid the bridges?" Claire asked tentatively.

"It'll be a lot of climbing," Toan warned.

Claire winced at the thought of her tired legs but nodded her head, "Please." They could tackle the bridges tomorrow after Claire checked them out as well. Even now, as they climbed each staircase, Claire sent her magic ahead before anyone touched it to check for dark magic.

If her men felt her do it, they didn't say anything but Claire felt the effects every time she sent it out, exhaustion creeping up on her faster than usual with her explosive magic use earlier. By the time they reached the platform with their room from the night prior, Claire was dragging her feet.

Toan hesitated before he left, as if he had something to say but was unsure of saying it. Claire almost wanted to let him go, unsure if she could take on any more today but she felt like that would be rude.

"What is it?" She asked, giving him a tired smile.

Toan hesitated a moment longer before speaking, his eyes scanning her over with the sadness in them that had Claire thinking Toan was thinking of her mother. "I have your mother's journals."

"What?" Claire's eyes widened. Her mother kept journals?

"I have your mother's journals." Toan said. "She gave me them for safekeeping instead of putting them in the Royal Library. I hid them around the Forest in case of an attack on the library but I kept one. This one she insisted I keep close at all times."

He reached in his shirt and pulled out a small leather-bound journal, the deep brown had lightened with age. It was a small book, unassuming but Toan held it like it was his entire world. Claire realized she was looking at it the same way.

She took it from him gingerly, as if the leather would disintegrate in her hands. "Have you read it?" She asked, looking up at him.

He shook his head, "No. I never have. Not even after she was gone. Her words were for you."

Claire nodded, swallowing down the sudden lump in her throat. She dropped her gaze back down to the journal, stroking the soft leather with her fingertips.

Everett placed a hand on her back as he spoke to Toan. "Thank you."

"Of course. I'll send dinner up shortly."

Everett guided her into their room gently as Claire kept her focus on the book. She sat at the edge of the bed, turning the journal over in her hands.

Desmond crouched before her, "You don't have to read it tonight." He said softly.

Claire nodded, "I know. But I think I want to." She looked into his blue eyes and then glanced up at Malcolm's golden ones and then Everett's green.

"We'll help you carry it." Everett said, "Whatever you read in there, we'll help you carry it."

Taking a deep breath, Claire nodded. With shaking fingers she undid the thin leather tie that held the journal closed. She was barely breathing. Would it explain why her mother left the Capital? Why had she bound Claire's magic so strongly it caused her to lose her sight? Would it explain why she left her in the woods or how she died or what happened to her father?

The questions spun so fast in her mind they made her light-headed. Soothing warmth down her bonds from her Triad forced her to take a breath. Then another. With shaking fingers she opened the cover, leather creaking softly from disuse. Tucked inside the front cover was a letter addressed to Claire.

Arielle Clarissa Mayfaire.

To my dearest daughter,

To be continued...

AFTERWORD

I know, I know, I'm sorry I had to do that to you... but you can pre-order Beyond Her Sight here *offers pre-order link as a small apology gift* and you can tell me all about your outrage in my Facebook group, Sunny's Rays of Sunshine.

Grab book three here, Beyond Her Sight, so you don't miss out on the next and final installment of Claire's story!

A huge shoutout to everyone who helped bring my second RH book to the world! To my beta and arc teams, your feedback is phenomenal and I couldn't have done this without you! To every reader of By Her Sight, your kind words inspire me every day!

To Author Stella Brie, your advice, help, and support is what inspired me to start this journey, thank you so much!

To my best friends who cheered me along every word count goal and every day I couldn't seem to get words on the page and read every review, thank you. I know you both think I'm a little bit crazy but only in the best ways.

OTHER BOOKS BY AUTHOR

Writing as Sunny Hart

Unitam Realm Series

By Her Sight

With Her Sight

Beyond Her Sight

All Her Feelings

Writing as Maddi Hart

Avoiding the Sack

ABOUT THE AUTHOR

Sunny Hart lives in the rolling hills of the Kentucky Bluegrass. She has spent her entire life expressing herself through writing and short stories until one NaNoWriMo she challenged herself to write a book to share with the world. By Her Sight is the first book Sunny has published but is one of many floating around in her head. When not writing, Sunny is spending time with her dogs and horse and working her 'day job' as a business strategy consultant.

For the latest news, updates, and giveaways, check out Sunny's Facebook group,
Sunny's Rays of Sunshine

To sign up for her newsletter and more, check out her website at authorsunnyhart.com